LOST

Without

YOU

LOST
Without
YOU

a novel

Annette Lyon

Covenant Communications, Inc.

Cover photograph by Maren E. Ogden

Published by Covenant Communications, Inc.
American Fork, Utah

Printed in the United States of America
First Printing: July 2002

08 07 06 05 04 03 02   10 9 8 7 6 5 4 3 2 1

ISBN 1-59156-019-5

Library of Congress Cataloging-in-Publication Data

Lyon, Annette, 1973-
      Lost Without You : a novel / Annette Lyon.
            p.   cm.
      ISBN 1-59156-019-5
      1. Mormon women--Fiction. 2. Separation (Psychology)--Fiction. 3. Widowers--Fiction. 4. Utah--Fiction. I. Title
      PS3612.Y557 L67 2002
      813'.6--dc21   2002022970

DEDICATION

To my husband, Rob, who had the faith when mine faltered and who never let me stop pursuing the dream burning inside me.

And to Mom and Dad, who filled my childhood with the magic of language and books, which kindled that dream in the first place.

ACKNOWLEDGMENTS

This book would not be what it is without the support of many people. I owe a debt of gratitude to Rachel Nunes, Shauna Andreason, Staci Call, and my sister Melanie, who read all or parts of my early drafts and gave honest feedback. Thanks also goes to the talented members of my critique group, who helped so much with the book—Stephanni Hicken, LuAnn Staheli, Sherri Schloss, Sandy Hirsche, Michele Holmes, and Lisa Olsen. I am also grateful to Valerie Holladay for mentoring me and giving the right advice to help me get here.

Thank you all!

CHAPTER 1

"So what are you saying?" Christopher asked, his eyes darting from the road to Brooke and back again. His hands gripped the steering wheel a bit tighter.

Brooke's voice lowered. "I guess I'm saying that you're not the one for me."

"I see," Christopher said quietly. He had always been a safe driver, but for the first time Brooke saw the speedometer well over the speed limit. Christopher's jaw tensed and his eyes practically bored holes into the windshield. Brooke couldn't help but stare at the look in his eyes, as if some other personality had taken possession of him. She hardly recognized the man sitting beside her.

They were in the middle of Provo Canyon for an evening drive, and there wasn't a good place to turn around. Christopher kept going, not slowing even at tight curves. Brooke's fingers gripped the edges of her seat. Christopher made it all the way to Heber City before turning around and racing down the canyon the other direction. He didn't say another word, and neither did Brooke. There was no point in discussing the matter or causing bigger wounds. They both knew it was over. But she wished he'd at least respond with some maturity. What was wrong with him?

They had dated for only three months, but Brooke had thought Christopher might be the one. That is until he had started acting moody and possessive over the past couple of weeks. Then he began hinting that she needed to change for his mother to approve of the match. The changes seemed benign at first. His mother preferred to be addressed as "Mrs. Morris." She hated hearing her son referred to as "Chris" in her presence. But when Mrs. Morris began suggesting changes in Brooke's hair and clothing—and Christopher insisted Brooke comply—she realized she had gotten more than she bargained for. Brooke had thought more than once that it was a case of the umbilical cord never getting cut, which was unacceptable for someone his age.

Breakups were never easy or fun, so she had expected Christopher to be hurt. But she hadn't counted on him reacting this way, swerving between lanes, barely missing a head-on collision with a truck when Christopher decided to pass a Jeep going only ten miles over the speed limit. It was like he'd gone from Jekyll to Hyde. What was he doing? He was acting like a wounded animal, or a selfish teenager at the least.

"Could you slow down a bit?" she asked.

Christopher glanced at her and pressed harder on the pedal, the dark look in his eyes now accompanied by a thin smile. A knot formed in Brooke's stomach as she mentally calculated how much longer the drive home would be. She knew that after he dropped her off they would probably never see each other again.

She would miss him, in a way. Not the Christopher of the last two weeks though. She would miss the one she had talked to at the ice-cream parlor until their pistachio ice cream had puddled and their fries were cold and hard. She had had two-and-a-half great months with him. It was this new side of Christopher that had destroyed everything. She couldn't have one side without the other, so tonight she would have to say good-bye to both.

As they crossed the light by Will's Pit Stop, the car sputtered and grew strangely quiet, then gradually slowed to a stop.

"We're out of gas," Christopher said tonelessly as the car rolled to a stop, the first words he had spoken in the last half hour.

Wham!

They jerked forward violently to the sound of crushed metal. After a moment of stunned silence, they whipped around to see what was left of the red sports car that had just rear-ended them. The front had caved in, making a mockery of what had been an elegant vehicle. The air bag had deployed, and as the driver got out, he coughed from the bag's fumes. Christopher jumped out of the car and ran to the back to assess the damage. His back bumper had a good-sized dent and a lot of paint had been scraped off, but otherwise his car seemed fine, especially in comparison to the other guy's.

"I guess you got lucky," Brooke said, joining him.

"Yeah, I guess so," Christopher said sullenly.

The other driver, no more than seventeen, let out a few colorful words and kicked the front wheel of his car. "Dad's gonna kill me," he said, pulling at his hair. "He's gonna kill me. And all because some idiot didn't speed up at the light like he was supposed to."

"Hey, I saw the light. I just ran out of gas," Christopher snapped.

The young man turned on him. "Oh, well in that case, I guess you're not an idiot. You're a total moron."

Christopher threw a few nasty and colorful descriptions back at the driver as he took his cell phone off its clip and called the police. Brooke returned to the car, wishing she could hide. The two cars blocked the intersection, and dozens of cars were piling up, their drivers staring at them. All because Christopher had been too upset to notice he was running low on gas.

A police car arrived shortly after, although to Brooke it felt like an eternity. She tried to stay in the background as the officer took care of the formalities of paperwork and clearing the accident, but he called out to her as she leaned against the car.

"Miss? Could you come over here? I need you to fill out a witness statement too."

She closed the gap and took the papers from his hand without a word, but as she turned away, he flashed her a smile. Brooke hated herself for noticing the dimple in his right cheek and the name on his tag, *G. Stevens*. Not tonight, she thought. She had just broken up. This was not the time to be thinking about men. Brooke set the papers against the back of the car and began filling them out.

"Your car still looks functional," Officer Stevens said to Christopher.

"Yeah, but I ran out of gas. I'll have to hike back to the gas station to get some," Christopher responded, the tips of his ears finally turning red from something other than anger.

Before long the tow truck arrived for the sports car. The paperwork had been completed, their car was pulled over onto the gravelly shoulder, and traffic had nearly returned to normal. All that remained was for Christopher to return with the gas.

"I'll stay with you until your boyfriend gets back," Officer Stevens said.

"Oh, he's not my boyfriend. At least, not anymore." *Why did I say that?* She had sounded like a schoolgirl. Here she had just broken up with one man, only to make a perfect stranger aware of it—as if this police officer was planning to ask her out. Hardly. And as if she wanted him to. He was probably married anyway, she reminded herself, although she hadn't noticed if he wore a ring. After all, she reasoned, he was far too good-looking *not* to be married. Except for the extra short hair. He'd look better if he grew it out a bit. But cops often had shorter hair. She wondered if it was to make them look more intimidating or something.

"Thanks for the concern, Officer," Brooke said, looking down to avoid seeing the dimple again. "But I think he'll be back any minute. I'll be fine."

"Just the same, I'll stick around for a minute or two. Until he gets back." He stood to his full height, and with a trace of disappointment leaned back against the car and said, "Looks like he's on his way now."

"Thanks again, Officer. It looks like crises are following me tonight, but hopefully this will all be over soon and you'll never have to see me again."

"Oh, I wouldn't mind seeing you again," he commented under his breath, then quickly stood up. "And here he is." At that instant Christopher came up behind the car.

It took him only a moment to transfer the red container's contents into the gas tank. Soon they were on their way. Christopher didn't say a word as he drove, changing lanes with abandon, cutting off cars, the engine straining before he shifted. Brooke looked over at him. His eyes looked like those of a stranger, as if something had snapped inside him. She tried to remember better times, but his cold glare made it impossible. He turned left at a light and narrowly missed getting broadsided by an oncoming car. Brooke gripped the armrest and hoped they'd make it without another more serious accident that evening.

They arrived at Brooke's twin-home complex without anything more hazardous than a few honks and curses from other drivers. Christopher stopped in front of her place and waited for Brooke to open her own car door. He had never opened it for her before, but he always walked her to the door.

"I'm sorry it had to end this way," Brooke said.

She reached over to hug him good-bye, but Christopher pushed her away with one swift motion. "Get out."

She fell back against the armrest. Her arm stung from the blow. She was too stunned to move. Christopher looked over, his eyes burning with anger, and she fought back tears.

"Good-bye, *Brooke.*" He said her name like a dirty word.

As she grabbed her purse and opened the door, she tried to ignore the throbbing spot on her arm. He grabbed her other arm and she turned to face him, hoping for a kind word.

"I'd like the bracelet back."

She removed his only gift and dropped it in his hand before stepping out of the car. He barely waited for her to close the door before hitting the gas pedal and racing off, tires squealing as he pulled out of the parking lot onto the road. Then she hugged herself for warmth, even though the evening wasn't cold. She turned and walked to her door, suddenly feeling very alone.

* * *

Christopher drove home, where his mother would be waiting for him. He knew something wasn't quite right; the feelings surging through his body and the thoughts filling his mind felt like something trying to take control over his body. He hadn't felt like this for years.

Mother couldn't see him like this. She would start asking about whether he had taken his medication. *Rather, my poison,* he thought. He was fine. He didn't need any medication. He hadn't needed it for nearly two years, but had taken it faithfully in spite of the side effects until March, nearly two months ago. He blamed his extra twenty pounds and receding hairline on those pills. Not to mention the headaches and nausea. And tossing and turning every night, unable to sleep. Poison, that's what those chemicals were. Brooke deserved a man without love handles or a shiny scalp.

A surge went through Christopher again, and he paused, looking over at the passenger seat where Brooke had been minutes before. He wanted nothing but her. He needed her. Everything had been going so well until she pulled that surprise out of nowhere tonight. He stroked the seat with his hand. No matter how much she'd hurt him, he'd win her back. The two of them would be together, in this life and the next. No matter what it took. He couldn't live without her. She would see soon enough that she couldn't live without him, either.

As he pulled into the driveway and turned off the car, he dropped his forehead onto the steering wheel and tried to even out his breathing so his mother wouldn't ask any questions. If his mother didn't shove the pills down his throat, she might trick him into seeing Dr. Hamilton again. He couldn't risk that. He leaned against the headrest and closed his eyes, breathing deeply while running his fingers across Brooke's seat. After a few minutes he adjusted the rearview mirror so he could peer into his eyes to see if he looked all right. He blinked, searching his eyes for anything his mother could find amiss. With one final breath, he got out and headed for the front door. He glanced at his watch. Mother would be watching one of those newsmagazine shows. If he came in with a smile and gave her a kiss on the cheek, she might not ask why he was home early.

Christopher reached for the doorknob, then gave one final glance at the passenger seat. Brooke was his; he would make her see that. He knew she was still in love with him. As he opened the front door of the house, he couldn't help but smile.

CHAPTER 2

Brooke locked the door behind her. She leaned against it and breathed out heavily. She kept replaying what had just happened in her mind, and none of it made sense. Christopher wasn't a rude person. At least, he hadn't been before. And he had never been physical with her until he had pushed her away in the car.

She put her purse on the kitchen counter and out of habit glanced at the calendar in the kitchen. Her sister Pat, and her family, were arriving tomorrow. They would stay with Brooke's mother across town, but that wouldn't keep the two sisters from seeing plenty of each other—and talking for hours. Brooke wished Pat was already there; she felt a particular need to unload all that was on her mind on a willing ear. If Pat's family hadn't been on the road right then, Brooke would probably have called her to talk about the breakup.

Brooke's eyes went to the next square on the calendar, and she sighed. On Sunday she and Christopher were supposed to go to a fireside. She took a pencil from the drawer and erased the words. If only it could have ended differently.

It was only eight o'clock. She couldn't go to bed yet. Not that she could have slept right then anyway with this wave of emotions flooding through her. She flipped through the television channels but found nothing of interest. A novel on the end table didn't appeal to her either. Her gaze finally rested on her piano, recently purchased from BYU's Music Department. It wasn't fancy, and it wasn't new, but it was hers. Christopher had thought it was a silly purchase and a waste of time.

Which is precisely why she never played around him or let him know that she sang—loudly—while she played. She had always wanted to be a real singer, but she hadn't done much with her voice since she was a teenager. At least, not since her high-school musical productions.

That was where Brooke had caught the theater bug, especially from playing the lead in the musical her senior year. After high school she had intended to pursue theater and voice further, but college, a mission, and a career had gotten in the way, and she had nearly written off all thoughts of the stage. Each year she directed a play for the fourth-graders she taught and that kept her busy.

Then the ad for the piano sale arrived in the mail. Since the purchase, she had spent many evenings singing her heart out, playing Broadway show tunes. She remembered much of the training her choir teacher had given her and tried to do the techniques. She didn't sound half bad, if she thought so herself.

Singing was just what the doctor ordered right now, Brooke thought. She went to the piano and thumbed through her favorite music book, singing tunes from the classic shows *South Pacific*, *Fiddler on the Roof*, and *The Music Man*. Then she pulled out a more contemporary selection, and for a few moments became the characters in *Les Misérables*, *The Secret Garden*, and *The Scarlet Pimpernel*.

The weight she had come home with lightened considerably as she sang. Then she went to bed, firmly deciding to keep herself so busy with Pat and the piano that she would have no time left to think about Christopher or men in general. Lying in bed, she made a mental checklist of things she could do that would fill the bill. Pat's visit would keep her busy for the next week, though she doubted that would be long enough to get over the night's events. It was creepy how much Christopher had changed—almost like the surprise bad guy at the end of a horror movie. *What had gone wrong?*

* * *

She woke up to the sound of the phone ringing. Brooke quickly cleared her throat so she wouldn't sound too sleepy, then noticed her mother's number on the caller ID.

"Pat?"

"Yep, it's me," Pat said cheerily. "We drove all night. It's a lot easier to just keep driving when the kids are asleep. Do you want to do lunch?"

Brooke sat up, adjusted the phone, and looked at the clock. It was almost nine, which was rather late for her to be sleeping, especially since she had gotten to bed earlier than normal last night. "Sure, but don't you want to take a nap or something? You must be exhausted."

"Oh, I slept most of the night. Rick drove almost the whole way. He fell asleep on the couch right after we got here, so I doubt we'll be seeing him most of the day."

They decided to meet later and take the kids out for Happy Meals, then go to a park, where, with any luck, the sisters would be able to talk.

Brooke enjoyed her leisurely morning, spreading out the morning paper, pouring herself some bran flakes, and cutting a banana into them. When she put the milk away, she once again noticed the small ad she had found the other day which she had put on the fridge with a magnet. It announced an open audition at a small local theater.

At eleven o'clock Brooke went to her mother's house north of the Provo Temple. As she helped Pat's three little ones get ready to go, she purposely avoided talking about Christopher until they left, which was no easy feat, considering how much their mother pried into Brooke's romantic life. Brooke managed to dodge most questions by heading off to find a lost shoe or the diaper bag. A pang of guilt went through her, but she brushed it aside. She needed to tell Pat about it first, and her mother would have to wait to find out when the whole thing wasn't so fresh.

But Brooke didn't get a chance to tell Pat much about it at the restaurant. They both had their hands full keeping track of the three children, wiping messes, and catching drinks just as they were about to spill. Seven-year-old Tammy dribbled honey sauce all over her shirt and hair. Two-year-old Amy spilled ice-cold root beer down her front and burst into shocked screams. Krissy, who was between her sisters in age, had blobs of ketchup dotting her white T-shirt.

After using several stacks of napkins to mop up the mess, Brooke and Pat gathered up the kids and herded them to the van. An hour at

North Park would undoubtedly prove more relaxing than the restaurant. At least there wouldn't be anything that could spill or stain.

At the park there were a couple of crises, such as when Amy scraped her leg, and later, when the older two refused to let her play with them, but aside from that the time went by smoothly. Brooke told her sister about her disturbing experience with Christopher and how she was so restless afterward that the only thing she could do was play the piano and sing. Against her better judgment she also told Pat about the audition notice.

"When is it?" Pat asked.

"Monday."

"You have to go."

"But I haven't prepared anything."

"So? It's just a community thing. It'll be fun."

"That's the last adjective I'd use for an audition. Try *terrifying* or *humiliating . . .*"

"You're going."

Brooke laughed. "Oh?"

Pat nodded, businesslike. "Yep. I'll pick you up and take you. Mom will watch the kids. And we'll go out for ice cream afterward."

"Ice cream?" Brooke said. "Well, I suppose I *could* go if I get ice cream afterward."

Pat looked at her watch. "Yikes. It's later than I thought. Amy's well past her naptime, and Krissy and Tammy are probably close to meltdown too."

Pat called to the kids that it was time to go home, and with a bit of coaxing they finally came. But just as they got to the van, Krissy began to bounce up and down.

"I gotta go, Mom. Real bad!"

"Can't you wait until we get to Grandma's?"

Krissy's eyes were desperate, and she bounced harder. "No. I gotta go *now.*"

"Fine. Come on," Pat said. "Let's go."

"I'll bring the van around," Brooke said. Pat handed over the keys and headed off in search of a bathroom.

The van had grown hot in the unusually warm May heat, practically stifling everyone's breathing. Brooke buckled the other girls into their seats quickly, but not in time to stop Tammy from finding a bag of peanut M&M's left in the van.

"Put those away," Brooke said. "The heat has probably melted them, and they'll make a big mess." From inside the van, Brooke slid the side door shut and squeezed her way forward to the driver's seat, where she collapsed and pushed her fingers through her hair.

"It's hot. I don't like being hot," Tammy declared. "Turn on the air."

"That's exactly what I'm about to do." Brooke glanced into the rearview mirror and caught Tammy popping M&M's into her mouth. "Tammy . . ."

She turned the key, but instead of starting, the van let out a loud, drawn-out wail. The vehicle seemed frozen, except for the high-pitched siren sound, which attracted stares from passersby. Brooke's face flushed red as she fumbled with the dashboard controls, frantically trying to figure out what she had done wrong. Nothing worked. It had to be the van's security alarm she finally realized, but what had set it off? And more importantly, how in the world could she get the thing to stop?

Amy, who had just fallen asleep in her car seat, awoke with a start and began crying at least as loud as the alarm, and Tammy joined her in a chorus of wails and sobs.

"Turn it off," she cried, holding her ears. "It's loud. I'm scared."

Brooke reached for the owner's manual in the glove compartment. "I'm trying. I'll turn it off as soon as I can figure out how."

With each wail of the van, Brooke's nerves wound a little tighter. Pedestrians gave her odd looks, and the cries of the children continued to escalate. By this time Amy was nearly hysterical, while Tammy thought it great fun to imitate the alarm to see if she could yell even louder. Brooke flipped the pages of the manual blindly, willing the right page to show itself. She couldn't think clearly; she wanted nothing more than for the alarm to turn off.

A tall man with short brown hair appeared a few feet away and walked with a determined step in their direction. He looked vaguely familiar, but then, how many men in Utah Valley had the same look? A few thousand?

When he reached the minivan, he mouthed, "Do you need help turning that off?" Brooke nodded in humiliation, wishing she could become invisible, but at the same time grateful for the help. She got out of the van so she could hear him over the noise. With her nerves on edge, she had to focus on understanding his simple instructions.

"Just lock the door, close it, and open it with the key instead of the Keyless-entry button."

It was worth a try. Brooke pushed the Power-lock button on the driver's side door and closed it. As the door left her fingers and shut tight, she gasped. "Wait!"

The man took a step forward, looking for what was wrong. "What?"

"If this doesn't work, they'll be stuck in the van. And in this heat . . ." she swallowed nervously. "I should have gotten them out before locking the door."

"It'll work. Trust me."

His voice was calm and reassuring. She tried to believe him. She did her best to brush off thoughts of the heat and the van's continued wailing and tried to steady her hand enough to get the key into the lock. Tammy suddenly pounded frantically on the window.

"Tammy, what's wrong?" Brooke yelled through the window.

Tammy held up the pack of M&M's and pointed to her throat.

"Are you choking?"

Tammy nodded, her eyes wide. Brooke said a silent prayer that the door would unlock; turning off the alarm didn't seem so urgent anymore. But with her hand shaking, she couldn't get the key into the lock. She glanced up at the window, where Tammy watched, tears streaking her face, her hands at her throat.

The man reached for the keys. With one quick motion, he slipped the key in. Brooke closed her eyes and held her breath. He turned the key and the wailing stopped as abruptly as it had begun. More importantly, the door opened. Before Brooke could do anything, he had opened the side door, reached inside the van, and pulled Tammy out. He turned her around, wrapped his arms around her, and after two quick thrusts, the offending candy flew out of the girl's mouth. She took a large gasp of breath, then collapsed in Brooke's arms with shaky sobs. Brooke let out a harsh breath of her own.

"Tammy, are you all right?" Tammy nodded, then buried her head in Brooke's shoulder for another hug. "What a relief!"

The man smiled at her. "I can imagine. I know how powerful those maternal instincts are. If it had been my child I would be a bit shaky too."

Tammy took a deep breath and pulled away, wiping at her eyes. "I'm better now."

Brooke watched her climb into the van. "Oh, these aren't my children. But I can't imagine being any more pathetic even if I had been their mother."

He laughed. "Don't say that until you're a parent. Those little ones can have quite a hold on you."

Tammy sat on the bench of the van and gave Brooke a look she had undoubtedly gotten from her mother. "Hey, we're not supposed to talk to strangers."

"I think this is an exception. This man just saved your life."

"Well, if you're not allowed to talk to strangers I'd better introduce myself. I'm Greg Stevens."

Brooke suddenly knew why he had seemed familiar. He was the police officer at the accident. Officer G. Stevens.

He held his hand out to Tammy. "And you are . . . ?"

Tammy giggled and shyly extended her hand. "I'm Tammy."

"That's a very pretty name. How old are you?"

"Seven. I'm almost done with first grade."

"Wow, almost a lady. You're tall for first grade."

Tammy bit her lip with pleasure.

"It's nice to meet you," he said, shaking her hand. He turned to Brooke and shook hers too. "You too . . . Don't I know you from somewhere?" He thought for a moment, then snapped his fingers. "Last night. Accident on University, right?"

"Right." Brooke could feel heat climbing up her face. "I'm really embarrassed. First you help with the alarm, and then Tammy . . . anyway, thank you. When it went off, I didn't have the slightest idea what to do. I don't even know what set the alarm off."

"Oh, you probably closed the doors, then locked them while you were in the car. If you lock the car and then try to start it, the alarm will go off." Brooke nodded, figuring that she probably hit the Lock button on the key chain somewhere between buckling up the children and squeezing into the driver's seat. Greg went on. "It's not that uncommon, especially when a person's not familiar with how the alarm works."

Brooke flushed, convinced that this handsome stranger saw her as an idiot blonde who couldn't take care of herself. No matter that her hair was chestnut brown. "Oh, this isn't my van," she said more quickly than she intended. She did not know this man, but somehow she wanted to be sure he didn't leave with the wrong impression. "I mean, if it were, I would probably know how it worked."

Greg shrugged. "Could have happened to anyone. It was nice meeting you again."

Brooke watched him head down the sidewalk, hating the fact that the dimple in his left cheek refused to leave her mind. She suddenly called out to his retreating figure, "By the way . . . thank you. Again, I mean."

He turned around. "No problem," he said with a final wave. She got back into the van and almost started it when Pat returned with Krissy.

"We barely made it," she said, helping Krissy into the van. She looked down the street and pointed. "Who was that?"

"Here's the keys," Brooke said.

With Krissy buckled, Pat took the keys, but looked down the street again. "Do you know that guy?"

"No."

"But you just waved at him."

Tammy jumped in. "The van started making this loud noise, and Brooke didn't know how to stop it, and that guy did, and he told her how, but he turned it off and got it open, but I had an M&M stuck in my throat, and he got me out and lifted me hard and got it out—"

"Are you all right?" Pat interrupted, maternal worry replacing curiosity.

"I'm okay. I won't eat any more of these candies though. But he was really nice, and his name is Craig."

"Greg," Brooke corrected, then blushed.

Pat eyed Brooke. "Oh?"

Tammy went on. "He called me a lady."

Brooke ducked around to get in on the passenger side. Pat put on her seat belt without saying anything, but as she turned the key, she spoke up. "So is he cute? Did he get your number?"

"No," Brooke stammered. "I mean, yes, I suppose he is pretty good-looking, but no, we didn't exchange any personal information."

Pat eyed Brooke and laughed as she put the van into gear. "Your ears are red."

Brooke stifled a smile of her own. "Hush, Pat."

* * *

Greg Stevens walked a distance from the park before he stopped and turned around. He gazed at the minivan, which was just pulling out of the parking lot. He watched it until it passed him and disappeared out of sight. What was it about that woman? He had seen her twice, and both times he'd had a compelling interest to be near her, to talk to her.

He shoved his hands into his pockets and closed his eyes tightly. His promise to Heather had been easy to keep for four years now; after all, he had no desire to even look at another woman since losing his wife. It had been four years last month. The longest four years of his life.

He shook his head and let out a sigh. It was time to pick up Gee-la. Pulling his keys from his pocket, he took a step toward his car at the curb, but stopped again and looked back to the park where the van had stood.

He didn't know the woman with the chestnut hair. And yet there was something about her . . .

CHAPTER 3

"You're not going to chicken out," Pat said.

"Who said I was going to chicken out?" Brooke said, pulling into the theater parking lot.

"Oh, I saw you eyeing your sheet music. Don't even think it."

Brooke found an empty parking space and turned off the car. She stared at the theater. "It's been so long that I'm terrified." Brooke let out a deep breath. "Well, here we go. Let's get this over with."

They headed for the theater. Brooke swung open one door and stopped. She looked at her sister. "When it's over, I'll need two scoops. Rocky Road and French Vanilla."

Pat laughed as they walked into the lobby, where they heard a piano and a tenor voice wavering on a high note. A forty-something woman at a desk handed Brooke a form to fill out and a numbered paper to pin to her blouse.

She and Pat entered the audition room, where a young man stood a few feet from a piano, singing his heart out for the director and two other people who all held clipboards and were jotting notes as they listened. His voice cracked on a high note, but he continued on confidently. Other hopefuls sat around the edges of the room, filling out their forms. Brooke wondered if any of *them* had a knot the size of an apple in their throats. They didn't look like they did.

Brooke stared at the sheet music in her hands, then at the room before her, then back at the music. She bit her cheek, unsure whether she could get herself to move one foot in front of the other and actually go in. Pat gave her a nudge, and the two entered the room. They walked around the edge and found two chairs. Brooke began to fill out the application form. Name, phone number, and address were easy enough.

"Experience: list your most significant productions, from the most recent."

Brooke groaned. Her last part was Anna in *The King and I* more than a decade ago. Before that was . . . she glanced at the application of the woman next to her. It was filled with productions and lead roles, all within the last three years. Brooke held her form at an angle so others couldn't see how glaringly blank it was. She turned in the form and returned to sit by Pat, where Brooke waited for her turn, knots forming in her stomach now too.

"My voice is going crack," Brooke whispered.

"Rocky Road and French Vanilla," Pat whispered back.

Several people auditioned before Brooke. One man announced straight out it was his first attempt at theater. The next three might as well have stepped off of Broadway. The woman beside Brooke was called up, and Brooke watched her practically float across the room. The woman handed the accompanist her music and gracefully took her place, as poised as a flower. *Exquisite* was the only way to describe her voice.

When they called Brooke's number, she didn't move. She didn't have the guts to do what all those others had just done. She couldn't do it. Pat firmly planted the sheet music into Brooke's hand and pushed her to a standing position.

With a deep gulp, Brooke pasted a smile on her face and crossed the room to the pianist. Somehow the room felt twice as large as it had when they first entered. With each step she could feel the eyes of everyone watching her. She wished the audition was closed, as they had been in high school, where only the directors watched. She handed the music to the pianist, then took her place at the same spot the others had. As she heard the opening bars, her eyes grew blurry, and before she knew it, her cue had arrived. She didn't have time to take a deep enough breath, so her first note, instead of sounding clear and bright, resembled a tortured mouse. Brooke tried not to wince. Her throat constricted tighter, squeezing at each note.

"That's enough, thank you," the director said. The pianist stopped, and after consulting with the two assistants at his side, the director made a few notes on his clipboard.

The blood that had rushed to Brooke's face now fled. She began to breathe again at the same moment she remembered that directors rarely listened to an entire song. Usually only sixteen bars. She had known that—a long time ago. The others had remembered to prepare only that much. She flushed again as the realization hit her. She must have looked like such an amateur.

Brooke left the theater still trembling, feeling weak after the adrenaline rush of the audition drained away. Pat couldn't have been more proud if Brooke had been her own daughter. "You did it. You did it!"

"At least it's over," Brooke said. "I made such a fool out myself. Whatever talent I might have had is gone now." With determination she drove for the ice-cream shop, her hands still trembling slightly as she clung to the steering wheel.

"You still have the talent," Pat insisted. "Look what you've done with your students."

Brooke laughed lightly, then found herself tearing up a little. "Making helpless fourth-graders do a yearly play doesn't exactly count." She wiped at her eyes.

"Uh, Brooke." Pat reached over, touched Brooke's arm, and turned to look out the back window.

"What?"

"I think that's for you," Pat said, jabbing her thumb behind her.

Brooke looked into the rearview mirror to see flashing police lights behind her. She hadn't realized she had been going so fast. With a groan, she pulled the car over and braced herself, hoping the police car would whiz past to its next call. She had never caused an accident before and had never had a ticket or even been pulled over.

The patrol car slowed to a stop behind her. "This is not what I need right now," Brooke said, frantically wiping at her eyes, figuring that the police officer would not react positively to a blubbering woman. Even so, a few more tears escaped and Brooke quickly looked in the vanity mirror to wipe them away before the officer walked up. She could see him in the mirror just a few steps behind her car. He had short brown hair. Brooke groaned as she rolled down the window and said under her breath, "Not him. Not again."

Something about the uniform and the gun made Brooke less than comfortable. His belt was surrounded by gadgets and pockets, and she wondered which one carried the bullets.

"Could I see your driver's license, ma'am?"

The voice was different than she expected. She looked up at him, and a broad smile crossed her face. It wasn't Officer Stevens. According to his tag, his name was *M. Smith*. Brooke happily handed over her license and registration, and didn't even care when he said he was going to give her a ticket.

While Officer Smith sat in his patrol car to complete the paperwork, Pat craned her neck over the back of her seat to look at him. "What was that about? Who did you think he was?"

"Just someone else."

"Who?"

Brooke flushed. "Remember the guy at the park?"

Pat looked impressed. "He's a police officer? Wow."

When Officer Smith returned, Pat leaned over Brooke to address him. "Do you know an officer named Greg?"

Brooke slapped Pat's leg, but Pat didn't seem to care.

Officer Smith nodded. "I do. Officer Stevens. In fact, people often ask if we're brothers. I guess we look alike. Do you know him?"

"A little," Pat said, as if she had actually met the man. "Could you tell him that the woman who was at the van is named Brooke Williamson?"

"Pat!"

Officer Smith nodded. "Brooke Williamson. Sure. If I remember, I'll pass along your message."

As they drove away, Pat said, "This is classic. I can't wait to tell Rick about this."

Brooke didn't find the situation nearly so amusing.

* * *

Brooke spent most of that Thursday running through the fourth-grade musical, a significantly shortened and simplified version of *Fiddler on the Roof*, to be presented to the school on Friday and to the parents the same evening. As expected, the rehearsal had its glitches: Tevye couldn't remember several lines, and Tseitel, the star of the "Matchmaker" number, couldn't be found. As one crisis after another surfaced, from ripped costumes to missing props and nonfunctioning lighting, Brooke had to keep reminding herself that she had gone through a half dozen similar dress rehearsals and had never had a disastrous performance—yet. She took a deep breath and tried not to think that there was always a first time for everything.

Brooke glanced over at the side of the auditorium where Melissa Ford's mother stood, arms folded and a scowl across her face. Mrs. Ford was her biggest trial this year. Brooke sighed and turned back to the stage, where Tricia, whom she had cast as Hodel, was helping a fellow actress adjust her costume. According to Mrs. Ford, Melissa should have been cast as Hodel. Mrs. Ford attended almost every rehearsal and never let Brooke forget about her presence. Brooke purposely encouraged and coached Tricia behind the scenes and hoped she would perform so brilliantly that her casting selection would be justified.

They had a few scenes left to go through, and Brooke nearly called for the next one when she saw the clock on the wall. It was time for recess, and while she thought they should really stay in this time, she welcomed the break. They could finish the run-through when they returned. Everyone was getting tense and bored, and pushing the reserves of ten-year-olds didn't usually prove productive.

"All right, everyone," she called out, "Put your costumes and props where they belong and head out to recess. Be back as soon as the bell rings. We need to finish the run-through and clean everything up before the safety assembly this afternoon." An enthusiastic buzz of murmurs and chattering immediately erupted as Brooke dropped her director's script on a chair and collapsed on the one next to it. She stretched her neck and rubbed one shoulder. Then she suddenly remembered that she had playground duty. With a deep breath to gather all her energy reserves, she stood up and headed for the door.

The first half of recess proved less than eventful, for which Brooke was grateful; she never enjoyed refereeing fights or nagging children to play safely. But as she walked past the jungle gym and headed down the small hill toward the blacktop, she heard a sudden cry behind her. She turned to find a small girl with pale blonde hair sitting on the ground, holding her hand to her head and grimacing.

Brooke peered back to make sure she was all right. Before she could say a word, blood seeped through the girl's fingers, dripping onto her yellow shirt and darkening her hair. Brooke rushed over and pressed her own hand against the wound.

"What happened?" she demanded of the girl's friend, whose eyes had grown three sizes.

The friend pointed to a little boy standing about ten feet away. "He threw a rock at her."

The boy's face had turned pale. "I didn't mean to hurt her," he cried, panicked.

Brooke gently pulled the girl's hand away to get a look at the cut, but there was too much blood to tell how large it was.

"Come with me," she said, and pressed her hand against the wound to stop the bleeding. She did her best to distract the little girl as they hurried to the nurse's office. "I'm Miss Williamson. I teach fourth grade. What's your name?"

"Angela."

"And you're in what—first, second grade?" The girl was so small that Brooke knew she couldn't be any older than first grade, but she knew that students liked being mistaken for being older.

"I'm in first grade."

"I loved first grade. Who's your teacher?"

"Mrs. Starr."

"I know her. How do you like her?"

Angela didn't seem to remember her injury any longer, which helped Brooke to relax as well. Chances were that the cut wasn't very large. "Mrs. Starr's all right," Angela said. "But I liked my kindergarten teacher better. Mrs. Mackay was really nice. I don't think Mrs. Starr likes me."

"Why do you say that?"

Angela shrugged. "She yells at me. She says I'm lazy. That I hear but I don't listen to what she's saying."

"*Do* you listen?"

Angela bit the inside of her cheek. "*Most* of the time I do. But sometimes she gets so *boring*. And sometimes she's wrong. One day she kept saying how an *r* after an *a* says its name, like in *farm*, and that you can't hear the sound an *a* makes." She gave Brooke a disgusted look. "I can hear the *a* in *farm*, can't you?"

Brooke had to hide a smile. "Yes I can," she said. This wasn't a lazy student, contrary to what Mrs. Starr might think.

"My dad teaches me better than Mrs. Starr, so I do my work in class, but when she starts teaching silly stuff I figure my dad's right and I stop listening."

Precocious girl.

"Tell me about what you like to do outside of school."

"I take ballet lessons. And I love cats, only my dad won't let me have one." She leaned in and whispered, "It's kind of a secret, but my Grandpa Miller's cat is having kittens, and he promised to talk my dad into letting us keep one."

"I won't say a word," Brooke whispered back as they entered the office.

At Angela's request, Brooke stayed close by while the school nurse examined the injury and stopped the bleeding. To Brooke's relief, the cut turned out to be tiny despite the amount of blood. The nurse called Angela's father, but couldn't reach him. She almost called the "emergency neighbor number" on her school record, but Angela wanted her father, so the nurse promised to keep trying his work number for a few more minutes. This comforted Angela, but to her dismay Brooke had to return to class before they reached him.

"Can't you stay just a little while? I'm sure my dad will come soon."

"I'm sorry, I can't. My class is waiting for me." Brooke gave her a small hug, then pulled back and patted her shoulder. "You'll be just fine," she assured her. "I want you to come by my classroom in the next day or two to let me know how everything turns out, all right?"

Angela nodded. "Okay."

Brooke left and headed for the auditorium. As she walked down the dim hallway, she returned to her *Fiddler on the Roof* mind set. She began ticking off items she still had to accomplish before the first performance: fix the tear in Hodel's scarf, get a few more bed sheets for the "Matchmaker" number . . . She didn't notice the man in uniform walking toward her until she ran headlong into him. He had short brown hair.

She stepped back. "Oh, excuse me," she said, hoping the man was Officer Smith. She glanced up at him. Officer Stevens. She hoped the hallway was dark enough that he wouldn't recognize her. He did.

"Hello again," he said, flashing a smile.

Brooke stumbled over her words. "Oh, hello. What . . . what are you doing here?"

"I'm here to speak to the school about safety."

"Oh, that's right. The assembly. I almost forgot about it. But aren't you here a bit early, Officer?"

"Call me Greg. But I'm only about fifteen minutes early, from what the principal told me," he said, checking his watch.

Brooke looked at her own watch. She hadn't realized how long she'd been with Angela. There would be no time to run through the end of the play, and chances were that she wouldn't be able to get the gymnasium cleaned up in time for the rest of the school to descend on it. "I didn't realize it was so late," she said, taking a few backward steps down the hall.

The door at the end of the hall opened, and Joshua, one of her students, appeared. "There you are, Miss Williamson. Mrs. Walker sent me to find you. We're all waiting for you."

"Tell her I'll be right there." She could picture Mary Ellen's growing panic at the prospect of directing alone.

"Okay." Joshua turned around and headed back through the door.

Brooke was painfully aware of her hot cheeks and the sound of her heart beating. She glanced at her watch again and took a step down the hall. "I'd better go. They're waiting for me."

"Wait," he said before she could turn away. "You've got something on your cheek." He reached forward and wiped at her cheek with his thumb, which came away with a smudge of mud on it. Her hand flew to her check and tried to rub off any remaining dirt, vehemently wishing for a mirror.

"You got it all," he said with a grin.

Brooke nervously ran her hands through her hair and discovered a large section that had come loose from her barrette. She fumbled with it for a moment, then gave up and removed the barrette completely. "I'd better go."

"It was nice seeing you again . . . Miss Williamson," he called after her.

A ripple went down her back as he said her name. "My name is Brooke," she began, but couldn't find any other words to say. Half of her wanted to say that yes, it had been nice to see him too, but instead she could think of nothing but finding a mirror to fix her appearance. So instead of saying anything, she gave a pained smile before turning around and bolting down the hallway so quickly she nearly ran into the door.

As she entered the auditorium, she ran her fingers through her hair a few times in hopes of making it look presentable. Mary Ellen insisted that she looked fine, so Brooke tried to brush off the incident and focus on marshaling the fourth grade into cleaning the auditorium.

She miraculously accomplished it with five minutes to spare, then grew nervous again at the prospect of seeing Greg on the stage, speaking to the school. She and the other two teachers, Mary Ellen Walker and Maggie Sorensen, got the fourth grade settled on the carpeted gymnasium floor just as the rest of the school began filing in.

But the assembly didn't start on time. Ten minutes after it should have started, the gym began to buzz with impatient students. The principal finally stood up with a microphone and apologized, saying their speaker was on his way and should arrive any moment. Brooke's eyebrows came together in confusion. She had just seen Greg—Officer Stevens—in the hallway. But her students didn't give her much time to wonder, as she had to break up two arguments and remind several groups of girls to stop talking so loudly.

Five minutes later a police officer appeared on the stage, introduced himself as Officer Berry and began his presentation. Officer Berry wasn't nearly as good-looking as Greg, Brooke thought, then banished the thought as quickly as it had come.

CHAPTER 4

Except for two missed entrances and a handful of forgotten lines, both performances of the play went off relatively smoothly. When the cast came out for their final curtain call, Brooke stood in the back of the gym and clapped until her palms turned red. She could never enjoy her students' performances while they happened; she was far too nervous for that. But now that another one of her productions had ended without any catastrophic glitch, she couldn't contain her excitement and pride.

"Weren't they great?" Brooke whispered to Pat, who stood beside her.

"Which part? When Perchik missed his cue or when the music didn't come on for the first song in Act Two?" Pat whispered back.

Brooke laughed with her. "Oh, I meant when the clothesline fell down during 'Matchmaker.'"

Pat began clapping harder as Tevye's daughters came forward for a bow. "Seriously, for ten-year-olds, I am really impressed. I'm glad I finally got to see one of your productions."

With the curtain calls completed, the student actors and parents milled about to find each other and share their excitement.

Tricia's parents came up, beaming with pride. "Thank you for working so hard with her," her father said, giving Tricia a squeeze. "She's done nothing for the past few weeks but memorize lines and sing her solo around the house."

Her mother's head bobbed with excitement and she added, "Her confidence has simply blossomed. I know these plays are a lot of work, but we want you to know how much we appreciate everything you put into them."

"You're welcome," Brooke said, giving Tricia a squeeze from the side. "I am so proud of you. Just wait until you get into high school. You'll blow them away, and they'll just have to cast you in all the lead roles."

Tricia giggled at the thought. "Thanks, Miss Williamson."

Maggie came over and put her arm around Brooke. "Too bad you won't be around next year, Tricia. I'm going to try to convince Miss Williamson to do *Hamlet*. You'd make a great Ophelia."

Brooke laughed. "I don't know about attempting Shakespeare."

As the crowd gradually thinned, Brooke looked at the empty stage. Folding her arms tightly, she sighed.

"Why the long face?" Pat asked.

Brooke shrugged. "It's just . . . last month Christopher and I spent a couple of nights together painting the set." She smiled. "It was fun."

Pat reached over and pulled her sister into her arms, and Brooke held her tightly as two bright tears squeezed out from between her lashes and fell down her cheeks. "I miss what it could have been," she whispered.

Pat nodded. "I know."

* * *

For the last half hour of school on Monday, Brooke held a cast party for the fourth grade. It wasn't anything big, only cookies, brownies, and a pitcher of lemonade, plus a few balloons, but she knew from past experience that students loved post-play parties. When the final bell rang and her students raced out the doors, only crumbs and a few cookie halves remained on the plates. She stood at the door and gave each student a high five, then returned to tidying up the room. She didn't mind cleaning up after the inevitable spill or two, especially when she considered how much the students enjoyed themselves—and how much she enjoyed watching them.

She popped a piece of cookie into her mouth, then began collecting paper plates, cups, and napkins from around the room. As she brushed some crumbs from a desk into the garbage can, she heard a small voice coming from the door.

"Miss Williamson?"

Brooke made a final swipe of the desk, then turned around. "Yes? Oh hello, Angela," she said, pleased she'd remembered the girl's name. She smiled and put down the garbage can. "How is your cut?"

Angela stepped into the room. She carried a small, lopsided cake smeared with pink icing. "It's okay. I had to get a few stitches though. At least they didn't shave off any of my hair. Dad says they do that sometimes."

Brooke grinned broadly and crossed the distance between them to look at the injury. "You sure got lucky," she said, looking at the three blue stitches below Angela's hairline. "Does it hurt?"

Angela shook her head. "Not anymore. At least, not unless I hit it when I brush my hair. I keep doing that." She made a little grimace. "I made this for you all by myself," she said, holding out the cake. "Well, except for putting it in and taking it out of the oven. Dad did that. I'm not allowed to use the oven alone till I get bigger. Anyway, thank you for helping me feel better when Jacob threw the rock at me."

"And thank you for the cake, Angela," Brooke said, taking the offering from the young girl's outstretched hands. "This means a lot to me. And I'm sure it'll taste as good as it looks."

A smile crept across Angela's face and she stood a bit taller. "I hope I get you for my teacher when I'm in fourth grade."

"I hope so too."

Angela took a step toward the door. "I'd better go. I promised Dad I'd hurry."

"Thanks again, Angela."

"You're welcome." Angela lifted a hand and waved. "Bye."

Angela disappeared, and Brooke eyed the cake with a smile. The icing had large chocolate crumbs in it, and an awkward hand had scrawled *Thank You* across the top in pink. For a seven-year-old, it was a pretty good attempt. Brooke set the cake on a desk so she could finish cleaning up, but decided to take a fingerful of icing first. No sooner had she stuck her index finger in her mouth, than another voice came from the door.

"Hello again."

She whipped around, her finger stuck ungracefully in her mouth, to see none other than Greg Stevens at her classroom door, this time in civilian clothes. She quickly licked her finger clean and desperately hoped she didn't have pink icing between her teeth.

"Um, hi. I . . . I didn't expect to see you. What are you doing here?"

He took a step into the classroom with a sheepish grin. "You'd think it was fate the way we've been meeting each other lately."

Brooke gave a nervous laugh in response. "Something like that." She went back to cleaning the room and wiped at her teeth with one finger. She could feel her cheeks getting hot.

"Hey, I've got an idea," Greg said, snapping his fingers as if it had just occurred to him. "Since we can't seem to escape each other, why don't we go out sometime?"

Brooke's hand froze as she reached for another cup. She turned toward him slowly, her eyebrows raised into an arch. "Excuse me?"

"How about Saturday night?"

Brooke leaned against a desk and folded her arms. "I'm going to keep running into you until I accept, aren't I?"

Greg shrugged in spite of the grin plastered across his face. "Looks like the fates have it in for us, if you believe in that kind of thing. Besides," he said with a mock threatening look, "I know where you work."

"Fine then," Brooke said in her best martyr's voice. "Saturday it is. Say, seven, seven-thirty?"

"Better make it eight-thirty. I have another commitment until then."

"Eight-thirty it is."

* * *

Brooke had been home not more than ten minutes when the phone rang. The caller ID registered Pat's number from California. Her sister had returned home just two days before. But she and Pat often had long phone calls after her trips, since they never got "talked out" when she visited. Brooke plopped onto the sofa as she answered the phone.

"Hey Pat."

"Hey big sister." It didn't take them long to get talking. Somewhere around the thirty-minute mark, Pat brought up Greg and getting pulled over by Officer Smith. "I still think you should have given him your number. Or given it to the other cop when he pulled you over."

"That has been remedied," Brooke said. "I'm going out with Greg on Saturday night."

"Oooooh," Pat squealed. "How did that happen? When did you see him again? How old is he? He's not much over thirty, is he?" Brooke laughed. Pat had a theory that for every year past age thirty a man remained single, he got progressively weirder.

"I don't know how old he is."

"I mean, you want someone close to your age, and you'll be thirty in a few months." Pat paused, considering. "I wonder if he's younger than you are. He could be, you know."

"It's not like a couple of years would make much difference anyway," Brooke said. "Besides, I'm tired of getting asked out by single men going on fifty. A man near my own decade would be nice."

Pat had a mind of her own and breezily changed the direction of the conversation. "You have to call me after your date. I mean, wouldn't it be great if he was the one? Talk about a romantic way to meet, helping you in a crisis at the van. He probably carries a gun, even when he's off duty. He could use it to defend you sometime."

"He's not John Wayne," Brooke interjected.

"Oh, I know," Pat said. "But can't you let your sister have a little fantasy now and then? I mean, if this worked out, the two of you could have some great stories to tell your kids, like how Daddy saved Mommy from a nasty gang of—"

"A gang of what, horse thieves?" Brooke laughed. "You've been watching too many movies, Pat. And I think you're jumping the gun just a bit."

"No pun intended?"

Brooke went on as if she hadn't heard the comment. "We haven't been on a single date and you're talking about our children. Don't you think that's a bit premature?"

Pat sighed. "I know. But I want you to find that special someone already. Maybe this Greg guy isn't the one, but I know there is someone out there, just waiting for you."

"At this rate he's been waiting a really long time." Some of Brooke's high-school classmates had children nearly the same age as her students.

"I'm sure there's a reason for that." Pat giggled at a sudden thought. "I know. Maybe your future husband is eight years younger than you, and you had to wait for him to grow up and get off his mission."

"Cute, Pat. Real cute."

"No, wait. Maybe you'll find him in another six years, and you'll realize he was in the first class you ever taught." Pat laughed uncontrollably now, and Brooke decided that the benefits of this particular call had come and gone.

"I should let you go, Pat."

Pat's laughter eventually calmed down, although Brooke could imagine Pat wiping her eyes and probably bursting into laughter again after hanging up. "All right," Pat said between giggles. "Let me know how your date goes. Make sure you find out if he's over thirty."

CHAPTER 5

As Brooke got ready for her date with Greg, she wished she had asked him how formally to dress. She picked through her closet for nearly an hour, taking out one outfit, holding up another in front of the mirror, putting each back again. She finally decided on a chambray shirt and a new pair of jeans, something she felt attractive as well as comfortable in. *Now watch, he'll take me hiking or something.* She shook off the thought, then added a spray of perfume and a bit of lipstick.

The clock seemed to move alarmingly fast, and with her last few moments she looked herself over in the mirror, wondering why she wanted to make such a good impression on this guy. She knew she could never make another first impression, but hoped she could undo at least some awkward impressions she had already made. She didn't want to think about why she cared to do even that much.

At 8:32 the doorbell rang, and Brooke hurriedly put on her pearl earrings as a final touch before opening the door. "Hello, Officer—I mean Greg," she said. "Come in." She backed up and motioned for him to enter. As he passed, she noticed that he wore a red button-down shirt and what looked like relatively new jeans. She had guessed pretty close; at least they wouldn't be hiking.

As she closed the door behind him, she noticed the cowboy boots on his feet. Her eyebrows went up. What kind of guy was this? *Tell me we aren't going to a rodeo.* He didn't strike her as the kind of guy who chewed on straw and ate half-raw steaks. But *cowboy boots?*

He brought his arm from behind his back, revealing a small bouquet of three yellow irises. "I'm a little rusty at this dating thing, but I got these for you. I hear that yellow is the color of friendship. And I've always liked irises."

"Me too." Brooke smiled and took the flowers. *Irises instead of roses. At least he's original. Christopher never bought me flowers.*

"I'll just put them in some water before we go." She headed toward the kitchen, wondering what he meant by being "rusty" at dating. *Please don't be divorced. I don't want to deal with that kind of baggage. What if he has a bunch of kids and an ex-wife?* She had never given a man with baggage half a chance. Usually she managed to find out such details before a first date. As she filled a vase with water, she reminded herself to calm down and stop jumping to conclusions— just enjoy the evening.

Meanwhile, Greg looked around the town house. "I really like the way you've decorated," he said. "Some women have nothing but frilly things on the walls. I can't stand that stuff. This is really nice. In fact, my place could use a feminine touch like yours."

Brooke never expected this kind of compliment from the men she knew. "Thank you," she said as she placed the flowers on the kitchen table and returned to the living room.

"Shall we?" Greg held out an arm and motioned for the door. Brooke snagged her purse from the couch, took his arm, and they headed out.

When they reached the truck and he unlocked it, Brooke put her hand out to open the door, but Greg stopped her. "I may be old-fashioned, but I think that's my job. If you don't mind."

Brooke couldn't keep a smile from crossing her face. "I don't mind at all." She took a step back and let him open her door.

When Greg had settled into his seat and started the engine, Brooke said, "So, where are we going?"

He pulled onto the street before answering. "I thought we'd do something a little more original than a movie. I've always thought that sitting silently in a dark room doesn't help two people get to know each other."

"All right, so where *are* we going?"

"Ever been country dancing?"

Brooke glanced at his cowboys boots, suddenly and painfully aware of the country music coming from the radio. "No, and I don't have the slightest idea how to either."

"It's easy. Just wait. Before the night is out, you'll be dancing like a pro." He saw her eyeing the radio. "Not much of a country fan I take it?"

"I've never really heard that much of it," she said, not adding that it was by choice.

As they sat at a stoplight, Greg popped in a CD. "I'll break you in easy then," he said with a smile. Guitar and a soothing voice wafted from the speakers. "Are you familiar with John Denver?"

"I've heard some of his songs," Brooke said with a nod. "You know, the classic ones everyone knows, 'Country Roads,' 'Rocky Mountain High,' and this one." She pointed to the stereo, indicating the song that was playing. "Wasn't it written for his wife?"

He nodded. "It's called 'Annie's Song.' I've always loved it." Greg shrugged. "Even if their marriage did end up in divorce."

"It did?" Brooke said in dismay. "I didn't know that. How sad. That ruins the song."

Greg waved the idea away. "Then I shouldn't have mentioned it. Forget I said anything."

Brooke eyed the stereo for a minute. "So you consider John Denver 'country'?"

"He's one of the all-time kings of country," Greg said emphatically.

"I've always thought of country music as those twangy songs that whine about their lost loves and broken saddles."

Greg pulled a face and laughed out loud. "To be honest, I still can't stand *those* songs. But country music has come a long way since then, and few artists bother with that kind of stuff anymore. I think you'll be surprised." He pulled into the parking lot of the dance hall. Out of habit, Brooke reached for her door. "No you don't," Greg said suddenly, almost sternly.

Brooke's hand pulled back as if she had touched something hot, and only then realized what she had done wrong. She felt a bit awkward waiting for him to come all the way around the truck to open her door, but at the same time enjoyed the pampered feeling. Christopher never opened her doors. The idea would have never even crossed his mind. *It's been a long time since anyone has treated me like a lady,* she thought.

Instead of heading for the dance hall, Greg opened the door of the extended cab and pulled out a pair of cowboy boots. "Here. Try these on. You can't country dance in those shoes."

Brooke glanced at her small leather flats as she took the boots from his hands. "Why not?"

"You'll understand once you've been on the floor a few minutes."

"All right," Brooke said, leaning against the truck as she switched her footwear.

"I hope they fit," Greg said.

Brooke slid her feet into the boots and felt around the insides with her toes. "There's a little extra room, but they feel all right."

"Good. Let's go." Brooke tossed her shoes into the truck and Greg closed it.

Brooke eyed the practically new boots as she tested them out with her weight. "Where did you get these?"

"Borrowed them from a neighbor across the street. She hasn't been dancing since her baby was born, so she let me borrow them for tonight." He took her hand and headed toward the doors of the dance hall.

Brooke entered with trepidation, and went onto the floor only after much coaxing. She told Greg she wanted to watch the dancing for a few minutes before trying it, but Greg insisted the best way to learn wasn't watching, but getting on the floor and doing it. As Brooke tentatively let Greg take her hand and lead her onto the dance floor, she felt odd; usually she had to coax her date to do something daring or out of the ordinary, not the other way around. But in those cases, she had been perfectly comfortable in her own little world, and was trying to bring someone else in to join her. This time she was the one standing in alien territory, and she suddenly understood why Christopher had felt so squeamish about his first time snowboarding. She no longer thought he had been such a wimp about it.

But then, she had always been somewhat of a control freak. Perhaps Brooke had over-compensated, dragging other people into situations where she felt comfortable and in command. The dark dance floor loomed before her, a place where she had absolutely no control. Greg took both her hands, and gently led her in and out of the basic step. Brooke got the hang of that one quickly enough.

"Relax," Greg called over the music. "It's supposed to be fun."

"It's hard to relax when you're concentrating," she said helplessly.

"You're doing fine," Greg insisted. And he was right. Not two songs later, Brooke could look around at other couples on the floor instead of clenching her jaw. When a couple about fifteen feet off starting doing lifts, she motioned toward them. "Don't do anything like that soon," she said, half-joking, half-serious, as Greg led her into a turn.

Greg shook his head. "Don't worry about that. I won't try that until at least, oh, your second time out."

Brooke's eyes grew wide. "You'd try *that* next time?"

Brooke blushed, realizing the implication that there would be a next time. Greg grinned. "Okay, maybe your third time out. Trust me, that's not too hard. I know a lot more impressive moves than that, although it's been a long time since I've done them. I'm a bit rusty."

"You don't look rusty to me." They danced for a few more minutes, Greg leading her into a new move every so often, sometimes with warning, sometimes without, and each time Brooke managed to follow along without too much trouble.

"You're doing really well," Greg said over the music.

"So far so good," Brooke said, glad she hadn't embarrassed either of them. She had even started to enjoy herself and let go a bit.

"The great thing about country dancing," Greg said as the song ended, "is that it doesn't matter if you're on the beat, so there's a lot less to think about."

"Less? It's a good thing there isn't more to think about. I've been concentrating so hard that my brain feels like Jell-O."

Greg took her hand and pulled her off the floor. A tingle raced through her arm and set her heart beating a hair faster. "Come on, let's take a break and get something to drink."

Brooke followed him off the dance floor to the refreshment bar, where he ordered two root beers. Brooke stretched her feet out in the boots. "You're right. I couldn't have done all that in my other shoes. But I couldn't tell you why. If I end up doing more country dancing, I'll have to get some boots of my own." Brooke turned to her root beer and took a long drink. She hadn't realized how thirsty she was.

"So, what kind of music do you usually listen to?" Greg asked after gulping down half his drink in seconds.

Brooke flushed before answering. "You'll think I'm silly."

"Hey, I risked you thinking I'm a complete hick by bringing you here. Take a chance."

"You'll laugh."

"I swear I won't." Greg raised a hand as if making an oath. "I promise."

She braced herself. "All right. My favorite album is ABBA Gold."

At first Greg's face registered surprise, followed by disbelief. "ABBA? As in platform shoes and disco?"

Brooke turned back to her drink. "Forget it. I knew you'd think it's silly."

"I didn't say it was silly. I just haven't known anyone who liked their music . . . this decade." Brooke shot him a look, but then they both laughed. "I'm kidding. To be honest, I don't know that I'd recognize more than one or two of their songs, so I can't give a fair opinion. But hey, you've indulged me tonight. Maybe you can educate me about the joys of ABBA sometime."

"I'd like that."

They danced for another hour or so before calling it a night. Leaving the dance hall, they decided to take a walk to cool off in the crisp night air. As they walked around the city streets, they talked about a variety of subjects. Greg asked about her teaching and as she told him about one of her student's oral reports he took her hand. While holding Greg's hand didn't seem at all odd, Brooke still got flustered and stumbled over her next few words. Greg gave her hand a gentle squeeze of reassurance, and Brooke soon felt at ease. The two of them continued to talk for a long time, as if they had known each other forever. But in the back of Brooke's mind she never once forgot that she didn't know this man. At all. She loved being with him, but wanted to know more about him—like what was behind his comment at being "rusty" at dating. But she didn't dare ask.

"Let's see. So far I know that you teach fourth grade and that you just broke up with that guy I saw you with at the accident," Greg said. "To be honest, I was afraid you might not be ready to date so soon. I almost didn't ask you out."

"No, I'm glad you did. It's good for me to get out and move on. Besides, the whole relationship was doomed. There were a lot of things that didn't feel right."

"Such as?"

"Specifically? For one thing, his mother. She has firm opinions on everything, and he stands by her side. I couldn't be with someone who wouldn't stand by me. Maybe I'm selfish, but when I get married, I expect to be number one. I refuse to take second place to anyone else, even his mother. It's not right." Brooke glanced over at Greg and realized that his mood had suddenly grown somber. His step slowed and then stopped. She chastised herself for mentioning marriage on a first date. She tried to lighten up the tension. "Don't tell me you live with your mother too," she said with a laugh.

Greg didn't laugh back. Instead, he gazed over her shoulder at the shadows, immersed in his own thoughts. For a minute Brooke panicked, hoping her marriage comment hadn't scared him off, then wondering if he *did* live with his mother.

"No, I don't live with my mother," Greg finally said. But his light mood was gone. He turned back toward the truck. Brooke replayed the moment in her mind over and over, wishing she had kept her mouth shut, at the same time not knowing what had caused the change. What had she said?

And she had learned almost nothing about Greg. He had asked so much about her all during their walk that she had done most of the talking, so all she knew about him was that he had had his thirtieth birthday last February, so he was acceptable under Pat's age requirement. Brooke herself would be thirty in August. He also said he had grown up right here in Utah Valley. From the way he said it, Brooke thought that he would have liked to move elsewhere, and she wondered why he hadn't. If he wasn't married, what was keeping him in the valley, let alone the state? Hopefully not his mother.

The somber mood lasted most of the way to the truck, and Brooke didn't want to ruin things more by prying into his personal life. Fortunately, when they reached the truck, his somber mood lifted, and his lighthearted tone returned. They talked and laughed as he drove her home. All too soon they stood at her door, and an awkward feeling arose in Brooke's stomach. She fingered her keys nervously, wondering how to act for the "doorstep moment."

Normally she didn't have a problem with it, hadn't since high school. Generally she had the control, and that was that. She had several versions of doorstep moments and could always pick the appropriate one for how she felt about her date. If she put her hand on the doorknob, her date would generally get the hint that she wanted to get inside. Now. Alone. She had also learned how to give the message quite confidently that she wouldn't mind something more than a friendly hug. But Greg had her heart beating so hard and her stomach doing so many flip-flops that she felt like a sixteen-year-old on her first date, and she didn't know how to act or what to say.

"I had a great time," Greg said.

"Me too." She fingered her keys again during the awkward silence that followed.

"So when do I get to hear some ABBA?"

Brooke looked up with a surprised smile. "Any time you're free." Once again she wanted to bite her tongue. Her voice had sounded desperate. Greg didn't seem to mind, or notice.

"How about next Saturday?"

Brooke hadn't expected anything so definite, or so soon. She hoped her surprise wasn't too obvious. "Sure. That would be great. What time?"

"Same time?"

"Eight-thirty? I'll look forward to it."

"I'll bring dinner, and you can spend the evening educating me about disco. Maybe we can even watch a disco movie, or Richard Simmons's *Sweatin' to Disco*, or whatever that one's called."

Brooke laughed. "Just because I like some disco music doesn't mean I like disco movies—or workout videos for that matter."

"Then I'll let you pick the movie."

"Fair enough. Maybe something with John Denver."

Greg vetoed the idea. "Nah. He wasn't much of an actor. I prefer listening to him in the mountains to watching him drive around with George Burns smoking cigars."

They lapsed into silence, and once again Brooke's heart began beating heavily with a life of its own. "I'll see you Saturday then," she said, wondering if she should turn to the door.

Greg leaned down. Brooke held her breath. She braced herself for a kiss, but instead he gave her a firm yet gentle hug before pulling away. "Good night," he said softly, inches from her ear.

"Good night." Brooke's trembling hands managed to slip her key in the lock and open the door. She went in and closed the door behind her, then leaned against it hard. It would be a long week.

CHAPTER 6

As Brooke walked in the door after school on Wednesday, the phone rang. She glanced at the caller ID out of habit before answering, then reeled back at the sight of the Morris family number. Her hand trembled as she lifted the receiver. Before she could speak, Christopher did.

"Hi, Brooke. It's me. I'm glad you're home. I have to talk to you."

Brooke dropped to the couch and strained to find her voice. "Hello . . . I . . . didn't expect to hear from you . . ." Her voice trailed off. For days she had pictured entire conversations between them if he ever decided to call, but now that he had, she didn't know what to say.

He paused. "I feel terrible about how I acted the other night. You were being honest about your feelings, and I lashed out. It was wrong, and I'm sorry." He let out a breath.

Brooke's heart beat heavily at the soft tone in his voice, which belonged to the old Christopher. Her stomach fluttered in a way it hadn't in weeks, in a way she thought it never would again for him. "Thanks, Christopher. That means a lot to me."

"I've missed you so much. But this last week and a half has been good for me. Gave me some time to think, and you know what? You're right, some things need to change. I'm willing to try if you're willing to give me another chance."

Brooke's fingers rubbed her forehead as she struggled with conflicting emotions. She had spent more than a week trying to keep the good times with Christopher out of her mind and focus solely on the reasons she had had to break off the relationship. She had to bury it all, since she had been so sure the two of them could never work. And she thought she had succeeded rather well.

But now . . . what if he was willing to change? Should she give him a second chance? When she didn't answer right away, he went on.

"Could I see you sometime? Even if you don't want to pursue 'us' again, I'd like a chance to end things on a better note."

"I'd like that." Anything to remove the sting from their last meeting.

"I thought we could go see a late showing of that new romantic comedy you wanted to see. Maybe Saturday night?"

Brooke nearly choked as ABBA and Greg came to mind. "How about lunch? I'm busy that evening." Images of Christopher and Greg stood side by side in her mind, both competing for attention.

"You're busy? With what?" He chuckled. "I mean, you don't have a date already or anything, do you?"

"Christopher, I just have plans—"

"You *do* have a date. Who is he?"

Brooke was not about to answer that one. Christopher would hardly react well if he found out that her date was the officer at the scene of their accident. "He came to Canyon Crest to speak at an assembly." She didn't need to mention that he didn't actually speak or that she had met him before that. She hoped it would be enough.

"Fine. A late lunch it is then."

* * *

Ten years ago Brooke would have loved a day like Saturday: two dates, both with good-looking men who were interested in her. But instead Brooke was a complete wreck all morning. For lunch with Christopher she purposely dressed in neutral colors, a white blouse and khaki slacks, and didn't do anything special with her hair and makeup. She didn't want to give him any hopes of their future until she had made up her own mind.

When the doorbell rang she said a silent prayer to give her strength and discernment of her feelings. She also needed help deciphering Christopher's true intentions. She put on a smile and opened the door to see Christopher grinning broadly and holding a large bouquet of red roses.

"Roses for a rose."

Brooke hardly knew what to say, although her mind went back to Greg's simple grouping of yellow irises. "They're beautiful. Thank you." Christopher leaned in for a kiss, but Brooke took a step back.

"What?" he asked, pulling back.

"We are not back together."

"Yet?" he added hopefully.

"Maybe," she said. Christopher's eyes dulled slightly, but Brooke tried not to look at them. Her future and their relationship hinged on a lot more than his hopes.

For old times' sake, Christopher took her to the ice-cream parlor, where they ordered pistachio ice cream and french fries. He talked of the night they met, and soon Brooke found herself laughing at the memories. He reached across the small table for her hands.

"Don't you see, Brooke? The past three months are too good to just give up on. This could be forever."

His hands were warm, and his touch made it hard for Brooke to swallow. She had to wrestle down the urge to kiss him, and instead forced herself to look into his eyes and speak with her mind instead of her heart.

"Not without some changes." She spoke in almost a whisper.

Christopher nodded. "Okay. For starters, I'm looking for an apartment right now. Mother doesn't like the idea of my moving out, of course. We had a pretty good fight, but I stood my ground. She sulked for days, but I didn't give in."

"Really?"

He nodded. "I know it's not a lot, but at least it's a start, right?" He squeezed her hands. "So can we give it another shot?"

She almost said yes, but instead surprised herself by saying, "Maybe. Let's take this one step at a time."

Christopher let go of her hands and leaned back in his chair, disappointment written all over his face. "But why? What else can I do to convince you?" He stared out the window in frustration until a thought apparently struck him. He turned to look at her. "It's that guy you're going out with tonight, isn't it?"

Brooke swallowed hard at his nasty tone. In her one date with Greg she had found something different from every other man she had dated—something definitely different from Christopher. She had a strong desire to explore that something. Besides, she wasn't ready to reenter the Morris world yet, not until she was sure things had really changed. She wouldn't have any proof of that until Christopher actually put down a deposit on an apartment and packed his bags.

"It's more complicated than that," she began.

"Yeah, I'll bet it is," Christopher muttered. Abruptly, he stood up and cursed under his breath as he snatched his coat. "Fine. Then go back to your new boyfriend and break his heart too." He kicked the leg of his chair and grunted. "I don't know why I bothered to try."

He stormed out of the restaurant, leaving Brooke alone to foot the bill and find a way home. When the server returned, Brooke asked for the check, embarrassment washing over her face like a wave. She wished Greg would show up out of the blue again. She could use his friendly face about now. She paid for the check and left the building, fighting tears of humiliation and anger.

Why had she even considered getting back together with Christopher? The shove in the car had shown her the true colors of Christopher Morris, a side that wouldn't be going away any time soon. She wiped at her eyes with the back of her hand and walked quickly, hoping others on the street wouldn't notice the tears burning trails down her face.

When she finally got home she collapsed on the bed and sobbed. The phone rang, but she didn't move. *Let the machine get it*, she thought. *If I hear Greg leaving a message, I'll answer.*

"Brooke, what a relief to finally find your number. This is the sixth 'Williamson' I've tried. This is Janet Lambert. I mean, Janet *Morris* Lambert, Christopher's sister. We met at the family's Easter dinner. I hope you remember me. I had to reach you before . . ." Her voice cracked. "Oh, Brooke, he's not well."

Brooke sat up straight. Her tears suddenly dried up. She leapt for the phone. "Janet, hi. What's wrong?"

"It's Christopher. He's having an episode, and from what we can gather, it seems like it may have been triggered by something that happened between you two. Do you know what it could have been?"

Brooke's mind spun in circles. *An episode? What does that mean?*

"Do you know what it could have been?" Janet asked again. "Did something happen between you two?"

Brooke ripped herself out of her thoughts. "We broke up about two weeks ago. Technically, I guess I did the breaking up."

"That would do it," Janet said with a weary sigh. "Did it have anything to do with his . . . problem? I mean, is that why you decided to break it off?"

"I don't know what you're talking about," Brooke said in a fuzzy haze. "Once he mentioned a thyroid condition and referred to something else taken care of years ago, but he didn't elaborate on it."

Janet sighed. "That sounds like him. It's been all we could do to keep him taking his medication. We insisted he live with Mother so she can keep an eye out for him, because he thinks he's cured. 'It's been two years since my last episode, Mother. I'm fine,' he always says."

"What do you mean, 'episodes'?" Brooke asked.

"I'm sorry, I thought you knew. Christopher has a bipolar disorder . . . manic depression. As long as he stays on his medication, he's perfectly fine, but it looks like he's been pretending to take it for a couple of months. When you figure he's been off his meds, and summer is coming—that's usually when those things—" She paused, then said, "Then add a trigger like breaking up . . ." Janet sighed deeply. "It was a disaster waiting to happen."

Brooke sat back, reeling, trying to digest all the new information, but still not knowing exactly what it meant. "So he's really depressed right now because of the breakup?" Brooke began, trying to understand. "And so he's having an . . . *episode?*"

"At least we think so. His symptoms started a couple of weeks ago, and he's showing all the same ones as before. He's irritable, secretive, staying up all night . . . We haven't been able to get him to a doctor to confirm it yet. We're all very worried about him and what he might try to do."

Brooke shook her head as if doing so might clear out the clutter of thoughts bombarding her mind. She thought of his violent behavior and aggressive attitude earlier that day. He really seemed like a different man than the one she had been interested in. Did she really cause this extreme change? "So I guess you want me to do something, like go talk to him?"

"Actually, no. It would be better for both of you not to have any contact, at least for now. I was just calling for your sake."

"For *my* sake? Why?"

"Well, to warn you. When he gets depressed he is obsessed with death. He feels it's the only solution. His own death . . . and possibly others'," she added hesitantly. "We're doing all we can, but thought you ought to know so you can take precautions. He's never seriously hurt anyone, but Carrie—you remember her, my younger sister?—she had to go to the emergency room during his last one two summers ago. It wasn't life threatening, but he beat her up pretty good."

Brooke thought back to the last few weeks. This news did explain his bizarre behavior, but that was secondary. Her heart beat with fear at what could have happened. "So why does he react this way? Is it the disorder, or the medication, or what?"

"It's fairly complex really. Not all people diagnosed with a bipolar disorder react so violently. A lot are fine with treatment. But given Christopher's already explosive personality, and . . ." Janet's voice trailed off. It was as though she couldn't even express the stress all of it had put her family through. "I just thought you should know," she finished meekly.

Hearing the pain in Janet's voice, Brooke realized how difficult it must have been for Janet to make such a call. "Thank you for calling, Janet. If you need anything, let me know."

"I will. I'm staying with Mother indefinitely, until this blows over. He keeps sneaking out of the house, so if you see or hear from him, please call me here."

"I will," Brooke said.

After hanging up, Brooke stared at the phone. She tried not to blame herself for causing Christopher's relapse. Looking back, she could see moments that pointed to something not being quite right with him, but not sure what to make of them she had shrugged them off.

She blinked, breaking her gaze, when she noticed the clock on her nightstand. She jumped to her feet. Greg would arrive in twenty minutes. She ran to the bathroom, shoving all thoughts of Christopher to the side. He had some serious problems, but she could do nothing to help him now. She refused to let him ruin her date with Greg. She glanced at the tub, wishing she could take a long soak. Instead, she hurriedly tried to mask the evidence of her tears with makeup, followed by fixing her wind-tossed hair. With five minutes to spare, she hurried to her closet and abandoned her neutral clothing in favor of a peach-colored blouse and a pair of jeans that she knew flattered her figure.

Even hastily getting ready to see Greg cheered her up, not to mention that the mere thought of him sent a ripple of goose bumps down her back. By the time the doorbell rang her mood had improved, and she hoped she could spend an evening with Greg without even thinking about her conversation with Janet.

She opened the door to see Greg, bearing dinner as promised. "I hope you like Chinese," he said as he stepped in.

Brooke recognized the containers from one of her favorite restaurants, a small place few people knew existed. "I love Chinese food." Before closing the door, she glanced into the parking lot as if Christopher might be lurking out there. She closed the door tight and bolted it.

She found a tablecloth and spread it on the living room floor, where Greg laid out the food. Brooke put her CD player on the floor and popped in her ABBA Gold CD, and Christopher finally faded from her thoughts.

As Brooke cued the CD to one of her favorite songs, she said, "Most people don't know this, but at one point, ABBA actually sold more albums worldwide than the Beatles. At least, that's what I heard somewhere." She turned up the volume as "Fernando" began and confessed, "I love this one." When the chorus came, she began to sing along, unaware that she did so. "'There was something in the air that night, the stars were bright, Fern—'"

Her voice caught when she realized that Greg was watching her. She blushed bright red and reached for her glass of water, taking a quick swallow.

"Sorry," she said sheepishly.

"Why? You have a great voice."

Brooke looked over her glass at him in surprise, wondering if he was being sarcastic, but his expression said otherwise.

"Have you ever sung professionally?" Greg asked.

Brooke shrugged and began pushing her beef-broccoli around her plate. "I'm not good enough for that. I took singing lessons in high school, and I've always been interested in the theater, especially musical theater." She waved off the idea with her fork. "But it's been years since I've been on stage, and even more since I've sung in public."

"But why? If it's something you love, why not do it? Especially since it's something you're obviously good at."

Brooke nearly snorted at his last comment as she remembered her audition. "I doubt everyone would agree with your opinion on that. The problem is that the older I get, the more I freeze up when I sing in front of people. When I sing in the car I can really let go, and sometimes I think I sound really good, but the minute I know anyone is listening to me, I sound like Kermit the Frog."

Greg reached for the two fortune cookies that lay on the floor between their plates, then held out his hand so she could take one. "Well, I think you should go for it. Get a teacher and try out for a play."

Brooke had to smile to herself as she took a cookie. She half wished that Christopher could overhear Greg's words now. "We'll see," she said. "Maybe sometime." She broke open her cookie and removed the white slip of paper.

Greg read his own fortune, then looked up. "'Look for the good in others.' Well, I just did that. What does yours say?"

She read it to herself, then laughed aloud. "I can't believe this."

"What?"

"'You will be rewarded by singing a different tune.'"

He chuckled, then popped a piece of fortune cookie into his mouth. "You'd better listen to that. It's your destiny."

"I don't put a lot of stock in fortune cookies." Brooke tossed the white paper to the side.

Greg retrieved the fortune from the edge of the tablecloth. "I don't know. It looks to me like you're a person who can't cheat fate. It didn't work with avoiding me, did it?" Brooke had to laugh aloud at that, and she shook her head. Greg persisted. "So it won't work with avoiding your talents either." He shrugged. "Hey, I hate to break it to you, but that's just the way it is."

Brooke gave him a skeptical look, but instead of a response, cued the CD to "Waterloo," another favorite. "You might recognize this one."

Several seconds into the song Greg began to nod. "I think I have heard this one." He wiped some sweet-and-sour sauce from his thumb and stood up. "Come on," he said, holding out a hand.

"What?" Brooke asked tentatively. Greg simply grinned and began moving to the beat. She stifled a giggle. "*What* are you doing?"

"What does it look like?" Greg asked. "And don't make me feel like an idiot. You'd better join me. I bet I can disco better than you can."

"Is that a challenge?" Brooke asked with a gleam in her eye. Soon the two of them were dancing around the room like John Travolta wanna-be's. As the song ended, they collapsed onto the couch in a heap of laughter. "I didn't know ABBA could be so much fun," she said between gasps. "I bet you can't dance like that to any of your country music."

"No, you can't," Greg agreed. He got a significant gleam in his eye. "But there are certain things you can't do to ABBA."

"Such as?"

"ABBA can't create . . . certain moods. Maybe I'll show you sometime." Greg grinned knowingly.

Brooke swallowed hard when she realized what he meant. She half wished he'd show her that night. She had imagined more than once what it would be like to kiss Greg Stevens, and wondered why he hadn't made the slightest move to try yet. *Not that a gentleman like him would. All in good time,* she had to remind herself. *Don't rush what could become a very good thing.*

Brooke tried not to hope that he'd do just that when he left; she didn't want to be disappointed if he didn't. As before, he gave her nothing more than a good hug before leaving, and as she closed the door behind him, she wondered if he wasn't attracted to her.

She went to the bathroom where she looked at the mirror and evaluated what she saw. Not bad, but definitely not twenty-two anymore. A few fine lines were beginning to develop around her eyes. She stood back a few more inches and squinted. At that distance they weren't so noticeable. She sighed and reached for her toothbrush.

As she got ready for bed, she consoled herself with the thought that at least he had wanted to see her again the next weekend, this time to convert her to country music. A thought struck her, and her head popped back up to face the bathroom mirror. A smile spread across her face.

Maybe then he'll show me what moods county music can create.

CHAPTER 7

As Brooke drove to work Monday morning, she turned up the volume on the car's stereo and belted out her best along with the cassette. The music playing was from one of her favorite Broadway musicals, *Into the Woods*. It was the story of what happens when several fairy tales collide in the forest. She had always loved Cinderella's part and imagined performing it. She often imagined performing the different roles. She thought Little Red Riding Hood's role as the sarcastic voice of reason would have been fun to play too, though she never pictured herself as the Witch, even in imagination. She was a bit more realistic than to even fantasize taking over the role that Bernadette Peters played on Broadway.

As Brooke sang along to "No One Is Alone," the mood of the song filled the car, and she pictured the devastated world around the four remaining characters on stage as they tried to piece their lives together and move on from the consequences of their actions.

"'Someone is on your side,'" she sang. "'Someone else is not.'" And suddenly, as a thought struck her, she stopped singing. Over the years Brooke had recognized a number of themes, symbols, and hidden meanings in the play, but this one had escaped her. Until now. Today the lyrics seemed to clash in her head like two cymbals.

Someone is on your side. Greg wanted her to pursue her talents. *Someone else is not.* Christopher wanted her to himself. *Christopher didn't encourage me to improve myself. He didn't want me to focus on anything but him.* Brooke realized that she never could have made that relationship work on her own. She felt even more confident in her decision to end her relationship with Christopher as she thought of how Greg encouraged her and introduced her to new things. He was interested in learning more about her and her interests, as well as sharing his own. She felt comfortable and optimistic when she was with Greg, not self-conscious and worried.

Greg had said she had talent. If that were true, she should pursue it. As Brooke pulled into a parking space at Canyon Crest, she swallowed hard to overcome the nervous knot in her stomach that formed as she made the decision. She would find a voice teacher. She didn't have the slightest idea where to look for one, but that didn't matter.

She spent most of her teaching day thinking about her plans, and wondered if she could find a teacher and perhaps even have a lesson before her Saturday date with Greg. If she could help it, he would not hear her sing any time soon, but she would love to be able to tell him that she had taken his advice to follow her dreams. At least partially. She didn't dare contemplate another audition too soon.

During lunch she walked through the library, where two mothers stood talking. Classes frequently had mother-helpers, and since the library stood in the center of the school, it tended to be a high-traffic area for mothers to take shortcuts to classes. The sight didn't surprise her, but their conversation stopped her cold.

"I always hate to lose promising vocal students, and Cindi was one of my best," the mother with strawberry blonde hair said.

The other mother nodded. "I imagine she'll want to start up again when she gets back from her dad's in the fall."

The first woman took out her planner and made a few notes. "In that case, I'll take her off Thursday."

The other mother apologized again, then left. Brooke approached the woman, her interest piqued. "Excuse me," she said. "I couldn't help but overhear you. You teach voice lessons?"

"Yes . . ." the woman answered slowly, eyeing Brooke curiously.

"Oh, I'm Brooke Williamson," she said, sticking out her hand to quell the woman's curious look. "I teach fourth grade."

The other woman shook Brooke's hand and nodded. "I'm Desaray Cahoon. I've heard of you. Aren't you the one who puts on the plays each year?"

"Guilty as charged." The bell rang, signaling the end of the lunch period. She glanced at the clock and hurried on. "I'm looking for a vocal coach. For myself."

"I generally teach younger students," Desaray began hesitantly. "My oldest student is about to graduate from high school."

"Oh, I wouldn't mind having recitals with young kids. I'm practically a beginner anyway. I took lessons in high school, but I've forgotten most of what I learned."

"All right," Desaray said. "As you probably heard, I have a new opening—Thursdays at four-thirty. Would that work for you?"

Brooke nearly did a Toyota jump. She nodded instead. "That would be a great time," she said, then fumbled through the papers she held, looking for a blank scrap. She wrote down her own name and number and asked for Desaray's number and address in return. Desaray opened her planner and jotted Brooke's name down on her Thursday schedule to make it official.

"All right then, I suppose I'll see you on Thursday," Desaray said. "Bring any sheet music you have and a blank cassette tape. Are you alto or soprano?"

"Soprano, in my better days. I don't know how high I can sing anymore."

"We'll get you back up there." Desaray scribbled a title on a page from her planner, ripped it out, and handed it to Brooke. "If you get a chance, you might want to buy that book. It's a great collection of Broadway songs for sopranos. My address is on the bottom."

"I already have that book," Brooke said. "I love it." She looked at the address and roughly pictured where Desaray lived. The halls began to buzz as students returned from recess. "Thank you," she called out as she hurried out of the library to meet her class. "I'll see you Thursday."

When she reached her class, she realized she didn't know how much Desaray would charge per lesson, but she brushed it off. Whatever the cost, it would be worth it.

* * *

Greg and vocal lessons took over Brooke's thoughts for the next few days. Christopher also managed to enter them here and there, like when she checked her caller ID and bolted her door each night. He left a few messages on her machine, each darker and more desperate than the last. Some referred to killing himself, others to her heartlessness. Sometimes she avoided listening to her messages, for fear of finding another one from Christopher.

More than once she had seen a tan car like his parked across the road from the school, and her stomach had turned over. No one had been sitting in the car, but the hair on her neck stood up nevertheless. She couldn't help but wonder if Christopher were watching her. She often peered around, wondering if he was hiding behind some bushes or a nearby building. She always hurried to her car and drove home a bit faster than she should have, then bolted the door as soon as she got inside. She was beginning to wonder if she ought to call the police, or her bishop, or someone.

On Wednesday evening she sorted through her sheet music, trying to decide what to bring along to her first voice lesson the following day. She was surprised to see just how much music she had accumulated with the intention of learning to sing the songs and play them on the piano. In addition to the book of Broadway show music Desaray had suggested, Brooke had a few books of music from Broadway shows, plus dozens of individual songs. She found several long-outdated tunes by Barry Manilow and Neil Diamond that as a kid she used to sing into the big, round Christmas bulbs that her parents always wound through the living room planter. She picked up her audition music and considered whether to include it, then tossed it aside.

* * *

Thursday afternoon she showed up at Desaray's home with a six-inch stack of music, which Desaray eagerly went through, setting some pieces aside as possibilities to start with. A few minutes later, Desaray let the stack drop to the floor beside the piano. "All right. Let's get started." Brooke expected Desaray to play some warm-up exercises on the piano while she sang along, but instead, Desaray went to the stereo, pushed the Play button and said, "Hit the floor."

"Excuse me?" Brooke asked, unsure what her new teacher meant.

"Just lie down, feet uncrossed, hands at your sides. First I want you to listen to some music as you practice breathing. You can use the pillow from the couch if you want." Brooke silently complied, but still wondered why she wasn't singing. Desaray seemed to read her mind as she returned from the stereo, the soothing New Age music floating through the room.

"Breathing is the most important part of singing," she explained. "It's the foundation for everything that comes after it, so it's best to focus on that before you confuse the issue with anything else. There are just too many other things to think about when you sing. You'll breathe for a few minutes before each lesson, and I hope you'll do it before you practice at home too. Today I want you to focus on using your diaphragm."

"All right." Brooke lay down, feeling a bit conspicuous.

"Pretend you've got a balloon in your belly. When you inhale, inflate the balloon to a count of eight with the music. Then exhale, slowly pushing the air out of the balloon, also to a count of eight. There's more to breathing than that, but it'll give you a good start and help you to relax. I've learned over the years that my students sing better after a few minutes of floor time. Helps to get rid of stress and to focus. Now close your eyes so you can concentrate and forget I'm here."

Brooke gratefully closed her eyes; she didn't feel so silly lying on the floor if she wasn't looking around the room. As she counted to the music, she found it surprisingly difficult to breathe in and out for a full eight counts each and realized this was why Desaray had had her focus on one deceptively simple task by itself. Desaray sorted through more music as Brooke lay breathing, occasionally giving Brooke reminders on how to do it correctly. A few minutes later, she told Brooke to get off the floor for warm-ups. Brooke caught a glimpse of the clock as she stood. She had been on the floor for over ten minutes. It felt closer to three.

Desaray popped a cassette into her tape player, sat down, then pushed Record. When she saw Brooke's questioning look, she said, "I want you to listen to your lessons at least once a week. It really helps to hear yourself. On the other side of the tape I'll record some of these warm-ups on the piano so you can do them anytime. All right. I call this one 'the hoot.' Do you know how to lift your palate?" Brooke nodded. "Good. This exercise will help strengthen that muscle, plus make a good space for the sound to resonate in. Pretend you've got an orange stuck in the back of your throat. Stretch your throat around it.

I'll play the scale, starting at the top and going down. It should sound sort of like an owl. I'll do it with you at first so you can hear what it should sound like."

Several exercises later, every muscle in Brooke's mouth and throat ached as if they had been through marathon training, including muscles she hadn't known existed. Desaray pulled out a few songs. "Now, let's hear you sing for real, so I can get an idea of where we're starting from."

Desaray selected songs somewhat randomly, most of which Brooke already knew or had at least heard before. The next thing Brooke knew, the tape player stopped, and she realized her lesson had gone several minutes overtime. Desaray turned the tape over and recorded the warm-up exercises, announcing each one on the tape before playing it. That took about five minutes, after which Desaray took the tape out and handed it to Brooke.

"There you go. Most lessons won't go this long, but I generally make an exception the first time. Remember to practice at least thirty minutes a day."

"I will," Brooke promised, putting the tape into her bag and gathering up her music.

Desaray handed her the pieces she had sung last. "You've got a great instrument in your voice," she said. "From what you said before, I didn't expect you to sound nearly so good."

Brooke's head came up in surprise. "Really?"

Desaray nodded. "Definitely. Of course, there's a lot to learn and work on, but the way I see it, people are either born with the instrument and simply need to be trained to use it, or they have to work on *developing* a vocal instrument and then have to learn how to use it. I was in the latter category. It took me years to get where you naturally are. You already have a beautiful instrument. I'm looking forward to helping you learn to play it even better."

CHAPTER 8

As he had for the last two weekends, Greg arrived at Brooke's door Saturday night shortly after eight-thirty. He had warned her to wear something comfortable and to bring along a sweater or jacket, but hadn't told her anything about his plans for the evening, except that John Denver would be on the agenda. As they walked to Greg's truck, Brooke thought she saw a man duck out of sight in the parking lot. Her heart beat a hair faster, and she craned her neck to see better, but couldn't make out more than a tan-colored car. It could have been any one of a hundred cars that looked just like Christopher's, but given its frequent presence at the school, she involuntarily sucked in her breath.

"Is something wrong?" Greg asked.

She squeezed his hand lightly and put on a smile. "Everything's fine. I just thought I saw someone I knew." Greg seemed to accept the explanation, but Brooke remained nervous. She remembered Pat's joke about Greg protecting her with a gun, and found herself holding Greg's hand a bit tighter.

Soon they were driving up Provo Canyon, where they found a large grassy area for the picnic Greg had packed. He returned to his truck for a boom box, some CDs, and a kerosene lamp for when it got dark. Brooke spread out the blanket, and Greg set out a bucket of KFC with the fixings, a thermos of hot chocolate, plus a box of miniature chocolate doughnuts.

Greg set the lamp on a picnic table. "The best place to listen to John Denver is close to nature," he explained as he situated everything on the blanket. "There we go," he said with satisfaction as he surveyed the feast. "Let's eat."

As before, they talked like old friends, with John Denver's music playing in the background. Sometimes Greg would offer tidbits about the songs: what had inspired John Denver to write this one, or what that one meant to Greg personally.

"I'd love to listen to this music for hours," Brooke said. "His voice is so simple. It's soothing somehow."

"Why don't you borrow these for a while then?" Greg handed her the case that held the two CDs.

"Are you sure?" She took the case carefully. "I mean, I know these mean a lot to you . . ."

"Take them for a week or two. Enjoy them."

"Thanks, I think I will," Brooke said. She put the case to her side, then decided to tell him about her latest accomplishment. "Looks like I'll be busy on Thursday afternoons for a while now."

Greg pulled a piece of chicken off a thigh. "Oh? How's that?"

"I'm taking voice lessons."

Greg lowered the chicken. "That's great! Sing something for me."

Brooke laughed. "Yeah right."

"Why not?"

"Because I'm just a beginner. Maybe someday I could invite you to a recital or something . . ." She flushed as she reached for a napkin, realizing the implication of what she had just said. Well, why wouldn't she be seeing Greg several months from now, she reasoned with herself. He was sweet and fun, not to mention handsome, and she loved being with him. Greg didn't react to her comment and instead insisted that she plan for an audition.

Brooke waved her hands away. "No, no, no. Not anytime soon. Not since my last audition fiasco."

"It couldn't have been that bad."

"Trust me. It was."

"I don't have any idea what you sounded like, but I can honestly say that from what I've heard, I think you've got a beautiful voice."

"Thanks." Brooke took a drink and quietly laughed at a memory that talking about the past had conjured up.

"What's that for?" Greg asked.

"I just remembered something I did my senior year in high school. One of my friends dared me to try out for the professional show at the Sundance Theater. I dared her back, so the two of us went together and humiliated ourselves. It was fun, even if I slaughtered the dancing tryout."

"What about the singing part?"

Brooke shrugged. "Oh, I did all right, I guess. That was when I was more involved with theater and voice. The experience is largely a blur in my memory except for a big white room with the judges at one end staring at me."

Brooke managed to steer the conversation into other areas, largely away from herself and toward finding out more about this man she was so attracted to. She managed to discover that he had served a mission in Sweden, played football in high school, and left college to attend the police academy. It didn't get past her that any of her attempts to ask about his family were skillfully sidestepped, although Brooke couldn't imagine why. What did he have to hide?

Greg put in a different CD, this one by Garth Brooks. "Uh-oh," Brooke said, eyeing the album. "That's *real* country music, isn't it? You barely got me liking John Denver. Are you sure I'm ready for the heavy-duty stuff?"

"Trust me, you'll like Garth," Greg said as he cued the music.

Two songs and a side order of coleslaw later, Brooke decided she was pleasantly surprised. "He's really good," she conceded. Greg got up to light the lantern. She listened to a few more bars and began swaying to the music. "I like this song," she murmured. "It's so romantic." As soon as the word left her mouth, she bit her lips tight, wishing she could take it back.

"I like it too," Greg added, a gleam in his eye. "Like I said, there's some things ABBA can't create." He blew out the match and reached for her hand. "Let's dance."

"We don't have boots," Brooke said as he took her hand, pulled her to standing, and drew her near.

"I think we'll manage," he said as the two of them gently swayed to the music. The lamp gave off the only light in the darkness. Greg's cheek brushed against hers, and Brooke liked the roughness of his evening stubble. She loved being with Greg, but still felt uneasy about not knowing him. She leaned back and looked up at him inquiringly.

He smiled back at her. "What?"

"Tell me, how has such a good-looking guy managed to remain single all these years?" Greg's smile faded, and he took a deep breath. He dropped his hands. "What did I say?" Her hands came up and covered her eyes. "I'm sorry. That's a sensitive topic. I've been single long enough to know that."

Greg shook his head and gave her hand a squeeze. "No, don't be sorry. You didn't say anything wrong. I'm the one who should apologize." He looked up into the darkness and drew in a deep breath. "It's long past time you knew a few things about me."

Brooke took a step back. "Such as?"

"Such as how I haven't spent my entire life being single."

"You're divorced?" She tried not to care. After all, beggars can't be choosers. And at her age she was quickly becoming a beggar. Besides, Greg would be a catch for anyone.

"No, I'm not divorced," he said. He took her hand and walked to the blanket.

"I don't understand."

"Let's sit down for a minute."

Brooke settled onto the blanket tentatively, then watched Greg sit down in front of her. "All right. I guess this is it," he said, clasping his hands together.

"This is what?"

"This is when you decide whether you want to pursue anything between us. I know we haven't been seeing each other for very long, but I am certainly not going out with you just to have a good time, and I'm guessing you're not either." Brooke nodded but said nothing as she waited for him to continue. He was right; she had stopped dating just for the fun of it several years ago.

"This is going to go down one of two very different roads, and you'll have to decide whether to even start moving towards that crossroad. It's best for you to find out a few things soon, before this—we—go any further."

A knot formed in Brooke's stomach. She had just dealt with a hideous revelation about Christopher. She didn't know if she could handle any other big revelations. She braced herself, not knowing what to brace herself for. "What is it?"

"Remember how you said that you would have to be the number-one female in a man's life?"

"Yes," Brooke said slowly, not liking where this was going. "But you said you don't live with your mother, and you aren't divorced."

"I'm not divorced. But there is still someone else. I guess, if you want to get technical, *two* someone elses."

Brooke racked her brain. What could he be talking about? Dogs? Maybe a sister. That wouldn't pose a big problem. The two of them could be friends. Greg reached into his back pocket and withdrew his wallet. He opened it and pulled out a picture, then with another deep breath but no word of explanation, he handed it to her.

Brooke took the picture and leaned toward the lamp to see the image better.

Angela.

Brooke's head snapped up, and her eyes grew wide. "How . . . how . . . why do you have a picture—"

"Angela is my daughter."

Brooke had to struggle to keep her jaw from dropping. She looked back at the picture, then back at Greg, first in disbelief, then in disappointment. "But I thought you said you hadn't been married. Unless . . . unless you and her mother were never—"

"I said I'm not *divorced,*" Greg interjected. "But I have been married. My wife died after Angela's third birthday. My daughter doesn't really remember her mother."

Brooke brought a hand to her mouth. "I'm so sorry."

Greg smiled softly and shrugged. "Thanks." He let out a pained laugh. "It took me almost a year to clean out Heather's things from the bathroom drawers, and another two years to clear her side of the closet. At times I still don't deal with it very well."

"That must be very hard," Brooke said, unsure what else she could say.

Greg nodded with a shrug. Silence followed, and Brooke considered the picture again. "So Angela is your daughter," she said softly, trying to digest the information. She handed the picture back, then put out her hand as if to explain herself. "I swear, when I stayed with her after she was hit with the rock, I had no idea there was any connection between you."

Greg chuckled as he put the picture back into his wallet. "I figured as much. I was on my way to speak at the school assembly, and when I got to the office, I found that my little girl was hurt. So I called for another officer to come speak in my place. On the way home, Angela told me about Miss Williamson, this really cool teacher who helped her."

"So it was you who helped her bake the cake," Brooke added, mentally putting the pieces together.

"I had nothing to do with that. It was her idea. I just supervised. She desperately wanted a way to thank you."

"Wait a minute. She gave me the cake, and then you showed up to ask me out right after she left. Why didn't you just come in with her?"

Greg snorted. "For the same reason I waited until now to tell you about her. You probably would have run for your life." Brooke had to admit that the possibility was a strong one. "I figured you wouldn't accept a first date if you knew me as a single father. Besides, I didn't see any reason to tell you until I knew whether you'd be interested." A smile curved the corner of his mouth. "Or whether I'd be interested, for that matter. But you need to know now, before we get any more involved . . . especially because of what you said about being number one. The fact is, I have a daughter, and she has to come first. That's just the way it is. And of course, there's her mother. I am sealed to her. So in a way, there are two females that were here before you. I know that's a lot to take, and I understand if you don't want to deal with any of it."

Greg's voice grew soft. "After she died, I promised myself and Heather—Angela's mother—that I'd take care of our daughter as best as I could. Angela has been the focus of my life ever since. I spend as much time as I can with her. This is the most nightlife I've had in years, but even now I've made a point to spend time with her, like at bedtime. Except for when I work nights I'm always there for the tuck-in. We read books and talk about the day. It's our special time together. Her bedtime is eight o'clock, which is why—"

"Why our dates always start at eight-thirty," Brooke filled in. "Because you always have a 'commitment' until then."

"She'll always be my commitment," he said with a firm nod. "My mother has been coming over to tend while I'm out with you.

Anyway, I thought you should know the situation now so you can decide whether to bolt from something that could get rather complicated."

"Thank you for telling me," Brooke said, unwilling to trust herself to say much more. Her mind was going in circles, and she didn't know for sure what she thought of the situation. Here she was really starting to care about a man with heaps of baggage. Yet she knew their relationship could go far, if she let it.

If being the operative word.

Greg looked at another picture in his wallet, and Brooke scooted closer so she could see it. He tilted the photograph so the light from the lamp spilled across the image. A bride and groom held hands and gazed into each other's eyes, with the Salt Lake Temple behind them as a backdrop. The bride had blonde hair with soft ringlets falling to the sides of her face. She wore a gorgeous dress that reminded Brooke of Disney's Cinderella. The bride looked at her groom with pure love and joy in her eyes. The groom, a younger version of Greg wearing a black tuxedo with tails, had the same expression.

Brooke's throat constricted at the sight. What would it be like to be with a man who had been married to—been in love with—another woman? A man who had lived the classic fairy tale and then was left alone not by divorce, but by the death of his bride? Brooke could hardly breathe, but she couldn't stand the silence any longer.

"She's beautiful."

"She was," Greg said with a nod, a slight mistiness in his eyes. "It's been four years now. A long four years." He closed his wallet. "You're the first woman I've dated in all that time." When Brooke's eyebrows raised questioningly, he explained. "I felt as if it would be betraying Heather if I even looked at another woman." His eyes locked on Brooke's with intensity. "But when I saw you, something happened inside. That's the only way I can describe it. Something clicked, and I just had to get to know you. So I wrote down your name from your witness statement at the accident and decided to find you again."

Brooke couldn't focus on what he had said. The image of Greg's bride burned into her mind, and she couldn't think of anything else. Until now she had looked forward to every moment she could spend with Greg, had imagined what the future might hold for them. But now . . . now she wasn't so sure. When she thought of Greg holding her, she pictured the woman who used to fill those arms. Greg reached for Brooke's hand.

"Are you all right?"

She nodded mutely, but as she looked at their intertwined hands, all she could see was Heather's hand instead of her own. She blinked hard and looked away. If this relationship was to work, she would have to rearrange her view of the future and make a place in it for Angela. And Greg's in-laws. And especially his first wife. She didn't know whether she could do all that.

Greg put his wallet away and smiled wanly. "Well, now you know. Like I said, I don't expect you to jump up and down at the idea of dating a single father. If you want to break this off now, I understand." But when Brooke opened her mouth to answer, he raised a hand. "I don't want an answer now. Frankly, I don't know that I'm ready for one tonight."

"You're right. It's probably a good idea to let it all settle for a few days."

Greg nodded, then motioned toward the truck. "Come on. I'll take you home."

They cleaned up their picnic silently. The drive was equally quiet, but when they reached her door, Brooke spoke up.

"Thanks for telling me about Angela," she said. "And about Heather. I'll bet she was a remarkable woman." Brooke pictured a paragon of virtue and wondered if she could ever live up to the memory of Greg's first wife.

"She was a great woman," Greg said with a nod. He paused, as if searching for words, then he bit his lower lip nervously. "Listen, Brooke. This whole thing is a little unnerving for me, so I can only imagine how you're feeling."

Brooke nodded reluctantly. "In the past I've written off men with anything messy in their pasts. And I can't deny that the idea of being number three isn't too appealing up front . . . ."

Greg shoved his hands into his pockets. "I understand. I should have known this would be a bit too much for you to take."

Brooke regarded him steadily. "It may or may not be. It's not exactly a young girl's dream to find a prince who already belongs to someone else." She reached out and touched his arm, then paused, a myriad of thoughts in her mind. "On the other hand, so far you do look a lot like a prince. I need some time. I'll call you in a few days."

"I'll understand if you want to run for your life." He brushed a stray wisp of hair from her face. "But I really hope you don't."

He reached behind her neck and pulled her close. Brooke caught her breath when she realized what Greg was about to do. He leaned toward her, and Brooke closed her eyes. His gentle kiss, though short, sent shivers through her frame. He pulled away all too soon, and Brooke was suddenly aware of a weakness in her legs.

Greg took her hand and stroked the top with his thumb. "Good night," he said with a smile that revealed his dimple. With a final squeeze of her hand, he turned and walked away, leaving Brooke behind him, breathless.

* * *

Greg arrived home and with a heavy sigh, closed the door behind him.

"What's that for?"

Greg locked the door, then turned to his mother. "I did it. I told her."

Linda Stevens set her magazine aside and rose from the couch. "And . . . ?"

Greg shrugged. "I suppose *shocked* might be the best word to describe it. I wish I could have waited longer to tell her. We've had such a good time together, and now it might be over."

"Did she say that?" Linda asked.

Greg shook his head. "She said she'd call in a few days, after she had some time to think it through." He took a deep breath and ran his fingers through his short hair. "I might as well brace myself for the worst."

She patted his arm reassuringly. "Don't say that. You won't know until she calls. Just give her the time she asked for. That's the best thing you can do right now."

"You're right, of course. But at the same time . . ." Greg sat on the couch and put his head in his hands.

Linda sat beside him. "Greg, what's wrong?"

He looked up and sighed. "In one way, it would have been simpler if Brooke had just dumped me tonight."

"I don't understand," Linda said.

"Mom, I keep thinking about Heather. How I promised her I'd never remarry."

"Oh, Greg." His mother took his hand in hers. "That was a long time ago. You were both young. A lot has changed since then."

"I know, but I promised. At the time I thought I would never lose her, at least not until—I don't know—we both had dentures." Greg gazed at the wedding picture on the shelf beside the entertainment center. "I've tried so hard to move on, for Angela's sake. But I'm not sure if I can."

Linda pulled her son toward her and hugged him tightly. "I think now that she's on the other side, Heather would want you to find someone else and be happy."

"I hope so." He gave his mother a final squeeze. "Thanks for coming over, Mom."

They stood, and Linda headed for the door. "Are you going to be all right?"

Greg shrugged. "I think so."

As Greg closed the door behind her, he heard the sound of small footsteps and turned around. Angela stood in the hall, holding her teddy bear to her chest, her pale blonde hair tussled around her face. She squinted at the light.

"What's up, sweetie?" Greg went to her and squatted down on her level. "Did you have a nightmare?"

Angela shrugged slightly. "No. I can't sleep."

"Why not?"

Angela stared at the fuzz on her teddy bear's head and shrugged.

"Come here." Greg took her hand, and together they went to the master bedroom and plopped onto the bed. He repressed the urge to jump into a discussion and instead waited for Angela to talk.

She picked at teddy-bear fuzz for a moment, then said, "Daddy, how can you know if the Holy Ghost is warning you?" Greg had prepared himself to answer a variety of childlike concerns, but this one took him off guard.

Angela continued. "I won't be baptized for another year, so I can't have Him with me all the time, but on Sunday Sister Penrod said He can still talk to me."

"That's right," Greg said, still unsure what the problem was.

Angela looked up. "She told us a story about a time when she was little and her house burned down, but the Holy Ghost warned her so the whole family got out in time." She turned back to picking fuzz.

Greg's brow furrowed. He still didn't know what was bothering his little girl. "And?"

"What if the Holy Ghost tries to warn me about something and I don't know it?" Angela's eyes welled up with tears. "I've had all kinds of scary thoughts all week about getting kidnapped, or the house burning down, or of you getting hurt at work, but none of them have ever happened. If it wasn't the Holy Ghost talking to me any of those times—just me thinking scary things—then how can I know when it's really the Holy Ghost?"

Greg thought for a moment before answering. "You need to remember how the Holy Ghost talks. He doesn't make you afraid, even when He's warning you. Instead, he'll tell you not to do something, or maybe to stop doing something, but you won't be afraid. If you feel calm and warm right here—" he took her hand and tapped her heart with her fingers—"then you can know it's the Holy Ghost, and not your imagination, even if it's a warning about something dangerous. You'll have to practice listening, though, so you can always know when to obey. Does that answer your question?"

Angela chewed on the inside of her cheek for a minute, then she nodded. "I'll try to practice listening . . . and I'll try to stop thinking scary thoughts." She looked at the bed and its fluffy pillows. "Daddy, can I stay here for a few minutes?"

Greg smiled and stroked her cheek. The poor thing had spent most of the night imagining all kinds of scary things and wondering if any of them was the Spirit speaking to her. "Sure. But just for a little while."

A broad smile spread across Angela's face, and she threw her arms around him. "Thanks. You're the best, Dad." She snuggled into his arms and breathed a sigh of contentment. Then she opened her eyes and looked up. "Daddy? Have you talked to Grandpa Miller lately?"

Greg looked at the mischievous smile his daughter wore and asked suspiciously, "Not for a week or two. Why?"

"Because he says Muffin had kittens and—"

Greg raised a hand and shook his head. "We've been over this before, young lady."

"But Dad, Grandpa says that if he can't find homes for them all, he might have to take them to the pound." Her eyes pleaded. "Please, Daddy? I'll take care of it all by myself. You won't ever have to feed it or clean the litter box or—"

"There is no way I'm having a litter box in this house. This is going to be an outside cat."

Angela grinned. "So we can have one?"

Greg laughed and ruffled her hair. "You know I can't say no, don't you? Fine. We can get one of Grandpa Miller's kittens."

CHAPTER 9

Brooke didn't call Greg "in a few days" as she had promised. More than a week passed, and while she knew he wouldn't begrudge her taking whatever time she needed, she also knew she had taken plenty of time already. Besides, she found herself missing Greg, wishing she had something planned to look forward to, some time to spend with him.

More than once she picked up the receiver and dialed the first few digits of his number, then hung up. What would she say? That she missed him horribly, that she wanted to dance to Garth Brooks and ABBA, but that she couldn't yet deal with the idea of a daughter? No, it wasn't so much the idea of a daughter, as much as it was the idea of a previous wife, someone he had given his life and heart over to, someone he had shared the most intimate of experiences with. Her Cinderella dreams didn't include someone who had already found his lady and ridden off into the sunset with her. For eternity.

She hadn't worked out her own feelings completely, but it wasn't as if she had wasted the last week. On the contrary, she had spent hours each day thinking about Greg and everything that surrounded him. On Sunday the telephone rang, and at her wits' end, Brooke jumped to look at the caller ID, not sure whether she hoped or dreaded to see Greg's name on it. Instead she saw her parents' telephone number.

"Hi, Brookey," her mother said when she answered. "I ran into Chris and his mother at the mall, and he said you two weren't together anymore. He looked terrible."

Brooke rubbed the back of her neck. Her mother never stopped pining for Brooke's wedding day. If Brooke wasn't involved with someone, her mother would play matchmaker. When Brooke did have a relationship, her mother continually poked her nose into it, wanting all the details, especially when a potential wedding date might be. "That's right," Brooke said. "It's been a few weeks now." She braced herself for more questions, which, as usual, she would do her best to dodge.

"Did you break up with him, or did he break up with you?"

Brooke hated that question. From past conversations, she knew that regardless of the answer, her mother would go into a fit. If Brooke had broken off the relationship, her mother would rant about how she might have lost her last chance for marriage. If he had broken it off, her mother would fume about the man, and men in general, who were blind and couldn't appreciate a good prospective wife when they had one dropped in their laps.

"It was sort of a mutual decision," Brooke lied. She had never more fervently wanted to keep the facts from her mother than with this relationship, especially with the recent revelations about Christopher's health problems.

"How on earth can a breakup be mutual? Someone must have initiated it."

"Mom, can't you just accept the fact that he and I would not have made a good match? It's over, and that's that." Brooke did her best to avoid talking about her personal life, but the longer she stayed single, the harder it was to speak with her mother.

"Is there someone else?" her mother persisted.

"No, there wasn't anyone else."

Brooke's changing the tense didn't get past her mother. "What about now? Are you seeing anyone else?"

Brooke held her breath as she tried to find an answer. "I've had a few dates here and there since we broke up, that's all."

Her mother sighed. "I wish you could understand how frustrating it is for me to watch you alone year after year."

"It's not as if I'm avoiding marriage," Brooke began. She had guarded any and all information about Christopher and found herself on the verge of lashing out. "Mom, I'd love to be married, but to the right person. I've seen enough to know that there are worse things than being alone. I'm sorry if that's hard for you, but it's my life. I'm not your little girl anymore."

The silence on the other end was palpable. "I didn't know you felt that way," her mother said in a whisper.

Brooke immediately regretted every word. "Mom, I'm sorry. I didn't mean—"

"No, I know exactly what you meant. I didn't realize you resented my concern for you." She paused, then added, "I'll try to keep out of your business from now on. I'll try to let you tell me when there's any news, and I won't ask for it."

Brooke could hear a sniff on the other end, but before she could respond, her mother hung up. Brooke knew she should have handled it differently. There had to be a better way to avoid talking about Christopher. And about Greg. And, Brooke realized, she had protected that information just as vigorously as she had that of Christopher. The knowledge of Heather and Angela had stirred her emotions for days. If her mother had learned anything about it, she would have insisted Brooke throw herself at him.

She looked at the phone in her hand, then with a determined finger, dialed long distance. She needed her true sounding board—Pat.

"Hey, how's the gorgeous cop?" Pat asked when she heard Brooke's voice.

"Pat, I think I just hurt Mom horribly."

"Does she know about Greg?"

"No. That's just it. I sort of told her to mind her own business. I didn't want to tell her about him."

"Hmm. I bet that didn't go over well. But on the other hand . . . why don't you want to tell her about him? I know she's nosy, but usually you give out at least the dry facts of your romantic life. Why not this time?"

"Because I'm not sure about the facts myself. I need an objective ear, and Mom's not the one to give it to me."

"Well, I'm dying for you to get married as much as Mom is, so I'm not exactly an objective ear, but I'll do my best." Pat's voice dimmed as she turned away from the phone to deal with two fighting children, then she turned back as cheery as ever. "So tell me. What's the problem with him?"

"There's not exactly a problem with him. It's more what he told me about his past."

"Let me guess, he used to be a drag queen."

Brooke laughed aloud at the image Pat's suggestion put in her mind, grateful her sister could lighten the mood. Brooke needed that now. "Hardly."

"Then what is it?"

"He has a seven-year-old daughter."

"Oh, that's not too unusual. Remember, once you hit thirty you get men with divorces and all kinds of histories."

"He's barely thirty, and he's not divorced. He was widowed four years ago."

"Oh." Pat paused as she thought through the information and readjusted her mental picture. "All right, so what's the problem?"

Brooke's eyebrows went up. "Weren't you listening? He lost the love of his life, and apparently I am the first woman he has so much as looked at since then. How can I even *think* of a relationship with a man who has shared everything with another woman? Who is *sealed* to another woman? Remember how I've always said I want a man's entire heart? Half of it already belongs to another woman, and the other half belongs to his daughter. Where could I possibly fit in?"

Pat let out a thoughtful breath. "I don't think it's quite like that," she finally said. "Don't take this wrong, but you might not be able to fully understand what I'm going to say because you're not a mother. When Tammy was born, I thought I could never love anyone as much as I loved her. The power of a mother's love is almost frightening. So when I got pregnant with Krissy, I panicked. I thought I'd never be able to love another child as deeply as I loved my first little girl."

"But that's ridiculous. Of course you could. Each child is different, and you'd love each one in a slightly different way."

"Exactly."

"Exactly what?"

Pat laughed. "I think you just answered your own question."

"Oh, so you're saying that he could love me as much as his first wife?"

"Or more, who knows? But you shouldn't let his feelings for her interfere with what may turn out to be the best thing that ever happened to you."

"Or the worst," Brooke said sullenly.

"Brooke," Pat articulated in her maternal, chastising tone.

Brooke sighed. "Fine. You're right, of course. But it's more than how much love a heart can hold. What if *I* can't deal with the idea of *her?* His first wife will be there in the next life, you know. And all I know of her is that her name was Heather and she was gorgeous. She's a total stranger to me."

"I think you just answered your own question again, Brooke," Pat said with another chuckle. "You're not letting me do any helping. You're coming up with all this on your own."

"I think I missed something."

"I'd be willing to wager that if you got to know who Heather was, that you'd be able to deal better with the idea of her. Look at pictures of her, home videos, anything. Ask him about her. You might have more in common with her than you think, and if she seems like a friend, she won't seem so much like competition."

"All right, I'll call him," Brooke said with determination, but then her voice failed. "When I get up the courage."

"Brooke," Pat cajoled again in her maternal voice.

Brooke sighed heavily. "Fine. I'll call him. I promise."

"Good girl."

"In the next day or two."

"Brooke!"

"Thanks for your help, Pat," Brooke said, ignoring her tone. "I'll let you know how it goes." As she hung up, she knew deep within her that discovering more about Heather would give her a better chance at handling the situation. Greg was beginning to mean too much to her to let him go now. Hopefully the details of his past and her feelings toward it would sort themselves out later. In the meantime, she needed to call Greg. But not tonight.

The phone rang as soon as she hung up. With the phone still in her hand, she answered without checking the caller ID.

"Brooke, why haven't you ever called me back?"

Brooke's heart stopped at the sound of Christopher's voice. She couldn't speak, but Christopher didn't give her the chance anyway.

"Why, Brooke? I've left so many messages. I don't know what else to do to win you back, but you won't give me a chance. What's wrong? Do you hate me?"

Brooke thought back to what Janet had said about Christopher being suicidal when he was off his medication, and racked her brain for what she should say. "No, of course I don't hate you, Christopher."

"Then you'll come back to me?"

Brooke closed her eyes tightly. "I don't think so. We can be friends, but that's all."

"If we're still friends, why don't you return my calls? Friends talk on the phone, right?"

Brooke didn't know what to say. Should she refer to his disorder?

"Brooke, would you please open your door for me?"

Her heart leapt to her throat, and she looked at the door. "Christopher, where are you calling from?" *Please don't say you're on your cell phone.*

Christopher let out an odd laugh. "Don't tell Mother or Janet. They try to keep me in the house all the time. But I sneaked out to come see you. I'm right outside. Open the door, okay?"

Brooke's hand flew to her mouth to stifle a yelp. She hurried to her door and peered through the peephole. There stood Christopher, or at least someone who looked vaguely like him. The wild look in his eyes, the greasy hair, and the disheveled clothing had turned him into a completely different person. She backed up from the door slowly, trying not to make a sound, knowing it was silly since he knew she was inside. The doorknob began to jiggle, and he kept begging for her to open up.

"Brooke, open the door right now, or I'll break it down myself! Then I'll use this nine millimeter, first on you, then on me. We belong together!"

Brooke turned off the phone, then ran to the half bath between the living room and kitchen. She locked the door, then realized with horror that she hadn't bolted the front door. She didn't dare go back, and instead sat on the toilet lid and trembled.

"Open the door, Brooke. Now!" Even from the bathroom she could hear him thrusting his body against the door. "Let me in, Brooke!" Christopher yelled angrily. "You *owe* me that much!"

With a shaky finger she dialed 911, praying Christopher wouldn't beat the door down before help arrived. When the operator answered,

Brooke did her best to stay calm and speak slowly so help could be dispatched as quickly as possible. Every second felt like an eternity as the operator continued to ask mindless questions. Didn't the operator realize the danger she was in? A bang on the front door made Brooke jump, sending another wave of tears coursing down her cheeks.

"They're on their way," the operator told her. "It shouldn't be more than a few more minutes now, but I want you to stay on the line until they arrive."

Quite suddenly, the banging and muffled yelling subsided. Brooke looked up, cautiously hopeful that it might mean Christopher had left. She stood up and leaned toward the door to hear better. She couldn't make out any distinct sounds. A couple minutes later— though it seemed like ten times that—she heard a tense, muffled voice outside the bathroom door.

"Brooke! Where are you?" The bathroom doorknob moved.

Brooke screamed. "Get out! I've called the police!"

"Brooke, open the door. It's me, Greg."

Brooke's entire frame shook, and even though she knew it was Greg's voice, she still pictured opening the door and seeing Christopher on the other side. "Greg, is that really you?"

"It's all right, Brooke. He's gone."

She tentatively unlocked the door. Greg opened it, and at the sight of him she collapsed into his arms and sobbed.

Greg held her tight. "It's all right. He's gone." He took the phone from her and talked to the dispatch operator, then hung up. "Come sit down."

He led Brooke into the front room where he sat her down on the sofa. He waited, letting her regain her bearings before asking her any questions. She wiped at her eyes and looked at the door, which stood ajar, the frame splintered.

"How did you know to come? You're not on duty." She glanced at his civilian clothes.

"Something told me to come over. I almost didn't. After all, you hadn't called since we talked in the canyon, but the feeling was so insistent that I had to. When I pulled in, I saw him at the door. Thought he was a burglar at first. He had just got the door open, but when I yelled at him he panicked and ran. I should have gone after him, but I had to make sure you were all right." He wiped a tear from her cheek with his thumb. *"Are* you all right?" She nodded as he continued, "You can press charges, and—"

Brooke shook her head. "No, I don't want to do that."

"But—"

"No." Brooke was so insistent that Greg didn't push further. She wondered if she should explain why Christopher had acted so crazy. She understood Greg's reasoning; even if Christopher couldn't be held totally accountable, he was still responsible for his actions. He probably needed psychiatric care more than legal confinement. Maybe she should see if Greg knew how to pursue that type of thing. She dismissed the thought though, because she was so emotionally exhausted from the day's events. Instead she laid her head against his shoulder and closed her eyes. "I don't know what I would have done if . . ." Her voice trailed off, and she shuddered. "Thank you for coming."

* * *

Brooke looked over her shoulder for Christopher for days, never once forgetting to bolt her door, which had been fixed the same day Christopher had broken it. One night the phone rang, and the caller ID showed the Morris family number. Brooke waited for the answering machine to pick up, and answered only when she heard Janet's voice. Christopher's sister apologized for what had happened, then told Brooke that he was in the hospital and back on his medication.

By Thursday, Brooke no longer jumped at loud noises, but she couldn't keep from glancing around for tan cars.

Brooke finally called Greg that evening, although little was resolved by the phone call. They decided to have dinner at his place Saturday evening. Brooke let Greg think the evening was his idea, a way to bring Angela into the picture. In reality, she wanted a chance to spend time at the Stevens household and follow Pat's advice to learn about Heather.

"Maybe I should come over after she goes to bed," Brooke said. "Angela might feel defensive about a new woman taking the place of her mother or even sharing her father with anyone else. It might seem like competition."

"That's the last thing I'm worried about. Angela keeps asking me when she can have a mommy. She doesn't have many memories of Heather. All she sees is her friends with their mothers and wishes she had one too. Up until now I haven't told her about the two of us, because I didn't want to get her hopes up that we'd get married—I mean . . ." Greg suddenly stopped short and groaned. Brooke hadn't fully resolved her own feelings about Greg's situation, and they both knew it. "The 'm' word is probably the last thing you needed to hear about now. Forget I said that."

"Don't worry about it," Brooke said with a forced laugh.

"I'd bet Angela would be thrilled to find out about dinner from you."

A slow smile spread across Brooke's face. "You're sure it won't be a problem?"

"I'm sure."

"Then I'll tell her tomorrow at school."

Friday Brooke wandered the playground during recess, looking forward to going to Greg's place for dinner the following evening. She found Angela playing on the swings with a friend. When Angela noticed her, she waved and ran over.

"Hi, Miss Williamson. Look, my stitches are gone." Angela touched the spot on her head. "My dad took them out. The doctor said he could. Dad had me lie on the couch, and he used these tiny scissors." She shivered at the memory. "Scared me to death."

"That would have scared me too. By the way, that cake of yours was really delicious."

"Thanks," Angela said with a shrug, although she was clearly pleased at the compliment. "I don't know how to make a real cake with flour and eggs and stuff. But Dad says mixes are hard to mess up." For the first time Brooke noticed how much Angela referred to her father, and wondered why she hadn't noticed it before, especially since she never mentioned her mother. Angela's face lit up at a thought. "Oh, and guess what! My dad let me have one of my grandpa's kittens. The gray one. I wanted to name it George, but then I found out it's a girl, so we named her Misty."

"That's great," Brooke said with genuine excitement. She remembered the joy of getting her first pet, a pair of mice she named Cookies and Cream. "I didn't tell your dad your secret, you know."

"I know that," Angela said with a giggle. "You don't even know my dad."

"Actually, I do. He's a friend of mine. I'm coming over for dinner tomorrow night, and I'm bringing dinner. Do you like pizza?"

Angela's face lit up. "Wow! I told Dad you were a really neat teacher. And now you're friends. That is so cool. Do you like my dad?"

Brooke flushed slightly. "I like him very much."

CHAPTER 10

Saturday night Brooke showed up promptly at six-thirty bearing a deep-pan pizza and a two-liter bottle of root beer. After ringing the bell, Brooke could hear Angela racing to answer the door inside.

"Daddy, she's here," Angela called as she opened the door.

"Put that cat back in the garage," Greg said as he followed her.

Angela came out of the door, squeezing past Brooke. She held little Misty, who meowed pitifully. "Isn't she adorable?" Angela cooed.

Brooke agreed, but she couldn't pet the soft, fluffy fur with her arms full. "We'll have to play with her later. How about after dinner?" Brooke leaned over and let Angela smell the pizza. "Do you like pepperoni and pineapple pizza?"

"It's my favorite," Angela said with wide eyes. Brooke gave Greg a grateful smile; he had tipped her off to Angela's preferences earlier. Greg took the pizza box and root beer from Brooke and led her into the kitchen.

"Angela and I were just putting the finishing touches on dessert."

A chocolate jelly roll sat on the counter. Pink ice cream spiraled inside. Angela returned the kitten to its box in the garage, then hopped onto a bar stool.

"Wash your hands after touching the cat and before touching food," Greg reminded her.

Angela hurriedly jumped off her stool, went to the sink and splashed some water on her hands before returning to her spot. "Brooke, watch this. Dad just taught me how." She picked up a sieve with powdered sugar using one hand and tapped it with a spoon in her other hand, sprinkling powdered sugar over the cake in a light, even layer. "Cool, huh? My grandma makes ice-cream jelly rolls all the time, and they're my favorite. We've never tried one at home though. I don't know if it'll taste very good." Angela wiped her finger along one edge of the platter where some ice cream had spilled and put her finger in her mouth. She caught her father's eye. "Oops. Sorry, Dad. I forgot."

Greg laughed, but made an attempt at a serious look. "Go wash your hand." He put the cake into the freezer, then got plates and cups out for dinner.

Angela washed up at the sink, then skipped to her place at the table. With everyone seated, Angela asked, "Dad, can I say the blessing on the food?"

"Sure, honey."

Everyone bowed their heads, and Angela began her prayer in a matter-of-fact tone, as if she spoke to a friend. "Heavenly Father, thank you for my dad, and our house, and my dancing lessons, and that Miss Williamson . . . I mean Brooke . . . could come for dinner."

Brooke braced herself, afraid that Angela might pray for something to come of her relationship with Angela's father.

"Thank you for the food, especially since I love pineapple and pepperoni pizza and root beer. Please bless it. Help us to be good. . . And bless Brooke that she won't be scared." Angela closed her prayer, then picked up her cup. "Can I have some root beer?"

Brooke's and Greg's eyes locked. What had Angela meant by her last request? Brooke wondered if Greg had told her about the experience with Christopher, but she doubted it.

Of course, there were her fears about what her future with—or without—Greg would hold. But Angela couldn't be referring to any of that. Angela hadn't known about her father's new "friend" until a day ago.

"Dad? . . . Hey Dad!" Angela waved her glass in front of her father's face. "I said, can I please have some root beer?"

Angela's voice broke them out of their thoughts, and Greg's bright smile returned. "Oh, of course, honey. Here you go."

For the rest of the evening Angela proved to be a perfect hostess. She made sure Brooke had plenty to eat and drink. When they finished their pizza, she helped her father serve the dessert, which

Brooke praised up and down. Then Brooke and Angela spent some time playing with the kitten in the backyard. All too soon Greg looked at his watch. "Look at that, Gee-la. It's past eight. You're supposed to be in bed by now."

"That's okay, Dad. It's a special night."

"You still need to get to bed. You don't even have time for a bath and tomorrow's Sunday."

Angela shrugged. "That's okay. I'm clean, see?" She held up her hands as evidence.

"Gee-la . . ."

Brooke glanced at the two of them. "What's this 'Gee-la' name?"

"That's what my family calls me," Angela explained. "Dad thought 'Angie' was too normal for a nickname, so he took the last part of 'Angela' instead."

"Sort of, but then I say it differently so it sounds more like a real name," Greg added.

"Gee-la." Brooke tried out the name on her tongue.

"Um," Angela said, twisting her shirt between her hands. "That's kind of a name that only Daddy uses, and my grandparents and Aunt Jane 'n' stuff." Greg shot his daughter a sharp look. Angela caught the look and added, "But not even my best friends use that name, and you're like one of my best friends."

"It's all right, Angela. I didn't know. I won't call you 'Gee-la.' I'll call you 'Angela' if you prefer." She leaned down to Angela's height and whispered, "Or maybe some day we'll come up with our own nickname just between the two of us. How does that sound?"

Angela grinned. "Yeah!"

"All right, little girl. Off to get ready for bed." Greg swept Angela off her feet and tickled her mercilessly. Angela howled in delight. He stopped long enough for Angela to come up for air, then said, "All right. Off you go." He set her down and gave her a gentle push toward the hall.

Angela turned around. "Will you still read me a book?"

Greg looked at his watch. "If you're ready in five minutes, I'll read two."

"You got a deal." Angela gave a thumbs-up sign before running down the hallway.

Greg turned back to Brooke. "I hope you don't mind if I go read to her . . ."

Brooke shook her head. "Of course not. You never miss the tuck-in. She comes first, right?" Brooke looked down the hall where Angela had gone, then at Greg. "She's a great girl. You're lucky."

"I know." Greg paused, then eyed Brooke nervously. "So are you all right with everything now?" he asked quietly so his voice wouldn't carry to Angela.

"I'm getting there," she said honestly. She wished he would kiss her again, but knew he wouldn't, not yet. Not until he knew where she stood. Since she wasn't so sure herself, that might not be soon. They sat in silence for a minute, and Brooke wondered if he was thinking about it too.

"Well, it looks like you'll have a little extra time to mull things over," Greg said.

"Oh?"

"My parents have been planning a trip to England and France for over a year. We'll be gone about three weeks and return the first week of July."

"That's only two weeks away."

"I know. If I had known I was going to meet you I would have planned things differently," Greg said helplessly.

Brooke shrugged and tried not to look too disappointed. She tried to picture her summer without Greg. It was impossible. "Don't worry about me. Like you said, it'll give me some extra time."

A few minutes later Angela returned wearing a long white night-gown. Greg's face lit up. "There's my angel."

Angela offered Brooke an explanation. "Dad thinks this night-gown looks like an angel's dress, you know, 'cause it's white."

Greg shook his head. "Oh, but it's more than that," he said, taking her into his arms. "You really are my angel, sent right from heaven. Of course, the nightgown doesn't hurt."

Angela rolled her eyes in mild embarrassment. She took his hand and pulled him to his feet. "Come on, Daddy. Let's go."

Greg gave Brooke's hand a squeeze. "I'll be back in a few minutes. Make yourself at home." He gestured toward the entertainment center. "There's the television, the stereo, books—whatever you'd like to amuse yourself with."

"Thanks."

Father and daughter disappeared, and Brooke looked around the family room. She stood up and crossed to the entertainment center, intending to put on a country music CD, maybe Garth Brooks, when she noticed a wedding picture in a gilt frame on a shelf, the same one as in Greg's wallet. Several photo albums rested beside the frame. Brooke glanced over her shoulder, wondering whether she dared look through one. She tentatively picked up the first one and brushed a considerable layer of dust from the cover. She settled on the couch and stared at the cover, which framed Greg and Heather's engagement picture. Several pages chronicling their courtship followed. Greg looked almost boyish in many of them, including several that looked like high-school dances.

She found pictures of Heather and Greg in a water fight. Another page showed the two of them covered in chocolate frosting. When she came to several pages devoted to Heather in the hospital, her hand stopped. She turned the pages slowly and learned of Heather's bout with leukemia. One of the last pages in the album showed Greg's proposal in her hospital room. A red scarf covered her head instead of thick, blonde locks. The next pages showed wedding preparations, including Heather selecting a wig to wear.

A tear fell onto the plastic page protector. Brooke wiped it off and sniffed. Heather had quite suddenly become much more real. Brooke turned back to a picture with Heather's baldness and wondered if Greg's wife had died from a relapse. Brooke put the scrapbook on the coffee table and retrieved the other two volumes in hopes of finding an answer to Heather's death. Both were equally silent on that point. Instead the books recorded Angela's birth and followed her through her toddler years, stopping abruptly after her third birthday. Brooke sniffed again as she closed the final scrapbook and placed it beside the others.

"I didn't think you'd want to look at those right now," Greg said suddenly from behind her. His voice startled her, and she jumped. Greg eyed her tears.

Brooke stood up quickly and wiped at her cheek with the back of her hand. "I'm sorry. I shouldn't have intruded."

Greg shook his head. "They're meant to be looked at. They just haven't been for a while." He sat beside her on the couch and eyed the

books. "Looking at those made it worse, right? I suppose you're close
to running now."

Brooke shook her head. "To be honest, it helps to know that she
was a real person. In fact, I'd like you to tell me more about Heather."

Greg's gaze was thoughtful. "All right. If you really want me to.
But first, Angela has a request. She wants you to say good night." He
pointed down the hall. "Around the corner, second door to your
right."

Hoping the dim hallway would hide her tear-streaked face,
Brooke went down the hall and peeked around Angela's bedroom
door. "Your dad said you wanted to see me?"

Angela lay in her bed, her fluffy pink comforter up to her chin.
She nodded. "Usually he sings me a song for a tuck-in, but would you
do it this time?"

"Sure." Brooke sat at the edge of her bed. This was one performance that wouldn't make her nervous. "What song would you like?"

"'Families Can Be Together Forever.' It's my favorite." She paused
and lowered her voice. "You know, because of my mom."

Brooke swallowed hard at the thought. "It's a pretty song, isn't it?"

Angela took Brooke's hand, then closed her eyes and settled into
her pillow as Brooke softly sang of eternal families. As she finished the
last phrase, Angela groggily opened her eyes. "Thanks."

Brooke leaned over and kissed Angela's cheek as if she had done it
every night of her life. "Good night, Angela."

She left the room and quietly closed the door behind her. When she
looked up, she saw Greg smiling in the hall. "I love hearing you sing."

"You set me up," Brooke said, giving Greg a light punch in the
arm. Greg winked as he took her hand, and together they returned to
the family room.

They sat on the couch, both eyeing the albums, but neither saying
a word for an awkward minute. Finally, with a deep breath, Greg
picked up the first one. "Are you sure you want to hear about Heather?"

Brooke nodded. "I'm sure."

Greg turned the pages and looked at a picture with a distant gaze.
"Heather and I were high-school sweethearts," he began. "She asked
me to the Sadie Hawkins dance our sophomore year, but I couldn't go
because my sixteenth birthday was still four months away. She was a

couple of months older than me, but she assumed I was older. Anyway, I was humiliated to have to say no, but when she heard the reason, she didn't want to ask another boy. So she had a video party at her house with me and a bunch of other friends from school and some youth from her ward that night instead."

Greg's eyes grew sentimental at the memory as he continued turning pages. "We dated most of high school. Here's our junior prom picture. And this one is from MORP, the spring dance after that. She and her friends took the 'prom backwards' thing literally." He laughed at the memory. "That was one of the most fun dates I ever had."

He pointed out some more pictures on the next few pages, then went on. "She refused to be exclusive—the General Authorities had counseled against it, she said. So every time I took her out twice, she would make sure to have a date with someone else in between. It didn't matter. It was no secret to our entire class that we were a 'couple.' But for her it was the principle of the thing. She broke up with me two days before my mission, saying she wouldn't ever wait for a missionary. She still wrote to me regularly, but not a romantic word the whole two years. I fully expected her to be married or on her own mission by the time I got home. Either way, I figured she wouldn't care for me that way anymore. But when I returned, everything was still there."

He looked up from the page and stared at the wall as if he could see the memories playing out before his eyes. "When I walked off the plane, there she was with my family. She stood away from the rest of the group, by a window. The sun shone through it and lit up her hair and face so she looked like an angel. And I knew. All my feelings rushed back, only stronger."

Greg's head snapped back to the book as his thoughts returned to the present. "Sorry. You didn't need to hear all that." He silently turned to the pages of Heather's illness, and almost passed them in silence, but Brooke stopped his hand.

"Was she sick when you got home?"

"She was sick, but we didn't know what it was then. She wasn't diagnosed for another month." A finger passed over a picture of Heather smiling in her hospital bed, surrounded by her family.

"That must have been very difficult for both of you."

"Especially for her. She always loved her hair. It had been waist-long since grade school, and losing it was one of the hardest things she ever had to go through. When it started to fall out she even tried to keep me from seeing her." He had a wan smile at the memory. "She thought I wouldn't love her anymore if I saw her bald."

"And yet you proposed then."

"I suppose that convinced her. We were married as soon as the doctors said she was strong enough to go to the temple."

Together she and Greg looked through all three books, including the one with pictures of Heather in a hospital gown holding a tiny red newborn. He swallowed hard at the picture. "Angela was born a few months after our first anniversary. It was one of the happiest days of my life." He gently traced the faces in the picture with his finger. "Heather wanted a big family. She used to say she wanted ten children, just to be in the double digits. We never expected that she wouldn't live to have more than one. Of course, with her treatments, we were thrilled that she got pregnant at all." He paused at the picture for another moment before closing the book.

As if he read her mind, Greg said, "I've kept meaning to put together photo albums for Angela, but I haven't been able to get myself to do it. That was one of Heather's hobbies, and I haven't been able to open the boxes with her scrapbook stuff in them." He closed the book and laid it on the table in front of them. "But I suppose I've put you through enough of that tonight." He tried to hide a sniff as he stood and carried the books back to their place on the shelf. Brooke's eyes had gotten misty too at the thought of the young mother, full of life and hope, her dreams ending so suddenly.

When Greg returned to his seat on the couch, Brooke asked in a whisper, "How did she die? Did the leukemia come back?"

The question clearly took Greg off guard. He glanced at the scrapbooks again. "No, it wasn't the leukemia," he said abruptly. He covered his eyes with his hands and shook his head. "I'm sorry, I—"

"No, I'm sorry. I shouldn't have asked."

His head came up, and he wiped at his cheeks. "That's all right. It's natural for you to wonder. But . . . I'd rather not talk about it."

Greg stared at the albums for another minute in silence. Then he sniffed, took a deep breath, and put on a smile. Brooke had a lot more questions, but figured they had both experienced enough emotion and revelations for one night. But for the moment, Brooke felt a little better about possibly being the second woman Greg might learn to love.

As soon as the thought crossed her mind, she shied away from it. She hadn't known Greg Stevens long enough to even toy with the idea of *love,* she reminded herself. She *cared* for him and would allow herself to explore what she and Greg had together. She hoped that what Greg felt for her might turn into love. She knew that her own feelings were starting to head in that direction—if she let them.

CHAPTER 11

As always, Brooke got a bit tearful saying good-bye to her class on the last day of school. But this year the melancholy was largely reduced by taking Angela out for ice cream at the end of the school day. Originally Brooke had expected that any time spent with Angela would also be time spent with Greg, but that quickly turned out not to be the case. Angela's Grandma Stevens had been tending when Greg worked evening hours, but lately that had become difficult because of her new calling as Relief Society president. So Brooke stepped in as Angela's evening sitter, and in no time Brooke and Angela considered each other great friends. Often Brooke put Angela down for the night and read and sang to her.

The days flew by. Brooke knew that all too soon Greg and Angela would be leaving for Europe, so she tried to make the most of each moment with them.

Grandma Stevens continued to tend Angela when Greg worked days, and Brooke quickly adapted from her school-year mentality to summer vacation. She planned on thoroughly enjoying some freedom. She knew how fast the summer could go, and before she knew it the next school year would be staring her in the face. Then she would have to buckle down with training workshops, faculty meetings, and plans for the next school year. As she did with the beginning of each year's vacation, she allowed herself some pet luxuries: reading a book into the wee, small hours of the morning, sleeping in, and taking ridiculously long bubble baths, followed by a bowl of Rocky Road ice cream.

One evening Brooke brought a video of *Sleeping Beauty* for Angela to watch before bed. Angela squealed. "I've never seen this one," she said, looking at the cover. "Dad and I usually get things like *Toy Story* and *Pinocchio*. They're fun, but I like princesses and stuff too. Can we watch it now?"

Brooke eyed the clock. "How about you get ready for bed, and then we can stay up late and watch it? It'll be past your bedtime when it's over."

Angela put down the video and headed toward her room. "I'll be back in one minute."

"Oh, and get Misty from the backyard and put her back in her box." Only recently had they let the kitten spend some time in the fenced backyard. Greg had grown a bit soft and even allowed the cat inside sometimes, although never at night.

Angela opened the back door and called for the young cat. When Misty didn't come, Angela stepped into the backyard and called louder. Her brow furrowed as she turned to Brooke, who stood behind her at the door. "She always comes when I call. What if she's lost?"

Brooke went outside and looked around too. "Let's check the front yard. Maybe she squeezed under the neighbor's fence or can't hear us."

Angela's face showed eager hope, but worry filled her eyes as she walked determinedly to the front door and opened it. "Misty! Misty-kitty!"

Calling for the cat, they went into the front yard. Angela searched the bushes and trees, and Brooke checked the rest of the yard. Brooke suddenly stopped short, a pit in her stomach. Misty lay in the gutter, obviously run over by a car and tossed to the side. Brooke glanced over at Angela, then back at the cat, just starting to grow out of its tiny kitten stage. She didn't know how to break the news. It wasn't her place, but Angela's father wasn't around, and there was nothing else she could do.

She walked to Angela, who peered up a tall maple in hopes of seeing her kitty in a branch. Brooke reached over and touched the young girl's arm. "Angela."

"Did you find her?" Angela's face fell when she saw Brooke's expression.

"I found her."

Angela's eyes grew wide. "Where is she? Is something wrong?"

Brooke involuntarily glanced toward the gutter. "Angela, I—"

Angela caught the look and ran to the gutter. She fell to her knees and burst into tears. "Brooke! Call 911! Maybe she's not dead yet."

Brooke knelt beside Angela and put her arm around her. "I'm sorry, Angela. It's too late for that. She's already gone."

Angela's lips quivered, and she could hardly speak through her tears. "But she can't be dead! She can't be!" Brooke held her close, and Angela sobbed into Brooke's shoulder as they sat on the cool grass. Eventually Brooke suggested that they find a box for the small body so that Angela could have a memorial service with her father later. Angela nodded through her tears and found a large shoe box that was just the right size. Angela insisted on staying right there as Brooke put the body in the box and cleaned up the gutter, then placed the box in the garage in spite of Angela's pleas to bring it in the house.

They didn't enjoy watching *Sleeping Beauty*. Angela eventually cried herself to sleep in Brooke's arms.

Greg arrived home moments after Brooke had carried Angela to bed, and she told him what had happened. He lifted the lid of the box, shaking his head at the sight of the pitiful form. "I knew she wasn't ready for a pet. I'll bet it broke her heart."

"Daddy?"

Greg and Brooke turned around to see Angela standing at the doorway. In two swift strides, Greg reached his daughter and held her close. "I'm so sorry about Misty."

Angela cried for a moment, then pulled away and wiped at her cheeks. "Daddy, is . . . is Misty with Mommy now?"

Greg rocked back. "I think so, especially if Mommy knows how much Misty meant to you. I think she'll take care of her for you in heaven."

Angela's lower lip quivered. "You think? You don't know for sure?"

"I'm not sure how it all works with animals, but I believe they have spirits and go to heaven, just like people."

Angela rubbed at one eye and another tear escaped. "If you're not sure about Misty, how can you be sure about Mommy?" She spoke in a whisper. "What if I never see either of them again?"

Greg picked Angela up and sat on the couch, putting her on his lap. He turned her so they could look into each other's eyes. "Gee-la, there aren't a lot of things I know for sure, but there are a few things I do know. I know that your mother is in heaven. I know she's watching over you. And I know you'll see her again."

Angela's eyes showed she wanted to believe. "How do you *know?*"

Greg touched his heart. "I've felt it right here. And you can feel it too." He reached for her little hand and placed it over her own heart. "Right there."

Angela looked at her hand on her heart, then up at her father. "Kinda like the Holy Ghost?"

Greg nodded, a slight curve spreading over his mouth. "Exactly like the Holy Ghost."

As Brooke drove home that night she couldn't stop thinking about Angela and Misty. There had been many times she had pictured herself as a mother figure to Angela. But with Misty's death that night, the point was driven home that Brooke was anything but a mother to Angela. Watching Greg comfort his daughter and Angela opening up to her father made Brooke realize just how little she knew about parenting.

Angela had been only three years old when her mother had died. Young, but old enough to have a few memories, memories held like treasures. Brooke suddenly felt guilty for picturing Angela calling her "Mommy" some day.

For weeks nothing had tarnished Brooke's life, not even her own feelings about Heather. Since the night she had asked Greg about Heather, Brooke had mentally put her on the shelf with the scrapbooks and hadn't thought much about her. She wouldn't have admitted it to anyone, including herself, but she had purposely avoided thinking about Heather. Everything Brooke had learned about the woman loaded the scales in Heather's favor, and left Brooke wanting. Heather had suffered through serious health problems and had come out meek but strong. She had attended nursing school and graduated at the top of her class. She was gorgeous. She was perfect in every way as far as Brooke could tell.

She had convinced herself that by learning about Heather, her concerns over the matter had been erased. Instead, her emotions had been conveniently shoved into a dusty corner in hopes they would simply be covered by cobwebs and disappear. Then Angela experienced another death, and everything about Heather returned front and center.

On Wednesday Greg and Angela dropped by for the evening, their last chance to be together, since the family would be leaving for their trip early the next morning. They baked cookies and played UNO. For a time, as she laughed with Greg and Angela, she almost forgot she wouldn't see them again for several weeks.

Too soon it was time to say good-bye. She held Angela close before letting her go to climb into Greg's truck. Greg took a bit longer. He squeezed Brooke's hand. "I'll miss you," he said.

"I'll miss you too. Don't go falling for some gorgeous French woman."

Greg laughed. "Don't worry, I won't. Unless I find one who can outdance you." A gentle kiss and a long hug followed, and Greg finally walked away, neither of them wanting to say good-bye. Brooke closed the door, then stood at the window and watched them drive away.

When their taillights were no longer visible, she drew the curtains shut and sighed. She wouldn't get to sleep that night unless she distracted herself. She thought about another hot bath, but brushed it off. She was not in the mood. Instead, she settled down at the kitchen table with a bowl of ice cream and the unread newspaper of the day. Flipping through it halfheartedly, she tried to think of things she could do to keep busy while Greg and his daughter were away.

She could call some of her single friends from the ward and have the Jane Austen video party they had been talking about for the last year. She could always read some more books. Maybe pick up that afghan she had been working on—or rather neglecting—for the last four years. She hadn't spent much time with her mother lately. They could go out for lunch together, if for no other reason than to help patch things up from their last conversation.

Last week she had gotten one of her mother's predictable answering-machine messages. Maybe a mother-daughter phone call would help. Or a lunch.

Brooke turned newspaper pages absently, scanning the headlines, here and there reading a paragraph or two. Then her eyes landed on a tiny announcement about auditions for a local theater's production of

Into the Woods. She nearly choked on a bite of ice cream, and she sat up to read the details. It was the same theater she had auditioned for last time. Open auditions would be held a week from Friday. Brooke mentally calculated. She had a voice lesson with Desaray tomorrow, which meant they could pick out an audition piece to work on for the week, and Brooke would have one more lesson after that for polishing.

She sat back in her chair and stared out the window before her. She had memorized the entire soundtrack of the play years ago. She thought through the cast of characters, wondering if she had any chance of landing a part, since the only minor parts were Cinderella's stepsisters, Rapunzel, and a couple of others. For the most part, all the roles were significant. Brooke would be happy to be a stepsister she decided. She hardly qualified to play Rapunzel. Even though the part was small, it required a high soprano voice, and Brooke couldn't hit Rapunzel's high b-flats to save her life.

If nothing else, preparing for the audition would keep her busy for at least a week of the Stevenses' trip. She could hardly wait to tell Greg about her audition. And she would tell him about it, she decided, even if it flopped. He was the one person who had hoped she'd chase her dream one day. Twice he had even told her about upcoming auditions he had seen announcements for. But she couldn't pass up her favorite musical of all time.

The next day she arrived at her lesson five minutes early, antsy to tell Desaray her decision and get to work. Desaray was thrilled at the news.

"I've been hoping you'd do something like this for some time now," she said. "You've got such a great voice, and auditions, no matter what the outcome, are always great learning experiences." She turned to the piano and began flipping through one of Brooke's songbooks. "So what part do you want to aim for? We can pick a song that complements your voice the best."

"Oh, I'd be happy with any of them," Brooke said.

"All right. Then, ideally, which one would you prefer to have?"

Brooke looked down at her hands, unwilling to admit her favorite role. "Ideally? My two favorite parts are Cinderella and . . ."

"And the Baker's Wife? She's sometimes considered the lead. She'd be a hoot to play."

"No, not the Baker's Wife." Brooke shrugged with a laugh. "It may sound silly, but I don't think I could pull off her kissing scene with Cinderella's prince."

"Then who?"

"The Witch."

Brooke braced herself for Desaray to laugh. They both knew that the Witch was the central character and most often was considered an even bigger part than the Baker's Wife. Desaray turned to a song in the middle of the book. "I think you'd have a shot at getting that part if you really want it. Let's try this song with your voice. It might work for getting either the Witch or Cinderella." Desaray leaned over conspiratorially. "Little Red Riding Hood is my favorite character, but she requires more attitude than vocal ability."

Brooke left the lesson with several new exercises specifically targeted at helping with her audition. Finally she had something to occupy her mind instead of Greg. So for the first time, she played her lesson tape on the way home. She listened to it over and over again each day that week as she did daily tasks. As she put on her makeup in the morning she listened to her own voice, then tried to stretch her own limits on each exercise. As she ran errands around town she popped the tape into the car stereo and sang along to the accompaniment. Instead of the expected thirty minutes of practice, Brooke found herself putting in a few hours each day. More than once she was tempted to put in the John Denver CD she bought the week before, but she tossed it to the side and put in her vocal tape instead.

The following Thursday when Brooke stood up from breathing at her lesson, Desaray began playing warm-ups. When she finished the last exercise, Desaray turned to her and put one hand on her hip. "What on earth happened to you this week?"

Brooke took a step back and scrunched up her face. "I forgot to raise my palate again, didn't I? Or was I flat?"

"Hardly. I've never heard such a huge improvement in one week. I knew you had an instrument in there, but . . . heavens, I don't know what to say. How much did you practice?"

"A lot more than ever before," Brooke admitted.

Desaray turned back to the piano with a shake of her head. "After hearing you warm up, I'm anxious to see what your audition piece sounds like."

As she sang, Brooke closed her eyes and pictured herself in her car, where she always sang her best. When she finished the song, Desaray nodded with satisfaction. "Fabulous."

Brooke bit her lip, not daring to hope. "Do you think I might have a chance?"

"Definitely. Provided you don't tense up at the audition, and that you sing for the casting director like you just sang for me." Desaray turned back to the piano. "Let's try it again. This time I want you to pretend you're performing it for the director."

Brooke pictured herself handing her sheet music to the pianist, taking her place before the director, and beginning to sing, just as she had before. The image was so real that her heart beat harder and she felt her throat tense up. She got only halfway through the song when Desaray stopped playing and shook her head. She wagged one of her pink manicured nails in Brooke's direction. "That's what I meant by tensing up. You need to relax." She pointed toward the carpet. "Hit the floor."

Brooke obeyed, her confidence flattened. So she could sing well relaxed, but how could she possibly sing well through nerves for an audition, let alone for an entire audience night after night?

After a few minutes, Desaray turned off the breathing music. "All right. Stand up. Let's try it one more time."

When Brooke finished the song this time, Desaray turned to her. Brooke hugged her arms to her chest as she waited for the verdict. "That time you were right on again. You can't let yourself tense up when you sing. Promise me something. Before you go into the audition tomorrow—and you *are* going—I want you to breathe for twenty minutes in your car. Deal?"

Brooke nodded. "Deal." Anything to avoid the painful constriction of her throat and the humiliation brought with it, she thought.

Desaray patted her on the shoulder and picked up the stack of Brooke's music from the top of the piano. "Just let it go. You've trained your muscles well enough that if you let them do their job, they will. Don't let fear get in the way."

CHAPTER 12

Brooke arrived at the theater parking lot with plenty of time to spare so she could breathe for twenty minutes as she had promised Desaray. She reclined the driver's seat and inserted a tape of classical music, then lay back and closed her eyes to do her breathing exercises. They helped her to relax somewhat, although she could never entirely get rid of the nervous energy bouncing around her middle. She kept eyeing the clock, finally getting out of her car to face the audition when she realized she had been sitting there for fifteen minutes. As she walked toward the steps of the theater, she held her music to her chest, thinking of the last time she had entered these doors. So much had changed since she left the audition in humiliation hardly two months ago. She felt as if she had lived enough in that time to fill two years.

The same middle-aged woman at the desk handed Brooke a form to fill out and waved her into the theater area. Brooke found a seat and began filling out the paper. She itched to sneak away, but she resisted the urge and instead focused on breathing deeply.

With determination she filled out her sheet and waited for her number to be called, and in an effort to distract herself, she looked around the small theater as she waited. She wondered how the director planned to put on *Into the Woods*, a show known for its elaborate sets, in the round.

Brooke didn't have to wait long for her audition, which turned out to be a good thing, because she didn't have a chance to get too nervous.

"Number eighteen."

Brooke crossed the room, handed the pianist her music, and took her place. She breathed in deeply twice before the music began. As she sang, Brooke felt almost detached from her body, as if she were watching herself.

I don't sound too bad.

"Thank you," the director said, more to the papers on his clipboard than to Brooke as he jotted down some notes.

A woman about Brooke's own age smiled and added, "If we need to see you again, you'll hear from us by tomorrow night. Callbacks are Saturday."

As Brooke made her way across the parking lot, she didn't have a firm idea of how well—or how poorly—she had performed. It had felt much better than the last time. She could actually breathe and get the notes out this time. Otherwise the experience resembled a haze. She collapsed in the driver's seat and closed her eyes, a smile curving her mouth. But she had done it. As Desaray had said, auditioning was a good thing, a learning experience, regardless of the outcome. She wouldn't worry about whether the phone would ring for callbacks. And next time would be easier.

"Next time," she murmured. Yes, there would be a next time. In an odd way, the audition had been fun; it brought back so many memories from performing in high school. Brooke turned the key and guided her car out of the parking lot. It didn't matter in the least whether she got a big part or any part at all. Even Sleeping Beauty would have been fine, even though she only appeared for literally five seconds at the end of the show. Only one thing could make the day better—telling Greg and seeing his face light up at the news, but she would have to settle for some ice cream with caramel sauce on top.

* * *

Brooke was invited to callbacks. She spent most of Saturday at the theater, which proved to be an ordeal—hours of being stared at and being asked to sing so many bars of various parts. More grouping and staring followed, then a bit more singing and playing a scene or two.

At one point the director, Mark, sat on the back row of the theater. "I want all you ladies to line up," he said. The dozen or so actresses lined up as ordered. "Jeremy will play Rapunzel's melody, and one by one, I want each of you to sing it." He turned to his assistant. "Kathy, I don't want to be prejudiced by seeing who is singing what part, since we hear Rapunzel without seeing her as often as not. So when I close my eyes, you point to them out of order for them to sing. Ladies, are you ready?" Brooke and the rest of the line nodded, and Mark closed his eyes. "All right, Jeremy."

One by one they sang Rapunzel's melody, and Brooke winced as her voice cracked on the high b-flat. No matter, she reminded herself. She wasn't there to get a part, just to get a learning experience and conquer her fears. When they had all sung the part, Kathy and Mark conferred for a few minutes. He nodded, and asked for the first, third, and sixth actresses pointed at to sing the part again. Brooke wasn't one of them. She had to swallow a knot of disappointment, but managed to keep any emotion from registering on her face. The director finally addressed the entire group of hopefuls.

"Thank you for coming. We'll contact you within the next couple of days if you have a part. Please audition again, regardless of the result. You're all very talented. It'll be a difficult decision."

As the actors dispersed, Brooke crossed the small stage to get her purse when the director called to her. "Wait a minute. I'd like to speak with Marci and . . . Brooke."

Brooke looked up in surprise. "Yes?"

Marci, another hopeful, who Brooke had known on sight would snag a part, crossed the stage area with Brooke. The director came down a few rows, sat down, put his hands on the seat in front of him, and leaned his chin on his hands. He stared at the two of them. Brooke was tired of being gawked at, but she kept her smile on anyway. "Would you two be willing to dye your hair?" he suddenly asked.

Marci's eyes widened a bit, but she smiled and nodded. "Sure, I guess."

"I guess so," Brooke said. "Why?"

"We've got this long, curly wig that's a gorgeous shade of red. I want the Witch to wear it for the second act, for when she regains her beauty. Are you familiar with the play?" Brooke nodded mutely. "Anyway, the wig isn't a full one. It attaches to the back of the head, which means the front of the actress's hair would have to be dyed to match. Probably permed too. I've decided I want the two of you for the Witch for the two casts. But before I make anything final, I had to know whether you'd be willing to perm your hair and dye it red."

Brooke and Marci looked at each other. Brooke wasn't sure she had heard right, but she came to herself just before the silence had become awkward. "Red?" Brooke said, then shrugged. "Sh-sure, I'll do it." She could think about the repercussions of having red hair later. Marci agreed readily, saying she had always wanted to try dying her hair, and this gave her the excuse.

Mark gave their hair another look as he bit the inside of his cheek. He nodded to himself. "Great. Anyway, if you guys want the part, it's yours."

Marci bounced lightly, then surprised Brooke by throwing her arms around her and giving her a hug.

Unable to get the grin off her face, Brooke finally regained the use of her voice. "Great! I mean, thank you. I mean, when do rehearsals start?"

"Next week. I'll call you both with details. You'll get a copy of the full schedule at the first rehearsal."

With that, he stood up and sauntered out of the theater with as little emotion as if he had just given Brooke the time of day rather than the incredible news that she had landed the lead role.

That night Brooke paced her living room, wishing she had something to do to use up her nervous energy, like go country dancing with Greg. He would be so proud of her, she knew, and wished she could call him. But since that wasn't an option, she satisfied herself by calling at least one of the people who would be as excited as she was—Desaray.

Her voice teacher had scarcely managed a "hello" before Brooke jumped in. "I got the Witch! Can you believe it? And it's all thanks to you!"

Desaray squealed like a schoolgirl, and Brooke did a little dance of celebration in her living room. "I knew you could do it if you didn't panic. So tell me all about it. Every detail."

Brooke willingly complied. Desaray had auditioned countless times herself, even judged auditions, so she knew the ropes as well as anyone. She could also appreciate everything Brooke went through, from the initial audition to the "cattle calls" of standing in line forever at the callbacks.

"I'll be there opening night," Desaray promised.

Each night at rehearsal, Brooke felt as if she lived a dream. The first week they did nothing but go over the music, since the play was an operetta. She hardly needed to look at the score since she knew the part by heart. Each time Mark cued her she got a thrill. The first two days she had to do some breathing beforehand to relax, but by the third practice she was enjoying herself thoroughly and could sing her part without her throat clenching up. Singing in front of an audience would be harder, she knew, but at least she was singing comfortably in front of other people. Mark spent much more time working with Marci, who had a beautiful voice, but wasn't familiar with the music of the play at all.

Brooke returned home after Friday's rehearsal not feeling tired at all, even though it was late and she had spent three hours at the theater. She'd been gone most of the day, and as she walked into the kitchen, she plopped the mail and her purse on the counter, along with the bright wig Mark had sent home with her so she could eventually get her hair dyed to match. She tried to picture what she would look like with flaming red, curly hair as she shuffled through the mail—mostly junk, except a bill and two postcards.

Brooke pulled out the postcards. One had a picture of Big Ben on the front, the other the Tower of London. She hurriedly turned them around. She read Angela's uneven handwriting first. "Dear Brooke, I liked the wax museum. Dad asked the information-booth guy a question, but he was wax! I miss you. Love, Angela."

With her heart beating a hair faster, Brooke turned over the other postcard. "Dear Brooke," it began, "Angela is having the time of her life. If you were here, I would be too." Brooke bit her lips with pleasure and read on. "Hope you haven't forgotten me yet. I wish I had an address where you could write to us, but I don't even know the hotel that we'll be staying at in Paris next week. Love, Greg."

Brooke instinctively turned over the postcard as if there would be more on the other side. She had struggled through nearly two weeks without Greg, and this single postcard made all her longings rush back, and she yearned for a long letter or a phone call. She turned back to the words and stared at the end of his message. "Love," he had said. He had never used that word before, but then, it could just be his way of closing a message. She picked up Angela's postcard. She had used it too, so it might not mean anything.

But she couldn't keep herself from murmuring, "I think I love you too, Greg Stevens."

* * *

To Brooke's relief, the last week of the European trip flew past, largely thanks to the daily demands of immersing herself in the play. She had to be fitted for her costumes, then for the prosthetic nose, teeth, and hands for the first act, when the Witch was ugly. Brooke arrived for her molds at a costume shop just as Marci came out.

"Have fun," she said, holding the door open for Brooke. "That's nasty stuff they put in your mouth."

Mark and Kathy, co-directing and apparently always on each other's tails, arrived at the same time. "It's not that bad. It's just like getting forms for braces," Mark said as he came up behind them.

"I rest my case," Marci said with a laugh.

A worker directed Brooke and Kathy to adjoining chairs, and moments later shoved a goop-filled tray into Brooke's mouth. When Kathy got a matching tray of goop in her mouth, Brooke's eyebrows went up. She waved her hand at Mark to get his attention, since she couldn't speak. He finally noticed her look and came over to explain.

"You're wondering why she's getting molds too? Oh, I forgot you didn't know. Kathy will play your double for the end of Act One, when the potion is getting mixed up. That's when you'll be getting all beautiful backstage, putting on the wig and evening gown. She'll only have a couple of lines, and she'll make sure the audience sees the witch nose, hands, and teeth. At the right moment, she'll slip offstage. That shouldn't be hard, because there's a lot of commotion going on right then, and the audience will be focusing on the Baker's father dying. Then you'll come on, this time with the hood covering your hands and draped over your face. When you drink the potion, you convulse a bit, drop the cape, and reveal your beauty. If we time it right, the audience won't know what hit them."

The attendant came to take the hardened mold from Brooke's mouth. She took the offered paper towel, wiped her mouth, then turned to Mark. "I always wondered how they made the switch. Is that how they did it on Broadway?"

"I have no idea," Mark said with a shrug. "Broadway won't share their secrets. I imagine they did something similar. This method is my own invention, but I think it'll work well, especially since you, Marci, and Kathy are all about the same height and have similar voices."

Kathy's mold was taken out and she wiped her face. "I don't remember that stuff being so nasty," she said with a grimace. "It started going down my throat. It was all I could do not to gag."

Brooke glanced from Kathy to Mark, then back again. "So why isn't Kathy playing the Witch with me or Marci as the double? She's got more experience."

"I'm the music director," Kathy explained as she dabbed at a few more bits of goo with a paper towel. "I've done my share of acting, and the thrill of being on stage is wearing off. I still do it when I'm needed, but lately I prefer to work backstage with Mark."

A worker called for Mark to come over to the counter and look at the impressions and schedule a time to pick up the molds.

"I want you to get your hair dyed this week," Mark said before heading for the counter.

Brooke's hand froze over her purse. "Already?"

Mark made a few notes in his planner and nodded absently. "I want to be sure we match the wig perfectly. That way we'll know how fast it'll fade and if we'll have to dye it more than once." Mark had been in theater for years. Brooke had no doubt he knew what he was doing.

"All right," she said, trying to picture herself with red hair. The reality of the hair color change hadn't sunk in until that moment. And Greg wouldn't know about it either—until he saw her.

CHAPTER 13

As she walked in the door at home, Brooke looked at the mirror and brushed her straight hair to the side. She tried to imagine it curly and red, then looked down at the mail in her hands. Behind two credit card applications she found a postcard, this one with a picture of Versailles on the front. It briefly listed a flight number and arrival time, then ended with a simple, "If you can't be there, I'll call you Sunday. Greg."

It didn't escape Brooke's notice that Greg hadn't written "Love" this time. Maybe they had been apart too long. After all, they had known each other only a short time before the trip. He might wish he could back out of the relationship, or at least be wary of her meeting his parents already. She looked back at the short message. He didn't actually say he wanted her at the airport. Did he secretly hope she wouldn't come? Angela had probably pestered him into sending the information.

Brooke supposed she might as well not overanalyze anything and just go. But as she looked up from the mail and saw her reflection in the mirror, she groaned. Going to the airport and meeting Greg's parents would be a big deal under normal circumstances, but with flaming-red, permed hair? What would Greg—not to mention his parents—think of her before she had a chance to explain?

A few days later she clenched her hands nervously as she watched the hair stylist pull out the dye. Mark had insisted she get the dye job as soon as possible so he could okay it and refused to let her wait until after the weekend. Brooke normally didn't have her hair styled after getting it cut, but this time Mark wanted to see the final product, so Brandi, the stylist, blow-dried and styled the new look.

"How do you like it?" Brandi asked as she pumped hair spray in a cloud around Brooke.

Brooke reached up and gently touched one of the bright curls. "It's . . . different." *I hardly recognize myself.*

"It's perfect," Mark interjected. "I'm glad your skin coloring works well with red. It doesn't look obviously dyed."

Brandi nodded vigorously. "I love the color. I might try it on myself next time."

For days, every time Brooke passed a mirror, she had to stop and stare. She felt like a stranger was looking back at her. She had tucked the postcard with Greg's flight plans into her bedroom mirror, and each time she glanced at her new look, she vacillated between going and not going to the airport. She knew that Mark would let her out of one rehearsal if she asked, especially since she knew her part better than most of the cast.

"I'll just leave it up to fate," she decided at last, tucking the postcard firmly into her purse. If Saturday's rehearsal went as long as usual, she wouldn't go. If Mark dismissed the cast early, she would meet Greg and Angela—and his parents—at the airport.

On Saturday Mark surprised the cast when he announced that he would be excusing the cast two hours earlier than normal. As everyone else packed up, Brooke snagged Jeremy. "Hey, would you mind going through my opening song with me? I still mess up on the list of vegetables in the garden."

"Sure." Jeremy dropped his bag and headed back for the piano.

Brooke breathed a sigh of relief, although she almost laughed at herself. She used to be the woman cowering before singing in public, yet here she was, begging to sing so she could delay going to the airport. Jeremy and Brooke went through the song three times. Jeremy glanced at his watch.

"Come on, Brooke. You know the piece cold. You deserve a night off."

"How about just once more through?"

Jeremy shook his head. "Brooke, the song is fine. Don't worry so much about it. I don't know about you, but I'm going to have fun tonight." He put on his jacket and left.

Brooke followed him out of the theater and slowly walked to her car. She sat in the driver's seat and stared at the clock, knowing she had plenty of time to make it to the airport even if she hit traffic. Finally, with a deep breath, she turned the key. "Here we go."

As Brooke drove down the freeway, she kept glancing at herself in the rearview mirror. *If only I had a baseball cap or something to hold my hair back with. Anything to make this loud hair less obvious.*

She arrived with nearly half an hour to spare. The airport clock read 8:14, and Brooke adjusted her own watch so it matched. After taking the elevator down from the parking levels, she wandered around the large room where others waited for passengers, first to the baggage claim on one end, then to the other side and back again. She sat down on a chair against the wall and flipped through a magazine, but couldn't concentrate on anything in it. Her toes tapped the floor restlessly. After checking her watch several times, she finally jumped to her feet and went to look at the large television screens again. To her chagrin, the plane was delayed fifteen minutes.

She counted shapes on the floor to distract herself, but each time the elevator behind her dinged, she jumped. Her nerves were frayed to the breaking point, and she knew that the whole thing was getting ridiculous.

Brooke needed to see Greg and his daughter. To see whether Greg still had any feelings for her, or if the past three weeks had changed anything. Maybe his parents had talked him out of dating again. Maybe seeing the romance of England and France had made their relationship pale in comparison.

The plane finally touched down, and Brooke found herself wringing her hands as she watched the passengers come down the escalator toward the security area and from there to baggage claim. She stood in a large group of people, all waiting like she was. She scanned the stream of heads for Greg, but at that distance, each looked the same as the last. A husband stepped off the escalator, passed by the security tables, and embraced his wife as two children clung to a leg each, unwilling to let go. Three young men in worn suits, obviously returning missionaries, were instantly swarmed by their families.

Brooke noticed a man holding a sign that read *Dr. Anderson* and wished she could hold a sign that said *Hair dyed for play*. She pictured the snide remarks Christopher's mother would have made had Brooke dyed her hair three months ago; the woman would have had a field day.

Brooke saw Angela on the escalator, the young girl searching the sea of faces.

"Angela, I'm over here," Brooke called with a wave. But Angela's brow furrowed, not seeing her.

"I can't find her, Daddy. I was so sure she'd be here," Angela said, leaning forward to talk to her father on the step below her.

A moment later, Angela emerged, holding the hand of a pleasant-looking woman who resembled an older Grace Kelly. Greg and a tall, salt-and-pepper gray-haired man followed close behind.

"I don't see her either," Greg said, scanning the crowd.

Brooke took a step forward and opened her arms to Angela. Only then did the young girl recognize her. Her eyes grew two sizes, and her hands flew to her mouth. She released her grandmother's hand and ran into Brooke's arms.

"I missed you so much!" Angela squealed. She pulled back and fingered a bright, curly lock. "But what happened to your hair?" she giggled.

"It's for a part in a play."

"I like it." Angela turned around and dragged Brooke toward the small group a few feet off. "See, Daddy, I told you she'd be here! And look at her hair!"

Greg moved around his parents. Brooke's stomach flip-flopped, and she braced herself for Greg's reaction. He pulled Brooke close. "I missed you," he said, then gave her a kiss and whispered, "I like your new look." He squeezed her hand, then turned to his parents. "Mom, Dad, this is Brooke."

"I'm Linda Stevens, and this is my husband, John. It's so nice to meet you."

John nodded and extended a hand. "Especially after hearing nothing but 'Brooke this and Brooke that' for the entire trip."

Brooke turned to Angela and gave her shoulder a squeeze. "Angela and I are good friends."

"Angela wasn't the one doing most of the talking," Greg said, giving her a smile that warmed her to her toes.

Greg's parents seemed sincerely pleased to meet her, so Brooke didn't feel the urgency to explain her hair. They hadn't reacted to it at all. But Angela had, and wasn't about to forget it anytime soon.

"Grandma, Brooke's real hair is brownish, but she dyed it."

Linda leaned over and whispered, "Angela, that wasn't very good manners."

Angela shook her head vigorously and rushed on. "No, it's not what you think."

"That's right," Brooke said, stepping in to relieve Angela. "I didn't expect to meet you looking like this. I don't usually have red or permed hair, but my director insisted I dye it this week."

Greg's eyebrows went up. "Your what?"

Brooke grinned. "My director. You are looking at the next Witch of *Into the Woods.*" She gave a small curtsey, and Greg applauded, then gave her such a big hug he lifted her off the floor.

"I knew you could do it!" He set her down, then ran his fingers through her hair thoughtfully. "You know, I always wanted to date a redhead. It was something of a fantasy of mine."

"Yeah right."

"No, really. I even asked Heather to dye her hair once, but she wouldn't do it."

"I wouldn't either if my director hadn't insisted on it."

"Wait till I tell my friend Tim," Greg said with a laugh. "We had a bet in high school about the first one of us to date a redhead. Neither of us won before we got married. I'll have to call him up and cash in."

"What do you win?"

Greg pursed his lips as he tried to remember. "A pizza, I think. That was the usual prize for bets."

They headed toward the rotating luggage carousels, Greg holding Brooke's left hand and Angela clinging to her right. Greg's parents took the lead, and Angela talked nonstop about the wonders she had seen.

"In England we even got to see the house where the Peter Cottontail lady lived."

"Beatrix Potter's home," Greg interjected.

"Yeah. And we went to this big castle place that people used to be thrown in when they did something the king didn't like."

"The Tower of London," Greg clarified as he scanned the bags for their own.

"Uh-huh, and we went to the wax museum, but I told you about that in my postcard."

Angela told about going to the Eiffel Tower and how they found out there had been a bomb threat the day they visited. "We could have been blown up!" she said with wide eyes. "Cool, huh?"

Then Angela changed her focus. "My other grandpa is taking us on a campout soon. We go to the Uintahs with my Grandpa Miller every year. You know, my mom's dad. This year he said that I'm getting bigger, so we can hike farther. We'll be gone for two days and one night. Hey, you can come too if you want." Angela's chattering finally stopped abruptly as she waited for an answer.

"Oh, I don't think so, Angela," Brooke said, reeling at the idea of meeting Heather's father. Greg had stepped to the other side of the carousel to pick up a suitcase and didn't hear the invitation. "I don't think your grandpa would like me to come on your special weekend."

"Yes, he would. I know it. Besides, it won't be as fun if I have to be away from you *again!*"

"We'll see," Brooke said in a noncommittal tone. She didn't want to disappoint Angela, but she knew full well that an invitation from a seven-year-old hardly carried authority. Which was just as well, since the very mention of Heather had sent Brooke's stomach churning. She hadn't thought of Greg's late wife for weeks, but now all the emotion surrounding her bubbled to the surface.

"I think we're set," Greg said, returning with their luggage. He glanced at Brooke, who put on a wide smile and hoped he wouldn't notice her flushed face.

His eyes narrowed. "Are you all right?"

Brooke nodded cheerfully. "Are we set? Let's go. Here, let me help." She picked up Angela's pink suitcase with one hand, and Angela held on to Brooke's other hand. Angela also insisted on driving back in Brooke's car with Greg. The Stevenses didn't object, and instead smiled knowingly as they said good-bye and went to find their car in long-term parking.

Angela fell asleep only minutes after they reached the freeway. Brooke glanced in the rearview mirror at her sleeping form. "Poor thing is exhausted."

Greg murmured in agreement. He reached over and squeezed her hand. "I didn't know whether you'd be here," he said. "Or whether you'd still want anything to do with me."

Brooke grinned. "Are you disappointed?"

"I'll give you two guesses." He leaned over and kissed her cheek. "Besides, how can I complain when I come home to my teenage fantasy?" He fingered her hair again. "So what's your schedule like this week?"

"Well, I have rehearsals every evening, usually six o'clock to at least nine, sometimes ten." When Greg blew out his breath, Brooke raised her eyebrows. "What's wrong?"

"I'm working like crazy this week, since I was gone so long. About the only time I have off is evenings, mostly for Angela's dinner and bedtime."

"Right when I'm rehearsing." Brooke gave a shrug that she hoped looked casual. "Well, we've been apart almost three weeks. What's five more days?"

"Seven," Greg corrected.

"You're working Saturday too?"

"Actually, no. My father-in-law scheduled our annual campout this weekend. It's just an overnighter, but I'll be gone Friday and Saturday." Greg thought for a moment.

Brooke nodded. "Angela mentioned it to me. I didn't realize it was this weekend though." She sighed. "Another week seems like forever."

"Unless . . ." Greg's voice trailed off.

"Unless what?"

"Unless you come with us."

Brooke let out a laugh. "You can't be serious."

"I'm completely serious. I'm sure Russell Miller would love to have you there. He keeps asking to meet you."

Brooke glanced sideways at him. "You expect me to believe that Heather's father wants to meet me?"

"He does. Really. Will you come with us?"

Brooke let out a hesitant breath, and shook her head. "I don't think so, Greg. I'm not ready for that, not yet."

"Will you at least think about it?"

Greg's dimple appeared as he smiled at her, and she caved in. "I'll *think* about it. But I'm not promising anything."

As she pulled into Greg's driveway, Brooke wished the drive could have been a bit longer, even if the hour was late. The trip from the airport hadn't come close to making up for three weeks apart, not to mention the upcoming week.

Brooke carried the sleeping girl into her bedroom while Greg brought in the luggage. When he walked her back out to the car, Brooke leaned against the door with a sigh.

"I wish our schedules worked out better this week," Greg said. "It's been too long. We'll have to figure out something so I can see you at least once."

Brooke nodded silently. All week she had been thinking up all kinds of things she could do with Greg, plus activities they could do with Angela. Now her expectations had evaporated, and she would have to wait another week before realizing any of them. Greg took a step closer and reached for her hands.

"I'll call you tomorrow, okay?"

Brooke nodded, trying to hide her disappointment. She forced herself to smile. "Okay." Greg leaned in and gave Brooke a long kiss, which awakened a swarm of butterflies inside her. When he pulled away, Brooke caught her breath. Greg was right. It had been far too long. As she climbed back into the car and drove away, she almost wished he hadn't kissed her like that. It made her want to be with him that much more; the next week would be twice as long.

CHAPTER 14

"I'm still not sure it's a good idea," Brooke said when Greg called about the campout.

"I mentioned it to Russell already, and he thinks it's a great idea. He's been on me for some time to date again. Go figure."

"What does Mrs. Miller think about it?"

"Celia Miller passed away while I was on my mission. It would just be us, Russell, and his daughter Jane. Come on, Brooke. Please come."

"I don't know . . . I've got rehearsal Friday night."

"I'm sure your director will let you miss a practice or two."

Brooke knew Mark would, but she still hesitated.

"I'll miss you if you don't come. And Angela will be broken-hearted," Greg insisted. "Please? We've been apart enough this summer."

Silence hung in the air as Brooke considered. "All right, I'll come," she finally said, wondering what she was getting herself into.

Greg called every morning that week, but Brooke didn't get to see him until Thursday, the night before the campout. Mark graciously let her miss two nights of rehearsals. The stepsisters and the princes needed extra work, he said, and Brooke would have been standing around doing nothing anyway.

Brooke went over to Greg's house Thursday evening so he could help her pack. "There's an art to putting together a backpack," he told her. She would have to take his word for it; she didn't know the first thing about camping. Technically she had certified each year at girls' camp back in her Young Women years, but that hadn't taught her anything. When she had been required to start a fire without matches and cook something on it, she'd managed only a meager flame and had quickly tossed a marshmallow on it before the "fire" went out. Somehow her leader had been willing to count the singed marshmallow as "something cooked." So Brooke certified, hoping she would never be put in a situation where her knowledge of building a fire with steel wool and a battery meant the difference between life and death.

Greg had said he would provide the food, cooking and eating utensils, sleeping bag, and tent. So Brooke just brought along the clothes and personal items he had suggested. When she arrived at Greg's, she found his truck and patrol car parked at the curb. The garage stood open, lights on, and Greg and Angela were inside arguing over something. It was dark out, and Angela wore bright red sleeper pajamas.

"Please, Daddy," Angela pleaded as Brooke walked up the driveway. "I'm so much bigger now. You said so yourself. Isn't that why you agreed with Grandpa to hike farther this year?"

Greg sighed. "Yes, you're bigger, but that doesn't mean you'd enjoy sleeping all by yourself." He glanced over at the sound of Brooke's step. "Maybe you can convince her," he said, tossing a rolled-up tent in her direction. When Brooke caught the bag, he closed the space between them, gave Brooke a light kiss, and put his arm around her shoulders.

"Convince Angela of what?" Brooke asked.

"That I'm big enough to sleep in a tent all by myself this year," Angela piped up. "Daddy has a one-man tent that he used when he was in college, and I want to sleep in it on our trip. He thinks I'll be too much of a scaredy-cat to sleep alone."

"Not exactly the term I used, but that's the general idea," Greg said.

Brooke looked the tent bag over. "Hmm. Are you sure you wouldn't be afraid? Not even a little bit? I mean, it'll be awfully dark, and you won't be able to have your night-light up there. It might be nice to have your dad next to you."

Angela folded her arms and gave Brooke a challenging look. "I've been camping since before I can remember. I know how dark it is up there."

"Oh, of course," Brooke said with an apologetic nod. It didn't matter that Angela had just passed her seventh birthday; she considered herself an expert in camping matters. "Do you usually sleep in your dad's tent on camping trips?"

"Yeah."

"That sounds like fun," Brooke said. "You know, I'll bet he'll miss having you with him in his tent."

Angela looked over at her father as if the idea hadn't occurred to her before. She seemed less antagonistic at the idea that his protestations were for his sake instead of hers. "Would you miss me, Daddy?"

Greg nodded. "Bedtime is one of my favorite times in the mountains. If you make me sleep all by myself, we won't be able to sing together or play our nighttime guessing games—"

"But we can still do all that stuff," Angela cut in. "In my tent, before I go to sleep."

"It wouldn't be the same."

"Please, Daddy? *Please?*" she pleaded, as if all her future happiness depended on his answer. He looked at Brooke, who shrugged with a look of surrender; she had tried.

Greg let out another weary sigh. "You're sure you want your own tent this year?"

"I'm sure."

"Fine. But I'll bring up my three-man tent just in case you change your mind."

"Oh, Daddy. That won't happen," Angela said with mock disgust, even though her face glowed. She jumped at him and clung to his waist. "Thank you! I'll show you how big I am. I'll even carry the tent myself."

Greg ruffled her hair. "All right, little girl. Then let's get packing. We've got a lot to do if we're going to make your pack light enough for you to carry your own tent."

Brooke set the tent bag on the floor beside the card table, which was laden with dehydrated foods, from ramen noodles to Cup-of-Soup mixes and boxes of single-serving hot chocolate packets.

"So how do you know when a backpack is light enough?" Brooke asked, picking up a packet of instant oatmeal with "Peaches and Cream" printed across the front. She grimaced at the thought of eating it.

Greg laughed at her expression. "That stuff really tastes pretty good in the mountains. I'd never eat it at home though. For some reason foods taste different when you're camping."

"The thin atmosphere must interfere with your taste buds," Brooke said, surrendering the oatmeal packet. She looked over the table and tried to picture herself eating any of the food on it, let alone enjoying the process.

"You do it with that," Greg suddenly said, indicating a household scale a few feet off.

Brooke had lost the thread of conversation. "You do what?"

"You use the scale to weigh yourself with and without the pack. That way you know how much your pack weighs. If you want to have a comfortable hike, it shouldn't be more than twenty-five percent of your body weight. That shouldn't be too hard, since we'll only be gone a couple of days. But it's good to check anyway. I've known a few Scouts trying to be macho who tried to make fifty-mile hikes with packs twice what they should be." He chuckled. "You should see them by the time they get home. It's a pathetic sight. I don't recommend doing it. If you want, I won't watch when you weigh yourself."

"Why?"

"Oh, I just assumed . . . I mean, a lot of women don't want to let other people know their weight. At least Heather didn't. Her weight was always a sensitive point . . . I mean . . . Sorry. I shouldn't have mentioned her again."

"It's all right." Brooke didn't mind hearing this kind of thing about Heather. Anything that made Heather seem less perfect gave Brooke less to live up to.

Greg began counting out hot chocolate packets for each backpack. Brooke stepped next to him and was about to ask how she could help when a car pulled up by the curb. In the dark she couldn't make out more than a sport utility vehicle, probably dark green or black. She knew instinctively that it belonged to Greg's father-in-law.

Russell Miller was more than his father-in-law, Brooke reminded herself. He was Angela's grandfather and Heather's father. In moments she would meet the father of the woman who used to fill the shoes she might be stepping into. Despite Greg's assurances that Russell Miller couldn't be more thrilled about their relationship, anxiety washed over her as she waited for the official introduction. She swallowed hard and tried to quiet her heart, which raced against her will as she watched a large man with a barrel chest and a thick, ruddy beard emerge from the car.

The passenger door opened, and a young woman stepped out. Her straight, dark hair was pulled back into a tight ponytail, and she didn't smile. She wore jeans and an oversized sweatshirt. Except for the hard line of her jaw, she bore a strong resemblance to the woman in Greg's wedding pictures. Brooke suddenly remembered Greg and Angela talking about an aunt, but she had forgotten that the sister would be coming along. She hadn't really thought beyond Russell Miller.

The Millers hadn't made it as far as the edge of the driveway before Angela swooped down upon them with a string of contagious squeals. "Aunt Janie! Grandpa! Guess what! Daddy says I can sleep in my own tent this year!"

Russell Miller picked her up in his thick arms and threw her into the air. She let out another one of her squeals, this one laced with a terrified thrill. When he set her down, she gave her aunt a tight hug. They walked up the driveway, Angela between them and holding their hands. Russell clapped Brooke on the shoulder and held out a hand of welcome. "So this must be the Brooke we've heard so much about."

Brooke wondered just what he had heard about her, and how much of that information he had liked. On second thought, she didn't want to know. But his broad smile, full of square teeth, warmed her up, as did the hearty squeeze of thick fingers when he shook her hand.

"She's got a good shake," he said to Greg with approval. "So many women have dead-fish handshakes, but you've got a good grip," he added, now smiling at Brooke. "That's always a good sign. I'm Russell Miller, but I guess you probably knew that." He gave her a wink, then took a step back and motioned to his daughter. "This is my daughter Jane."

"Nice to meet you, Jane."

"You too," Jane said, hardly looking at Brooke. She planted one hand on her hip and arched an eyebrow. "What's this Angela tells us about sleeping in her own tent? Tell me you're not serious."

Greg shrugged. "I tried to talk her out of it, but she's got the Miller stubborn streak." Jane didn't seem amused, so Greg continued in hopes of soothing her concerns for her niece. "Don't worry, Jane. I'll be in my three-man tent right beside her, so she can sleep with me when—" He caught Angela's expression and corrected himself—"*if* she decides to."

Jane sighed in resignation as if that would have to do. Russell and Greg moved together to the table and began packing methodically. Brooke could tell they had done this many times before.

"Have you done much camping?" Jane asked suddenly as she sorted oatmeal packets into piles. Brooke wasn't sure by Jane's tone whether she cared one way or the other.

"Not really," Brooke said with a shrug. "This will be a learning experience for me." An awkward silence ensued, and Brooke spoke up. "I hope I'm not intruding on your trip. I almost didn't come for fear of ruining a family tradition."

"I suppose Greg has the right to invite whoever he wants to," Jane said flatly. She placed a pile of oatmeal before each pack, then turned her attention to putting toilet paper rolls into plastic bags.

"Greg finally managed to convince me to come when he said it was Angela's idea, that she had her heart set on it."

Jane's eyebrows went up, and she looked at Angela, who was busy trying to fill her own pack, while her father and grandfather undid all her work. "Really?" Jane's tone implied a level of disbelief, which Brooke tried to ignore. She needed to stay pleasant, not get defensive. She wanted this woman to like her, although at this rate she would settle for Jane not *disliking* her. Already Brooke knew she had lost points, although she didn't know why.

Brooke began to wonder if coming on this trip was a big mistake. After all, she still didn't know whether she could deal with the entire package that a prolonged relationship with Greg would entail. This trip meant more than simply meeting members of Heather's family. It meant spending two days and a night with two perfect strangers who had every reason to hate her, and one who apparently already did.

Not that she could blame Jane. The more she thought about it, the more she realized that she would probably feel defensive of her own sister's place if she stood in Jane's shoes. Granted, in the same circumstance Brooke would have at least been civil. But even knowing that didn't make the situation any easier to handle. At least Russell seemed happy, if not outright thrilled to meet her. Somehow she felt as if she could spend two days and a night three times over with *him* without any problem.

* * *

The following morning Brooke arrived at Greg's home bright and early at six-thirty. She felt a little odd without any makeup and a tight French braid, which she hadn't worn in her hair since college. Russell and Jane were already there, eating breakfast in the kitchen. Jane wore no makeup either, but then, she had flawless skin and dark lashes, so she didn't look like the blank piece of paper that Brooke did without mascara.

Angela lay asleep on the family room sofa, a half-eaten muffin in one hand and crumbs at the corners of her mouth. She wore old jeans and a T-shirt that she had decorated herself with puff paints, and which showed obvious wear, probably her special camping shirt.

"What happened to her?" Brooke asked, eyeing Angela.

Greg laughed. "She was so excited for the trip she stayed up half the night. She got about three hours of sleep. She crashed as soon as she got dressed this morning." He pulled Brooke close and gave her a quick kiss of hello. "By the way, good morning."

A wave of crimson rushed over Brooke's face as she realized Jane was watching. She brushed her thumb across her lip as if somehow that would erase the kiss as well as that look on Jane's face. Greg and Russell didn't seem to notice the sudden shift in tone between the two women.

Greg motioned toward the spread of food on the counter. "Jane brought two different kinds of muffins, bran and blueberry, and a ton of fruit." He handed her a plate.

"Good morning," Brooke said to Russell and Jane. Russell had just taken a big bite out of a muffin, so he nodded and winked instead of answering. Jane didn't bother to acknowledge her. "This is a great spread, Jane. I didn't get much of a breakfast. Frosted flakes was all since I wanted to be on time, so this is a pleasant surprise. Thank you."

"Mmm hmm," Jane murmured. Brooke assumed it was her way of saying, "You're welcome," without having to actually speak. Brooke turned to Greg with questioning eyes, but he was busy downing the pile of fruit on his plate and didn't seem to notice. Maybe this was normal behavior for Jane.

Brooke filled her plate, then ate quietly at the table while Jane told her father about her latest date.

"He is just so fun. We've only been out once, but already I can tell we have a lot in common. Can you believe that his favorite ice cream is pistachio too?"

Brooke looked up sharply, spilling juice on her T-shirt. She had met only one person in her life who considered pistachio ice cream his favorite.

"So who is this guy?" Greg asked.

"His name is Christopher Morris. He used to work at this big software company, but he was let go with their last layoff, so he's between jobs."

"Christopher Morris?" Brooke asked casually as she wiped at the juice with a napkin.

"You know him?" Jane asked.

Brooke nodded, unsure how to get out of the mess she had just created for herself. "We used to be friends," she finally said, hoping that Jane wouldn't ask more. She didn't. Instead, she continued to talk about their last date and their plans for the next. It seemed almost too coincidental that Christopher would be dating Jane. Brooke wondered if Jane knew all of what Christopher was going through. Maybe she did and it didn't bother her. Maybe Christopher decided to get help after all, but somehow Brooke couldn't believe he could have changed so fast. She worried about Jane, despite the woman's harsh treatment of her. Maybe she should warn Jane. *Or maybe I should just mind my own business.* But the thought continued to nag her until she was determined to talk to Jane when she got a chance.

Twenty minutes later they were ready to leave. All the packs were in the back of Greg's truck, and all that remained was to wake up Angela so she could take a final potty break. Russell did the honors. He gave her nose a kiss and demanded that Sleeping Beauty awake.

Angela scrunched up her nose and rubbed the tip. "That tickles, Grandpa," she murmured, covering her nose with her hands and letting out a tired laugh.

"Better get up, or I'll do it again," Russell said, then proceeded to tickle her all over.

Angela sat up quickly. "I'm up, I'm up! Stop, Grandpa!" she gasped between gales of laughter. Jane shooed her off to the bathroom, and when she emerged, Jane took her hand. They walked outside, and Jane began walking toward the Millers' car. Angela pulled the other direction.

"Our car's over here, Gee-la," Jane said, gently tugging Angela's hand.

"But I want to ride with Daddy and Brooke this time."

Jane stopped dead in her tracks and glared at Brooke. Brooke held her breath. Jane had been distant up to this point, but this was the first sign of outright hostility. Brooke could have almost believed that Christopher had passed along some nasty comments about her to Jane, but she reminded herself that Jane had seemed genuinely surprised that she knew him at all. Not interested in the least, but surprised.

Angela looked up at her aunt. "Can I please ride with Dad?"

Jane answered without taking her gaze from Brooke's face. "Yes, I suppose you can ride with your daddy if he says it's all right."

Angela released Jane's hand and trotted over to the truck. She stopped at the curb with a hop. "I'm driving with you guys," she announced to Greg as he opened the passenger door for Brooke.

"All right, if you want to," Greg said. "But I thought you loved riding up with Grandpa and Aunt Janie."

"Oh, I do," Angela said, climbing up and settling in the center of the bench. "But I've driven with them lots of times. I've never driven into the mountains with Brooke."

Greg looked at Brooke, who couldn't conceal a pleased smile despite Jane's stormy reaction. Even if Brooke herself didn't know where this relationship or her heart was headed, at least Angela's acceptance was not one of the many issues she would have to face.

As soon as they entered Provo Canyon and began to leave most of the signs of civilization behind, Greg popped in a John Denver CD. Angela leaned over to Brooke. "This is our camping music," she explained. "Daddy says it's not right to drive in nature without listening to John Denver."

"So I hear," Brooke said. Greg returned her smile, then looked back at the road. Angela sighed contentedly, then leaned against Brooke's shoulder. By the time they reached Heber, Angela was sleeping deeply. Brooke adjusted Angela's limp form, putting her own arm around Angela's shoulders to make her more comfortable. She gently stroked the soft cheek and brushed the silky ringlets out of her face. Greg noticed the gesture out of the corner of his eye and let out a contented sigh, then turned his attention from the cab of the truck back to the road.

"What was that for?" Brooke asked.

"Nothing," Greg said. When Brooke continued to wait for an answer, he shrugged. "I've just never seen you looking so . . . don't get this wrong, I mean it in the best way . . . I like seeing you . . . maternal."

Brooke had to admit that she enjoyed the feelings that caring for Angela called up from somewhere deep down. She had always loved children. That was one reason she had become a teacher. But those feelings were different from what she felt for Angela. Now that Greg mentioned it, she realized that if she had to put a name to them, "maternal" fit quite well. Brooke looked in the side mirror at the Millers' car, and instead of giving Greg an answer, she let out an involuntary sigh.

"Okay, my turn. What was *that* for?" Greg asked warily. "I shouldn't have said that. I'm sorry. I keep forgetting. Move slow. Give you time."

"That's not it."

"Then what is it?"

"Why does Jane hate me?"

"She doesn't hate you, she—"

"I'm not blind, Greg. I'm sure she'd get a lot of pleasure from gouging my eyes out with a hot poker."

Greg stared at the road. "I suppose it's because you're not Heather," he said after a minute. "She probably thinks you're trying to replace her sister."

"I couldn't replace her. I didn't even know, her for crying out loud."

Greg reached over and took her hand. "She's a great girl, really. Just give her a chance."

"I'll try. But . . ." Her voice trailed off. "There's something else . . . Remember that guy who broke in?"

"The one you broke up with the night we met?"

"Right. That's the guy Jane has been gushing about all morning."

Greg stared at her in shock, then back at the road, shaking his head.

"I need to warn her, Greg. The man is not stable. He's bipolar, and Christopher in particular needs medication but has stopped taking it. After he broke in they got him into the hospital, and I'm sure he's back on his medication now, but . . . I need to tell her, but how, when she hates me? She'll think that anything I say is just bitterness because we broke up."

"You're right. She probably would right now." Greg thought for a minute. "But maybe the two of you will hit it off on this trip, and you'll find a good time to tell her."

"Maybe," Brooke said, but inside she couldn't help but think it would take a miracle.

CHAPTER 15

The hike to Mumford Pond wasn't exactly the "milk run" that Russell had described, at least for Angela. When she began lagging behind, he pretended he was tired and called for a break. They sat on logs and rocks on the edges of the trail to rest.

Angela turned her pack to Jane. "Can you get my trail mix out?"

Jane quickly complied, unzipping a side pocket. "There you go," she said, handing over the oversized plastic medicine bottle Greg used for keeping food dry on camping trips. Brooke decided she could use a drink of water while they were stopped, but didn't want to bother anyone to get it for her. As she unlatched the belt of her pack and set it down, Jane scoffed. "We don't take breaks without our packs. It wastes time getting them back on."

Brooke stood up slowly from retrieving her canteen. "I'm sorry. I didn't know we were on a schedule."

"We aren't," Greg interjected. "We can take all the time we need. If Brooke wants a break from the weight of her pack, she can have it. You too, Gee-la. Do want to take your pack off?"

"She doesn't need to take off her pack, do you?" Jane said. Angela looked from her aunt to Brooke and back again. In the end she shook her head. Russell shot his daughter a look, but Jane turned away. *Okay, this is getting a little immature,* Brooke thought.

After a few minutes of awkward silence, Russell slapped his thighs and stood up. "Well, I'm ready to go on. How about the rest of you?"

Without a word, Jane stood up and waited for them to move on. Russell took Angela's hand and told her to follow behind him. Greg came next so they could pace themselves according to Angela's energy. Jane purposely got in front of Brooke on the narrow path, then slowed her pace to a crawl. Soon a sizable gap grew between the two women and the rest of the group. When Greg and Russell were out of immediate earshot, Jane spoke up.

"He won't marry again, you know, so you might as well give up your little chase."

"Excuse me?"

"It's nothing personal. Even if you were his type, it wouldn't matter. He wouldn't marry Miss America if she landed in his lap."

"And why would that be?"

"Because of Heather's death. He's got too much guilt over it to ever be disloyal to her memory. He'll never remarry. He told me so the day of her funeral."

Brooke stepped up her pace to catch up with Jane. "Not that it's any of your business, but neither of us has any definite plans yet."

Jane negotiated a hairpin switchback, then answered. "That's probably a good thing. I mean, I wouldn't want you getting your hopes up. He's too torn up about being responsible for her death."

Brooke's eyebrows furrowed deeply. How could Greg have had anything to do with his wife's death? Brooke ventured to ask the question she hadn't dared ask Greg. "How did Heather die?"

"She was shot."

Brooke gasped. "How?"

Jane stopped to look at Brooke with a smug look. "Admit it. For a split second you wondered if Greg pulled the trigger, didn't you?" She turned back to the trail. "My family's tragedies aren't any of your business. I'm not about to go into details."

Jane hurried forward and soon caught up with the rest of the group, where she put on a cheery voice and helped Angela get out a package of cheese and crackers to munch on. Brooke held back slightly and eyed Jane. She didn't know whether to believe her. She could believe that Greg had said he would never remarry, but people say things in the depth of mourning that change later.

Another thought nagged at her. Did Greg really blame himself for his wife's death? And what circumstances had surrounded the shooting? Greg's silence on the matter took on a whole new meaning.

She shook her head to clear her mind. Her thoughts had gotten too jumbled, her emotions too fuzzy to be sure of anything. All she wanted for the next couple of days was to get along with Greg's sister-in-law. To at least be cordial with her so she could warn her about getting involved with Christopher. At the very least, she hoped to avoid any new fireworks, although she had to admit the odds of that were unlikely, since she couldn't tell what would set Jane off.

They reached their campsite shortly after lunch. Brooke sat on one of the logs surrounding the fire pit. As they stretched their legs out, Jane told a story about some girl she knew who went hiking with new boots and ended up with feet full of blisters. She laughed so hard at the story that Brooke let out a silent sigh of relief that she hadn't bought the boots she'd seen at the mall two days before. She had been tempted to buy the rather expensive pair for the trip, but now realized that her old sneakers did a much better job than the new boots would have, since they wouldn't have been broken in, no matter how expensive they were.

"Well, I could use a rock-stop about now. How about you, Geela?" Jane asked.

"Sure," Angela said, taking her aunt's hand. "What about you, Brooke? Do you need to take a rock-stop?"

"A what?" Brooke asked. She had no idea how much vocabulary this family had managed to develop for their mountain trips.

"We're going to go to the bathroom," Angela said in a whisper.

Greg broke in to explain. "The environmental handbooks say to dig a hole, but a shovel can eat into your pack weight pretty quickly, not to mention being a bit time consuming when the urge hits. But the Uintahs have a ton of big rocks half exposed that can easily be lifted out of the ground, and when you pull it out, *voila!* There you have your hole. When you're done, you replace the rock and the hole is covered up."

"Hence 'rock-stop,' " Brooke said with understanding.

"So do you need one?" Angela asked.

"I think I'm all right for a little while," Brooke said. She had no desire to spend more time that absolutely necessary at such private activities while roughing it. *Call me a wimp,* she thought. She wouldn't care. She didn't think she would mind the dirt and smoke though, or much of anything else about camping. She was actually beginning to love the experience so far, but she preferred her own clean—not to mention private—facilities to the great outdoors, and would take as few "rock-stops" as she could manage.

"Fair enough," Jane said. She found her roll of toilet paper in her pack, which, like nearly everything else, was in a resealable plastic bag to keep out any moisture, then headed off with Angela.

Russell and Greg soon left the fire pit to set up camp. They knew how unpredictable the weather could be in the mountains, so they put up the tents right away so they'd have shelter if—or more likely *when*—it rained. Brooke was assured that the ground cloth and the "fly," as Russell called the extra covering over the tent, should keep the rain out.

Jane and Angela returned a few minutes later, and Angela hung around and watched the men for a while, but soon got bored and wanted to go exploring around the pond. She begged Brooke to come along, but Jane's challenging glare made it easy to decline.

"I think I'm a bit tired from the hike still," Brooke said. "Besides, you haven't had any time alone with your aunt for a bit. Why don't you guys have some fun, just the two of you? I'll get my turn later."

"Okay." Angela's disappointment was short-lived as she turned to take Jane's hand, and her face lit up as they began running through the trees. "Let's go see what's this way!" Angela said, and they disappeared into the woods. Brooke let out an audible sigh.

"You all right?" Greg asked. He sat beside her on the log.

Brooke glanced behind them. "Where's Russell?"

"Taking a nap in his tent." Greg leaned forward, his arms on his thighs. "You didn't answer me. What was that sigh for?"

"She won't give me a chance," Brooke said, indicating toward the direction Angela and her aunt had gone. "Jane is determined to get rid of me. She even had the nerve on the trail to say that you—" Brooke stopped suddenly.

"That I what?"

"Never mind," Brooke said with a shake of her head. "Jane wants to get rid of me, that's all. It was a mistake for me to come. I can tell that already."

Greg put an arm around her and pulled her close. "It was not a mistake. If Jane is determined to be miserable, let her. And if she is too jealous to see what a great woman you are, so be it. I can't justify how she's treating you, but I can imagine how she probably feels. Chances are she doesn't dare get to know you, just in case she finds out she likes you. That would be like betraying her sister."

"She'd be betraying Heather?" Brooke echoed, remembering Jane using the same words about Greg.

He nodded and went on. "Don't worry. Hopefully time will take care of it." Brooke nodded, although she wasn't sure. She wasn't thinking so much about Jane as much as what Jane had said on the trail. She felt compelled to ask.

"What about you?"

"What about me?"

Brooke had to know. "Do you feel like you're betraying Heather?"

The toe of Greg's worn hiking boot pushed around some pine needles on the ground. He looked up. "It took me years to even look at another woman. I don't feel disloyal to Heather, but I can't explain why. Things would have been very different a couple of years ago if I had tried to date back then. A few months ago, even. But not anymore."

"That's not exactly what I'm talking about," Brooke said, wondering if she was opening a Pandora's box that should be kept closed. "Back on the trail Jane said something . . . about Heather's death."

Greg's eyebrows came together. His focus shifted back to the pine needles. "What did she say?" he asked, his voice tense.

"I know it's a sensitive topic. If you don't want to talk about it—"

"*What* did she say?"

Brooke swallowed hard and wished she hadn't mentioned it. "That you blamed yourself for Heather's death."

Greg's jaw worked as he thought, and he nodded slightly. "Did she tell you how Heather died?"

Brooke didn't want to answer. After a pause, she said in a voice that was scarcely audible, "Only that she was shot."

Greg lowered his head and closed his eyes tightly.

"I'm sorry. I shouldn't have brought it up."

Greg ran his hand through his hair, then blinked a few times to ward off the moisture filling his eyes. "No, you need to know. I should have told you before, and now is as good a time as any. One night I was really ill. I couldn't get to sleep. Around one o'clock in the morning I had a violent attack of nausea, and when I raced to the bathroom, Heather woke up. She stayed up with me for the next two hours. When I said offhand that I wished we had some cold and flu medicine, she said she'd go get some. I didn't like the idea of her going by herself in the middle of the night, especially since we lived in a bad part of town, but I felt so terrible I let her go."

He took a minute before going on, and when he did, he wiped at his eyes with the back of his hand. "About half an hour later there was a knock at the door. It was a police officer coming to tell me my wife had been shot at the convenience store."

Brooke gasped involuntarily. "Oh, Greg . . ."

"When I arrived at the hospital she was already dead. I didn't get to say good-bye. At least Russell was there. He was a paramedic back then. He was in the ambulance holding her hand when she died." He paused and stared at his hands. "So now you know why I feel guilty."

"No I don't. How could any of that be your fault?"

He wiped at his eyes again and took a deep breath to even out his voice. "Everyone knows convenience stores aren't exactly safe havens at night, especially in our neighborhood. I should have gone myself. Or at least I could have been man enough to deal with the pain until morning."

"There's no way you could have known. Things like that don't happen too often around here."

"Often enough. There had been an officer shooting two blocks from that store only a month before." He shook his head. "I shouldn't have let her go." He turned to Brooke with a teary smile. "Well, that's about it. That's how I was widowed. For that matter, that's why I joined the force."

"How's that?"

"The robber shouldn't have been on the streets. He thought his girlfriend had cheated on him, and he killed the other guy. Then he got off because an officer didn't do his job right. The crime scene was contaminated, so the evidence that would have convicted him wasn't admissible. And the guy walked. The officer is to blame for that criminal shooting my wife."

Greg looked up at the tops of the pine trees, which pointed heavenward. "I swore that I would do everything in my power to keep another family from losing their mother and wife. So I dropped out of college and went into the police academy." He let out a cynical laugh. "And wow, what a huge difference I've made, writing all those traffic tickets and responding to neighbor complaints."

"You've done more than that as a police officer," Brooke insisted.

"I suppose. But I haven't made a difference, not really."

Greg gave his eyes a final swipe with the back of his hand, then stood up. Brooke rose to her feet beside him, wondering how she fit in with Greg's future. It was clear that his pain still took up a tremendous amount of room in his heart. Was there room for her?

CHAPTER 16

While Angela and Jane were gone on their walk, Greg and Russell tried their hand at catching trout for dinner.

"We should have gotten you a fishing license too," Greg said as he cast his line.

"That's all right," Brooke assured him. "I prefer eating fish to catching them."

Russell reeled in his line and cast again. "I hear you are quite the country dancer."

"Not really. I've only gone once."

"Let's fix that right now." Greg wedged his pole between some rocks and stood up, holding his hand out to Brooke. "May I?"

When Brooke hesitated, Greg said, "There's no one here to impress." As he led her through the moves she had learned on their first date, Russell began clapping and whooping in time, making his own music. When Greg spun her out, however, Brooke slipped on a wet rock. With a yelp she landed in the knee-high water, then burst out laughing. Greg and Russell did too when they were reassured that Brooke was only wet. Very wet.

"I guess I don't have my mountain legs yet," Brooke said between gasps.

"Russell, would you watch my pole?" Greg said. "I'll go back to camp to help Brooke dry off."

Brooke was going to put on her spare jeans, but Greg gave her a pair of sweatpants from his backpack to wear, saying she would get warmer a lot faster with them. She changed into the pants inside her tent, cinching the drawstring so they'd stay on. Then she put on the thick wool socks Greg handed her through the tent opening. Her plastic-soled slippers went on over the socks so she could walk around camp and follow Greg back to the lake.

"I feel like I'm wearing clown pants," she said, pulling the sides out.

"Well, you'll be glad you're wearing those when the sun goes down. They'll keep you warmer."

Brooke squeezed Greg's hand. "Oh, I like them. They smell like you."

"Thanks, I think," Greg said with a laugh. He stopped and eyed her critically.

"What?" Brooke asked, looking down at herself. "I know I look silly, but—"

"We need to go dancing again, don't you think?"

"Definitely. But I'll need to get my own boots."

* * *

The rest of the day flew by. By the time the sun began to set, Russell had gutted and skinned the fish, and Greg had a fire started in the fire pit. Greg glanced at his watch, then in the direction Jane and Angela had gone. "I'm surprised they're not back yet."

"Let's start cooking the fish. They'll be back any minute I'm sure, and hungry to boot," Russell said, pulling out his cooking supplies from his pack.

Just then, Jane ran into camp, out of breath. "Greg!" she gasped. "I can't find Angela. I've looked everywhere. She went off for a rock-stop and never came back." Her voice was hoarse, her face ashen.

Greg jumped to his feet, dropping a piece of firewood to the ground with a thud. "Where were you?" He was ready to run into the forest, but Russell stopped him.

"It'll be dark soon," he said. "Get your flashlight. Jane, you and Brooke stay here and mind the fire in case she wanders this way."

After Jane explained where she and Angela had been, Russell grabbed his own flashlight, compass, and map of the area. The two men were off. Jane slumped onto a log by the fire pit, then put her face in her hands and began to sob. Brooke hesitated a minute, but finally sat beside Jane and put her arm around her.

For a split second Brooke wondered if Christopher could have followed them up the mountain and taken Angela, just to punish Brooke—and Greg too, for that matter, for taking Brooke away from him. But it was a ludicrous notion, so she brushed it off. "They'll find her," she said to Jane, tears building up in her own eyes.

Jane didn't answer except to nod briefly. She didn't seem to mind Brooke's arm around her shoulders.

The two women sat alone together for a long time, waiting. "What time is it?" Brooke asked when it was full dark.

Jane tilted her wrist so she could read the hands of her watch in the firelight. "After nine." She put another log on the fire and checked the water level in the pot. Angela would need hot cocoa when they got back.

Brooke rubbed her arms up and down and kept looking toward the west for Greg's and Russell's figures. Finally a twig cracked. Both women jumped to their feet and held their breath in hope. Moments later, a beam of light was visible, then Russell appeared, holding the flashlight with Greg cradling Angela's small form in his arms. His coat was open and she was wrapped against him inside it.

"Angela!" Jane's voice cracked as she ran to her niece. "Are you all right?"

Angela managed a nod. "I'm cold."

Jane jumped over the logs at the perimeter of the fire pit. "I've got hot water ready for you." She prepared a cup of instant hot cocoa and passed it to Angela, then sat back down and began crying all over again.

Greg refused to leave his daughter for even a moment, so Russell retrieved some warm clothing for Angela from her tent. Soon she was wearing her red sleeper pajamas, two pairs of wool socks, a sweater, plus Greg's coat. Once warmed up, she sat on her father's lap sipping her cocoa, and quickly became her old self again.

"Gee-la, can you talk about what happened yet?" Greg asked. He hadn't bothered to ask what happened, not until his daughter was safe and warm again.

"It was scary," Angela said, though strangely calm and matter-of-fact after such an experience. "I just went for a rock-stop, but when I was done I couldn't find Aunt Janie anywhere. I kept walking 'cause I thought I knew which way to go. When I didn't see her after a minute, I yelled, but I couldn't find her. I got really scared." She lifted her head to sip her cocoa. "And then guess what, Dad? I felt something right here in my heart." She tapped her chest with her fingers. "It told me to stop walking and wait right there by this big rock, and to keep calling for help."

Russell interjected. "You know what? That's probably why we found you. You were walking farther and farther away from us, so you needed to stop."

Greg nodded. "Then when we heard you, we found you, even though it was dark."

"I was really cold on the outside. But you know what, Dad? I was warm inside. I knew you'd come for me." She smiled up at her father. "That was the Holy Ghost talking to me, wasn't it? He told me what to do, and I listened."

Greg's eyes were shiny in the firelight as he nodded. "That's exactly right, Gee-la."

They sat around the fire in silence for a few moments, each with their own grateful thoughts. Finally Angela spoke again. "Did you start reading the book without me?"

Jane shook her head. "No. But I don't think we'll finish if we start it this late."

"Can you read some anyway?"

"Of course."

So they sat around a crackling fire and listened as Jane used a flashlight to read aloud from a Louis L'Amour book, one more tradition of the annual trip. Jane's voice brought to life a story of a young boy and girl traveling alone, and Brooke was so caught up in their adventures that before she knew it, her face and hands were cold and it was so dark she could hardly see. After a couple of chapters, Jane put the book away, promising Angela they'd read some more tomorrow before heading home.

As they sat there, not willing to leave the warmth of the fire, the wind shifted and sent a cloud of smoke right in Angela's face. With a series of sputters, she ran coughing around the fire pit, seeking refuge in her grandfather's arms. She had scarcely settled into his lap before the smoke shifted and consumed her again. She ran back to Greg, buried her head in his chest, and wailed, "Daddy, the smoke is following me!"

"You know what they say, 'Smoke follows beauty,'" Greg said.

"And 'Beauty' was a horse," Angela said with a giggle, finishing the old camping joke. The smoke shifted again, making it safe for Angela's face to emerge from the folds of Greg's sweatshirt. She snuggled close to her father, and he pulled her tight. She stared at the fire in contentment while the adults chatted and tried to keep warm.

Brooke wished they had a second campfire behind her; as soon as her front was almost too warm, her back was cold, so she would turn around, only to get her front cold again. She set her wet jeans and shoes near the fire, hoping to dry them, then sat down on a log again. A minute later Greg jumped up and hit them away with a stick.

"Why did you do that?" she asked, looking from her shoes to him in confusion.

"Look for yourself," he said with a chuckle, pointing at the shoes with the stick. "Some sparks landed on the soles. I figured you wouldn't want melted shoes." Brooke inspected the damage and then put them to the side.

"Thanks."

Russell rubbed his beard with pleasure. "It's sure nice to have you up here with us," he said. "It helps keep the experience fresh."

"Let's see, first I fall in the lake, and now I nearly melt my shoes. Having me here must show what pros you all are, and how little I know about camping."

"Sparks on your shoes is no big deal. Jane did the same thing last summer. Didn't you, Jane?" Russell said.

Jane looked up but gave no response. Instead, she wrapped her arms around herself a bit tighter and stared into the orange fire.

Russell began to tell a story about one of Greg's first camping trips. "He was all of ten years old, but thought he was a pro," he began.

"Not this story again," Greg said. To Brooke he explained, "My dad got a kick out of telling the story to Russell, and now I can't come into the mountains without hearing it, no matter which side of the family I go with. The story gets better every time."

"Anyway," Russell said, determined to relate the tale, "the story goes that Greg insisted he heard bears and downright refused to go to bed. He wanted to stand watch in case they attacked. I always wondered what he planned to do if they did—throw rocks?" Russell gave another rumbling chuckle. "Next morning his dad found the poor boy soaking wet in his tent. Greg had given up standing watch when it started to rain, which it does most nights up here, and ended up practically a trout in his own tent—bear food for sure!"

Brooke couldn't help but laugh, and Greg flushed slightly. "I was a kid."

"And a Webelos Scout who thought he had to prove himself," Russell added.

"I gave up when the lightning started. That was the coldest night of my life," Greg said. He put another piece of wood on the fire and shivered at the memory. When Angela took a long breath, Greg looked at her resting in his lap and stroked her hair. "Do you want to go to my tent, Gee-la? You've had a big day."

Angela's eyes opened to look at him, then closed slowly, and she shook her head. "No. I still want to be in my own tent. But not yet. Will you tell me a story?"

"Grandpa, I think we've got a request for another story," Greg said.

"I want one of your stories, Daddy. Tell me one about Mom. The one about the first time you saw her."

Greg looked up at Brooke. She forced a smile and tried to look as if she didn't mind or notice Russell's and Jane's eyes boring into her to see her reaction, each hoping for a different one. The only person who seemed at ease was Angela, who didn't seem aware of the silent undercurrents flowing around her.

"How about a different story tonight," Greg suggested. "Like the one about the day you were born?"

"I want to hear about Mom. Tell me again about how pretty she was."

Greg gulped and ran his hand over his growing stubble. "Well, let's see." He looked to his father-in-law for help. Russell shrugged, but nodded, as if saying he might as well go ahead and tell the story. Angela apparently wasn't about to give up. Greg deliberately looked away from Brooke so he wouldn't have to see her eyes. Jane grinned smugly across the fire pit.

"Your mother was one of the most beautiful women I had ever seen," Greg began.

Angela sat up with indignation. "*The* most beautiful, Daddy. You're messing it up." Clearly, Angela had heard this story countless times and wouldn't settle for an altered version. Brooke braced herself for the rest.

"Sorry. She was *the* most beautiful woman I had ever seen. Is that better?"

Angela nodded and settled back into position. "Better."

"She had the hair of an angel and the bluest eyes in the world. You've got the same hair and the very same eyes. You were as beautiful as an angel when you were born. That's why we had to name you after an angel." Angela breathed contentedly, eyes closed, and Brooke wondered if the little girl would soon be asleep. Greg stroked her cheek, encouraging that very thing.

"My family had just moved, and I didn't know anyone at my new high school. I met a friend in algebra class, and his girlfriend wanted him to come to her dance concert. Well, he didn't want to go alone, so he roped me into going with him. Your mom was dancing in the same concert. That's how we met."

"Tell me about her dance," Angela said, her eyes closed and her voice soft.

"All right." Greg breathed out heavily before going on, still avoiding Brooke's eyes. "I was getting pretty bored in the concert until a girl in white did a solo. I sat right up and started watching. And I decided I had to meet her after the show." He leaned over to see if Angela was sleeping, but she opened her eyes.

"Go on, Daddy. Don't forget the heaven part."

"Of course. In that white costume she looked like something straight out of heaven. At the end of the concert I fought the crowd to reach her. I stood at a distance as she hugged her family." His voice grew soft as he remembered. "Then she looked at me, and there we were, face to face. All she said was, 'Thanks for coming,' but that's all it took. She had my heart from that moment on. There was never anyone else."

Angela's breathing had turned deep and rhythmic, but Greg no longer seemed aware of his daughter or anyone else. He gazed into the flaming fingers of the fire as if reliving the past. He blinked a few times, and a tear trembled, then fell down one cheek. He brushed it away with the back of his hand, and as he looked up, he was suddenly ripped back to the present.

He caught Brooke's eyes, which shone with moisture in the light from the fire. Greg swallowed hard. "I'd better take Angela to her tent," he said hoarsely, then carried Angela away, leaving Brooke at the fire with the Millers. Russell gave her a sympathetic smile, and Brooke tried to return it and act as if hearing about the woman Greg still held on a pedestal hadn't bothered her in the least.

Jane stifled a yawn, and Brooke jumped on it. "I'm a bit tired myself," she said, standing up and wiping off the back of her sweat-pants. "Even a sleeping bag sounds pretty good."

Jane, who had watched Greg disappear into the darkness beyond the fire, nodded. "I suppose we all ought to go to bed. The fire is pretty much out anyway."

Brooke stood up and stretched her neck and achy legs, then picked up her shoes and pants. "Good night."

Jane swept past Brooke without another word, but Russell stayed to put out the fire. As Brooke passed him, he squeezed her arm. "You're good for him," he whispered. "And he really does care about you. Don't let what he said get to you. She's a part of him, of course. Always will be. But she's in the past. He needs to learn how to live in the present. You can teach him that."

The tightness in Brooke's throat turned to burning in her eyes. With a slight nod and a "Thanks, Russell," she turned away and hugged herself as she headed for her own tent, a brown dome-style that Russell had lent her. By the light of the moon and her little flash-light she could easily make it out between the trees. She shuffled along the rocky ground in her slippers, anxious to get inside and zip the tent flap shut, as if that might keep her emotions outside and protect her from the complications of her relationship with Greg. For weeks she had continually wondered whether she could handle competing with Heather. Now she felt certain. No woman could compete with the memory of perfection.

Somehow she would have to get through the next day. Then she would tell Greg she couldn't handle it—ever. The very idea tore her apart, but how could she put herself through a relationship where she cared more than he did? Where he loved the memory of another woman more than he loved her?

Angela's small tent stood beside Brooke's, and since Greg hadn't returned to the campfire, Brooke assumed he was still inside. Some movement at Angela's tent door confirmed her suspicions, and she hurried toward her tent to avoid a confrontation. She almost made it, but stumbled over a rock and silently cursed the mountains for having so many.

"Brooke," Greg called out. He struggled to secure Angela's tent flap.

Brooke hastily unzipped her tent and tossed her armload inside. "Good night," she called with a forced cheery tone. "See you in the morning. Thanks again for the socks and pants." She ducked low to go in, but Greg reached her and took her arm before she disappeared.

"Brooke," he repeated, his voice urgent. At his touch, Brooke had to close her eyes to steel herself. She straightened and turned around, but couldn't get herself to look at his shadowy form. Instead, she gazed behind him at the pale shape of Angela's small tent.

"Yes?"

"I'm sorry."

"It's all right. Like you said, Angela comes first, and she wanted to hear about her mother, and after all, Heather was your one and only love. I'll see you in the morning." Brooke turned toward her tent, but Greg's grip on her arm tightened.

"No."

Brooke looked at the ground. "No what? No, you won't see me in the morning or no, Angela doesn't come first?"

"No, Heather isn't my one and only love. I don't want you to worry about that."

Brooke stared at him. "How can I not worry about it, Greg? I can't compete with her memory. Everything I've ever heard of her makes her into an angel. Except for that fact that she didn't like her body, she's sounds perfect. She might as well have been translated with the City of Enoch. And after watching you talk about her today, first about her death, and then the story tonight, it's clear that your heart is still with her. You feel guilty about her death. And you just said yourself she's the most beautiful woman you've ever seen, that there could never be anyone else. How am I *not* to worry about it?"

"I didn't say there could never be anyone else," Greg said softly. "I said there never *was* anyone else."

Brooke sniffed and hugged her arms more tightly around herself as a chilly breeze swept around her. "So what are you saying?"

"I'm saying what I never thought I would ever say to another woman." He paused as if getting the courage. He swallowed hard and glanced at the bright moon above them before looking back at her. "I love you, Brooke."

"But what about—"

Greg took her by the shoulders and looked at her squarely. "But nothing. Didn't you hear me? It's not easy for a guy to say those words. Are you going to make me say them again?"

Brooke looked at the ground and shook her head. "How can I believe them? A few minutes ago I heard the most . . . the kind of eulogy every woman dreams of. She's still in your heart."

Greg pulled Brooke close and wrapped his arms around her. Her emotions wouldn't be held in any longer, and soon her tears had made a wet spot on his shirt. She cared for Greg even more than she had realized, but she couldn't be with him. Not when he would constantly compare her to Heather, and she would be found grossly wanting.

"Of course she's in my heart," Greg whispered after a moment. "I won't deny what Heather and I had together." He pulled back slightly and tilted Brooke's chin up. "But does that mean a man can't have a second chance at love?"

A long silence consumed them as Brooke's thoughts and emotions ran headlong into each other. A thrill of hope went through her as she remembered what he had tried to tell her moments ago. She looked up at Greg, her eyes silvery with moisture. "Say it again."

"What?"

"Say it again. Last time I didn't hear it the way I was supposed to."

Greg smiled widely. "I love you, Brooke."

"And I love you, Greg."

He let out a laugh of triumph, then pulled her face to his for a long kiss. He pulled back and whispered, "Now you say it again."

CHAPTER 17

Brooke couldn't get to sleep for a long time. She blamed it on the rock jutting into the small of her back and the lack of a pillow, but she knew better. She couldn't sleep because Greg Stevens loved her and she loved him. Somehow things would work out. She would help him get over his guilt about Heather's death and help him live in the present, as Russell had said she could. To her surprise, she no longer felt quite so jealous of Heather. Now Greg's first wife represented a part of Greg's heart that Brooke could help heal. She let herself dream of what might come, deliberately shutting out all thoughts of Jane.

She had just begun to nod off when a whimpered cry ripped her from the borders of sleep.

"Help me out! I can't get out! Daddy, help!"

Brooke sat bolt upright and listened, then slipped out of her sleeping bag, unzipped the tent flap, and grabbed her flashlight. After shoving her toes into damp shoes, she hurried over to Angela's tent, where she unzipped the flap and shined the flashlight inside. She found Angela clawing at the back of the tent and crying for her father.

"Angela?"

Angela whirled around with wide, startled eyes. Her red face revealed streaks of tears. "Brooke!" She threw herself across the sleeping bag and into Brooke's arms. Brooke knelt at the tent opening and held Angela as her choking sobs gradually subsided.

"Are you all right? What happened?" Brooke asked softly as she rocked the young girl.

Angela's breathing gradually evened out. "I had a nightmare. I wanted to go find Daddy's tent, but then I couldn't find the zipper to get out." She pressed herself into Brooke's arms. "I got so scared."

"Look over there," Brooke said, pointing to the back of the tent where she had found Angela. "You were trying to get out over there."

Angela looked toward the back of the tent and then the front. "I thought that was the door."

"You must have been turned around."

"Sometimes I do that in my bed at home." Angela shuddered. "I thought I would never get out. Daddy says I have a little *clau-stro-pho-bia*." She said the word slowly. "I get scared of being closed up."

"You know what? I was a bit claustrophobic when I was your age too."

Angela glanced up at Brooke shyly. "Really?"

"You bet. I know how scary it can be. I remember one time in second grade when all my friends were playing a dog-piling game with lots of huge pillows. When my turn came to be on the bottom, I thought I was going to die."

"Yeah, that's what it feels like!" Angela said. "No one else in my family gets scared like that, though. Even Aunt Janie thinks I'm silly." She leaned close into Brooke's arms and let out a contented sigh. "Thanks for saving me."

"No problem, Angela."

Angela sat up slowly in Brooke's lap. "Would you . . ."

"Would I what?"

"Would you call me 'Gee-la'?"

"But I thought only your family could call you that."

Angela nodded. "Yeah, but . . . I don't have my mom anymore. Dad says I'll see her again, but not until I die. And I don't remember her much. If she was alive, I bet she would be holding me right now. I want someone like my mom to call me 'Gee-la.'"

Brooke didn't trust herself to answer right away. Angela sat up straighter. "Hey, maybe Daddy will decide to marry you, and then you can really be my mom."

Brooke held Angela a bit closer to avoid meeting her eyes. Even if things did work out like that between her and Greg, she doubted whether she would ever feel comfortable having Angela call her "Mom."

"I don't know about that, but I'll call you 'Gee-la,' if you're sure you want me to."

Angela nodded. "I'm sure." She paused for a minute, then added, "Would you sing me a song? Like at bedtime?"

"Sure. Which one do you want? 'Families Can Be Together Forever'?"

"'I Am a Child of God'?" Angela asked. "It's my other favorite."

"Mine too, Gee-la."

As Brooke sang, she stroked Angela's hair and looked out of the tent flap into the night sky, glittering with bright stars. She glanced over at Greg's tent, then stopped. He sat at the opening, watching the scene with a smile on his face.

"Thanks," he called softly.

* * *

Brooke didn't get much sleep the rest of the night. Once she managed to stop thinking about Greg and Angela, the cold air and the rock in her back finally did their part to keep her awake. She tossed and turned, wishing she had some kind of pillow besides her arm. It began to rain, and Brooke quickly became grateful that Greg and Russell knew the mountains well enough to bring a fly for the tent. As the rain beat harder and harder, Brooke knew it was the only thing keeping her dry. Although she wondered if she would ever get to sleep, she must have dozed off at some point, because she awoke abruptly to Russell's deep voice straining at the high notes of "In the Leafy Treetops."

She didn't realize how warm her sleeping bag had kept her until she tried to get out of it. The morning chill bit her skin sharply, and she let out a loud yelp as she sought cover back inside the warmth of her bag.

"Sounds like Brooke's awake," she heard Greg say with a laugh.

Quick footsteps approached, and soon Angela's voice called out, "Hurry, Brooke! I found a squirrel! Come see it!" Then, "Oh, never mind. It ran away. Are you coming out soon?"

"Don't bother her, Gee-la," Greg called from a distance. "She just woke up. Give her a minute."

"I'll be out soon," Brooke said, determined to get out and face the cold. But as she looked over at her clothes, she groaned inwardly. She could imagine how cold her jeans would be in contrast to the warm sweats she already had on. Her hand darted out and grabbed her clothes, then stuffed them into her bag in hopes of warming them up a bit before putting them on. Sure enough, they were freezing, and as they touched her legs, she once again had to stifle a yelp.

"Oh, that's cold," she said between her teeth. But it wouldn't get any better anytime soon she knew, so she braved the chill and threw on her clothes, then emerged from her tent.

Russell and Greg already sat around the fire pit, where a crackling fire gradually gained strength. Brooke slipped an old college sweatshirt over her T-shirt, then rubbed her hands up and down her arms. As she found a seat beside Greg, Angela bounded over and sat on her other side.

"Good morning, Angela," Brooke said, putting an arm around her for a side hug.

Angela leaned in conspiratorially and shook her head. "Last night you said you'd call me something else," she whispered rather loudly.

Brooke nodded with the memory. "That's right. I almost forgot. Good morning, *Gee-la,*" she said, pressing her forehead against Angela's. The young girl giggled with pleasure.

Brooke looked around. "Where's Jane?"

"Taking a rock-stop, probably," Angela said. A rustling in the trees interrupted them, and they turned to see Jane emerge from the tall pines, triple combination in hand. Brooke stared at the book for a moment, taking in what it meant. Jane hadn't been taking a rock-stop at all. Unaware that anyone had noticed her, she went to her pack and slipped the volume into it. When she came to the fire pit, she brushed off part of a log and sat down, holding her hands out to the small flame for warmth.

"Sleep well?" Greg asked.

Jane nodded with a shrug. "As well as can be expected. Nights are the only part of camping I can't stand." She stretched her neck to one side and then the other, as if trying to work out the kinks brought on by the cold night.

Brooke didn't say anything. Jane seemed to be in a good mood for once, and she didn't want to be the cause of it ending. They sat around the fire for some time as the flames grew hotter, eventually creating enough coals to put on some water to boil for breakfast. Unable to sit still, Angela kept jumping on and off rocks and logs, racing up and down the campsite, looking over the pond. She came back with starry eyes and a story about a bird she had heard singing across the pond.

As they ate a breakfast of instant oatmeal and hot cocoa, Jane read another two chapters from the book they'd read the night before. All too soon breakfast was consumed and cleaned up, and everyone set to breaking camp. The chill of the morning quickly lifted as the sun heated the air. Brooke felt the heat beat onto her back as she stuffed her sleeping bag into its sack. She took off her sweatshirt and wrapped it around her waist. They took down their tents, packed their backpacks, and put out the fire, and were soon ready to head down the trail they had come up not twenty-four hours ago.

"I wish we could have had a longer trip," Greg said as he surveyed their now-empty camp.

Russell looked out over the pond beside Greg. "Hey, at least we managed to squeeze it in. What with your world trip last month, it's a wonder the P.D. let you come at all." The group headed en masse toward the trail, when Russell stopped at the head.

"Wait a minute," he said. He stopped by a tree and pointed to a wooden sign where someone had carved *Mumford Pond* and nailed it to the trunk. "Let's get a picture of everyone by the sign." He reached back to a side pocket of his pack and withdrew the cheap plastic camera he saved for camping trips. "All right," he said, waving at the group to gather in front of the tree. "Everyone line up in front of the sign."

"I want to stand between Brooke and Aunt Janie," Angela said, taking a spot directly beneath the sign. Greg stood beside Brooke.

As Russell raised his camera, Brooke took a step forward. "On second thought, Russell, let me take the picture. After all, this is the *grandparent* campout, and if you're not in the picture, we're missing the most important part. Besides, I'm not family."

"But you *will* be, right?" Angela piped up. Brooke flushed pink, and Jane looked away with flashing eyes. Angela seemed oblivious to the reactions. "We need Brooke in the picture too. Hey, I know. Grandpa, you take one picture with Brooke in it, then Brooke can take another one with you in it."

Everyone seemed to relax at the suggestion, and Brooke stepped back into place. After pictures, they took off toward the trail. Brooke made a point of walking behind Jane. After their time waiting together last night, Brooke hoped Jane would see her more as an ally, and this might be Brooke's best—or only—chance to warn her about Christopher.

They walked for several minutes before Brooke spoke, because Jane seemed upset, as she had much of the trip. Brooke knew that coming on the campout in the first place hadn't helped matters.

When the two women were nearly a full switchback ahead of the rest of the group, Brooke decided to speak. "So Jane, how long have you been dating Christopher?"

Jane glanced back at Brooke over her shoulder. "A couple of weeks. Why?"

"Just wondering. You see . . . I thought you might want to know that I dated him for a while and it turns out that he's . . . not well."

Jane stopped and turned around. "Brooke, don't try to break this up. He's a nice guy. What has he ever done to you?"

"For starters, he broke into my house and threatened to kill me."

Jane stared at Brooke for a moment. "You're kidding, right?"

"I wish I was."

Jane headed back down the trail without answering. She picked up her pace, and Brooke had to hurry to keep up. "I don't normally get involved with other people's relationships, but I thought you ought to know. Christopher is bipolar and isn't consistent with his medication. His sister told me he gets obsessed with death at times, and I can believe it."

Jane whirled around. "My personal life is none of your business." She turned away, taking huge strides as she fumed down the trail. Brooke knew better than to try to keep up, and instead walked slowly so Greg and the others could catch up.

"Where's Jane?" Greg asked as they reached Brooke.

"I told her about Christopher. She got mad and went off by herself."

Twenty-five minutes into their hike they heard a loud cry farther down the mountain. Russell stopped to listen. Another cry followed, this one laced with a few colorful words, followed by a call for help.

"Jane? Are you all right?" Russell called out.

"What do you *think?*" came the faraway reply. Russell began hurrying down the trail, nearly tripping on protruding rocks as he made his way a bit more quickly than he should have around switch-backs.

Angela took her father's hand. "Daddy, is Aunt Janie hurt?" she asked him softly.

"I don't know sweetie, but I'm sure Grandpa will take care of her. Let's hurry up and find out."

Although they picked up their pace, they didn't catch up with Russell and Jane for several minutes. When they did, they found Jane lying on the ground, gripping her leg and grimacing as her father gently probed her ankle. She sucked air between clenched teeth, and a tear squeezed out of one eye.

Russell sat back on his heels. "It's already swelling a bit. It might be broken," he said, looking up at Greg as they approached. "Or sprained. Looks like she twisted it pretty good."

"Would you stop talking as if I'm not here?" Jane hissed, then clenched her jaw as she tried to move her foot.

"Do you want me to go for help?" Greg asked.

Jane shook her head. "I'll make it all right," she said, trying to stand up. She winced in shock at the pain and fell to the ground in a heap.

"I'm going," Greg said, making a move to pass them.

Jane held up her hand. "What's the use? We're not that many miles from the trailhead, and it's all downhill. I can limp my way down faster than you can find help and get back to us." She reached for Russell's hand, and he helped her up. Her left foot dangled limply. She hopped to one side of the trail to retrieve her pack, nearly losing her balance in the process.

Russell steadied her. "You can't carry your pack in your condition."

"Then who will, Dad?" Jane growled. "Let me carry the thing already. I'm not an invalid."

No one noticed that Angela had wandered off until she returned carrying a thick stick about four feet long. "Here, Aunt Janie. I found a walking stick for you. I bet this will help you walk easier. I saw it work in a movie once."

Jane took the stick, her face softening slightly. "Thanks, Gee-la. That's just what I need." Jane looked to her father, then to Greg. "At least there's someone here who thinks I can do it."

Jane hobbled down the trail, carefully selecting each step before taking it so she wouldn't fall again. Russell helped her around the switchbacks, although Jane hated to admit she needed the help. What should have been a brief hike turned into an all-day ordeal. At first Jane tried to support some of her weight on her hurt foot, but soon the pain grew too intense. When her foot began to seriously swell, she loosened her shoe, but eventually that wasn't enough, and she had to take the shoe off altogether. By the time the parking lot was in view, Jane's face was a portrait of misery. She had her arms around both Russell and Greg, and she hopped slowly on one foot, taking breaks every twenty feet or so.

"All right, we're here. Let's find you a doctor," Russell said when they reached the cars.

Jane protested. "It can wait. We can't skip going to Granny's malt shop for shakes and disappoint Angela. It's a tradition."

Russell let out a groan of exasperation. "You've got a broken foot, for Pete's sake. Tradition can go hang."

"Angela *has* to go to Granny's."

"Fine. Since we're in two cars, why don't I take you to the emergency room while Greg takes Angela to Granny's?" Russell explained the situation as if giving instructions rather than offering a suggestion. Jane looked at Angela, then at Brooke, and swallowed hard.

"Sure, I guess so, Dad. At least Angela will get to go."

Brooke couldn't look at Jane's face. For the first time Jane would be missing out on sharing a tradition with her niece. If that were the only problem, Brooke wouldn't have felt so bad. *But now Jane thinks I'm replacing her as well as Heather.*

Before helping Jane to the car, Greg leaned down to explain the situation to Angela. "We'll still go for shakes, Gee-la, but since Aunt Janie is hurt and needs to see a doctor, she and Grandpa won't be able to come. Is that all right?"

Angela patted her father's arm. "Don't worry, Daddy. We can bring her a shake."

"Great idea. I'll ask what kind she wants."

As promised, Angela brought back a shake for her aunt, chocolate with marshmallow. She held it in her lap the whole way down the canyon, cradling it like a treasure.

Several minutes into the drive down the twisting road, her brow furrowed and she looked up at Greg. "Daddy, what's going to happen to Aunt Janie's foot? They aren't going to cut it off, are they?"

Greg gave her hand a reassuring squeeze. "No, they won't do anything like that. But I imagine they'll have to take some X-rays." When Angela's face didn't register understanding, Greg explained. "They're like pictures of your bones, so the doctors can see if one is broken."

"Then what? If she has broken a bone, I mean?" Worry filled Angela's voice.

"Then she'll need to wear a cast, which will keep her bone still while it heals."

"Then will she be all right?"

"She sure will."

Greg changed lanes and kept driving, the truck humming down the road. But Brooke looked at Angela and noticed that Greg's reassurance hadn't wiped the worried look from his daughter's face.

"Gee-la, what's bothering you?" Brooke asked.

Angela swallowed hard and traced a finger along the outside of the shake where moisture had condensed. "People can't die from broken bones, can they?" A fat tear tumbled down one cheek, but she didn't brush it away. She blinked hard instead, sending more big tears down her face. "Mom died. And Misty. Neither of them were sick or anything. I love Aunt Janie so much, and—" her voice caught and she buried her head in Brooke's sleeve.

"I'm sure Aunt Janie will be just fine," Brooke said.

"That's right," Greg agreed. "In fact, she'll probably be home by the time we get there to drop off the shake, and we can find out about everything the doctor said then. Does that sound all right?" Angela nodded.

Greg let out a sigh, hoping they had calmed his daughter's fears. "So you're all right now?" Angela started to nod again, but then slowly shook her head. "There's something else?" Again she nodded. "What is it?"

"Daddy, are—are you going to die like Mom did?"

"Oh, cutie," Greg said, putting his arm around Angela and pulling her close. His voice had a ring of sadness to it, as if he thought he had comforted his daughter on this point years ago. But her recent experience with Misty's death had brought her fears to the surface. "You don't need to worry about that. Of course everyone will die someday, but most people live a long, long time. And I, for one, plan on being around until I'm at least Grandpa's age."

"But you can't *know* if you will," Angela countered. "I mean, you thought Mom would live to see me all grown up. And Grandma Miller died before I was born. So you could die too, couldn't you?"

Greg eyed Brooke as if she could somehow give him the answers that would comfort his daughter. "You're right. I don't know when I'll die," Greg began tentatively. "But somehow I don't think Heavenly Father needs both your mother and me right now. I think I'm supposed to stick around and take care of you for a long time yet." Greg tried to laugh in an effort to lighten the mood. "I mean, I know you're practically a grown lady now, but you do still need me at least a little bit, don't you?"

Angela laughed back, then sniffed as she gave her father's arm a slug. "Of course I still need you, Daddy. I'm only seven."

When they arrived at the Millers they saw no sign of Russell, Jane, or any camping equipment. "Looks like they're still at the hospital," Greg said. "Why don't we leave the shake in the freezer and write a note so Aunt Janie knows it's there?"

Angela pulled open the freezer door and found a place for the shake, but as she turned around, she looked worried. "Do you think something's really wrong after all, since they're not back yet?"

Brooke shook her head. "I doubt it. Sometimes emergency rooms make you wait for a long time. They might still be waiting for a doctor to see her. Come on, let's get you home and in the tub. I'm sure your grandpa will give us a call as soon as they're home."

CHAPTER 18

On Monday Angela called as Brooke was getting ready to leave for rehearsal.

"You and Daddy were right," she said. "Aunt Janie just broke a couple of bones. She has to wear a cast for a while, but the doctor says she'll be fine after it comes off. She'll even be able to hike again, but not this summer."

"That's great news, Gee-la." Brooke wished she could do something to help Jane, but didn't dare extend the offer. She reluctantly eyed the clock, wishing she didn't have to rush off to rehearsal.

"Well, I'd better go," Angela said. "I asked Daddy if I could call you to tell you about Aunt Janie after he went to work, and he said I could as long as I didn't talk your ear off. He says you're busy and have things you need to do, so I wasn't supposed to take lots of time, just tell you about Aunt Janie." She finally took a breath, then paused. "When do I get to see you again?"

"I'm not sure. We'll find a time soon though, I promise."

"What about right now? Grandma Stevens is here, but she won't mind."

Brooke wore a pained smile. "Oh, I wish I could. But I'm on my way to rehearsal, and I won't be back until after your bedtime."

"Oh." Then Angela added, "Hey, do you think Daddy will let me see your play when it starts? Even if it's after my bedtime? I mean, I know you play a witch. Would I get too scared?"

Brooke laughed. "I don't think so. It's not that kind of a show. I'm not a very scary witch, and in the second half I don't even wear witch clothes, so I'm sure I could convince your dad to let you come. But it's not for a couple of weeks yet."

As Brooke drove to the theater, she was troubled. She had begun to care for Angela so much it scared her. If things didn't work out between her and Greg, she wasn't sure she could give up her friendship with Angela. Already she felt protective toward her and wanted to give her a little of the nurturing she hadn't been able to have from her mother. Brooke found the prospect of becoming Angela's mother equally exciting and terrifying.

Nearly losing Angela for good in the mountains made Brooke protective and defensive of the little girl. If anything ever happened to her, Brooke knew it would break her heart. She entered the theater rehearsal room, dropped her bag on the ground, and sat down beside it. This must be at least something like what a mother felt toward her own child, she thought.

The concept brought her head up with a start. She *wasn't* Angela's mother, and she had feelings this strong. What had Heather felt toward Angela? What did she *still* feel toward her? And more importantly, how much would Heather resent Brooke for stepping in and taking her place? Brooke knew that she would resent anyone taking the minimal place she had managed to establish in Angela's heart. How much stronger must Angela's real mother feel, watching this all from the other side? She wondered if things were different from over there.

Brooke pulled her knees up and rested her forehead on them. She had never had such a complicated relationship before. Brooke *couldn't* gain acceptance from Heather, who meanwhile possibly sat in pain as she watched Brooke parade into her former life and take over. Brooke thought of the incident at the tent in the mountains, how she had comforted Angela. It should have been Heather.

Brooke shook her head, but couldn't think clearly. Should she feel guilty for helping Angela that night? Of course not, she reassured herself. But on the other hand, Heather might feel differently. And if she pursued her relationship with Greg, the day would come when she would have to face Heather. Could she do that? What was that like, and how would it work out? Would Heather see things differently than Brooke was looking at them now? Would Brooke herself?

Mark came into the room, which had gradually filled with the cast. "Okay folks, let's get started." Brooke stood up and blinked quickly to get rid of the excess moisture that had collected in her eyes. Mark referred to his clipboard of notes, then continued. "We've got a lot of territory to cover today. Brooke, since we missed you last Friday, I'd like to start off with your 'Stay with Me' solo."

Mark turned to the rest of the cast. "I also want to work on the finale for Act One with everyone who is in that, and then the transformation scene at the end of Act One. It's still too rough. Then we'll take Act Two from the top and see how far we can get with whatever time we have left, all right?" He looked around the room, and Brooke nodded, hoping no one had noticed her emotion.

Jeremy played a few warm-up exercises for the cast to get their voices ready to sing. Brooke did her best to keep her thoughts from Heather and Angela. The warm-ups helped, but running through her solo had the opposite effect. It was the scene where Rapunzel, whom the Witch had raised from a baby, wants to leave her. So the Witch sings "Stay with Me," a heartrending song of a mother in the agony of losing her only child. As she sang to Rapunzel, Brooke felt as if she were Heather giving up Angela. As the scene ended and Rapunzel ran offstage, Brooke couldn't contain her tears.

Mark stood up and applauded. "That's the best I've ever seen that scene. Let's not touch it again tonight. I don't want you to peak early." He consulted his notes. "All right. Everyone in the Act One finale, take your places!"

Grateful that she wasn't in that number, Brooke slipped into the women's dressing room to fix her makeup as best as she could before going out again. She couldn't shake the image of Heather in her mind. "I'm sorry, Heather," she whispered. "I never wanted to hurt you."

She didn't have a whole lot of hope of anyone not noticing her puffy eyes. Fortunately, when she returned to rehearsal, Mark kept tinkering with the choreography of the finale, allowing Brooke to wait in a chair and let her face get back to normal before she was needed. She wanted to call Pat right away and let out all her thoughts and feelings about Heather. In fact, she nearly made some excuse to leave, but as soon as the thought crossed her mind she shook it off. She couldn't take this to Pat. This was one thing Pat could not be objective about. Brooke sighed. She would have to work this one out on her own.

Kathy rushed in the room, her cheeks flushed, and plopped beside Brooke. "How late am I?"

Brooke glanced at her watch. "Twenty minutes."

Kathy rummaged through her purse and found a bag of chocolate candy. "It was such a crazy shift that I had to stay and help pick up the slack, but when the girl who was supposed to replace me had to go help with an ambulance call, I couldn't leave." She ripped open the bag and popped a few candies into her mouth. "This is the first thing I've eaten all day since toast this morning."

"You're a nurse?" Brooke asked.

Kathy nodded and offered some candies to Brooke. "In my other life. Which reminds me. I met someone you know."

Brooke's eyebrows went up as she cupped her hand to catch the candy. She popped one in her mouth. "Oh?"

"Yeah. Jane Miller."

Brooke nearly choked. "Really?" she tried to keep her voice neutral. She hoped Jane hadn't passed along any of her nasty opinions about her. She didn't want her time with Kathy poisoned by Jane's comments. "How did you meet Jane?"

"I met her Saturday night when she came in with her broken foot."

Brooke breathed a sigh of relief. If Jane had been in the same frame of mind when she arrived at the hospital that they had left her in, Kathy couldn't have liked her, let alone believed anything nasty Jane might have said about Brooke. "So how did you make the connection?"

"Oh, I kept her talking. You know, to keep her distracted from the pain. But she turned the conversation on me. It came out that I'm working on a show here, and she said she knew one of the girls that plays the Witch. And there you go."

"I don't know her that well," Brooke began. "I'm just dating her brother-in-law."

"You must love her. She was so funny. I just loved working with her."

That brought Brooke's head around. "You *loved* working with her?"

"Absolutely. She was a joy to work with. I wish all my patients were that easy."

Brooke wanted to meet that version of Heather's sister. But how could she soften Jane enough so they could both get to know each other? Their real selves, not the ones who were set up to be at each other's throats. She wondered if she should go over to Jane's place and talk with her. She decided to check out her calendar and see when she could do it. Jane might blow up at her, but then again, she might warm up, even a bit. It was worth a try.

* * *

When Brooke arrived at the theater opening night, she could hardly see straight for nerves. Her hands shook as she put her keys into her purse and made her way to the women's dressing room. Sitting before the large mirror, she took a deep breath before putting on her witch makeup as the other female cast members milled about her. There was the Baker's Wife humming warm-up exercises, Cinderella panicking because she couldn't find her other golden shoe, and Jack's Mother trying to squeeze her generous self past them all to reach her costume on the other side.

Brooke's throat began to constrict in the familiar way it had every time she got nervous. She kept swallowing hard as if that would dissolve the tension, but instead she got more and more nervous. Soon the audience began to arrive, and their buzzing grew increasingly louder, like a beehive. Brooke put her hands over her ears and willed herself not to cry. This was the night she had dreamed of for years she reminded herself. She was about to debut in a leading role, and she was about to choke.

She wished Greg would show up, then changed her mind. She didn't want him seeing her on stage opening night. What she wanted was the reassurance he could bring with him. If he were by her now, he would tell her how beautiful her singing voice was, how he knew she'd do great.

A knock sounded, and when Cinderella covered her half-dressed form she opened the door. "Wow, who are those for?" she squealed. "Brooke, look what just arrived for you." She drew back from the door to reveal a huge bouquet of red Columbian roses. The roomful of women gasped.

"Who are they from?" someone asked.

A smile broke across Brooke's face as she took the vase. She didn't answer the questions peppered at her until after she read the card tucked into the greenery, even though she knew full well who had sent them. "Pretend you're singing ABBA," the note read, "and you'll blow them away. Wish I could be there to give these to you. Consider yourself kissed. All my love, Greg."

Brooke looked up from the card with a smile.

"Who, who?" came the chorus of curious actresses.

"They're from Greg . . . my boyfriend." Brooke hated calling him that. It sounded like something out of junior high, but she didn't have anything else she could call him.

Squeals filled the dressing room. "He's gorgeous, isn't he?" Rapunzel said with clasped hands. The youngest member of the cast, she had her head constantly in the clouds as she dreamed of the romance that would undoubtedly find her in years to come.

Brooke gave the vase full of blooms one final sniff before leaving the dressing room. Her knees felt weak as she walked into the wing to wait for her first cue. The music started, and her toe began tapping the familiar rhythm. She practiced some of Desaray's breathing techniques, and even though she couldn't "hit the floor" to do them, they helped a bit. She swallowed hard, then closed her eyes and said a silent prayer before making her first entrance.

When she walked on stage into the lights, she opened her mouth to sing, and any remaining tension melted away, leaving in its place an uncanny sensation. She felt as if she had stepped into someone else's skin for the night. Every bit of energy she put into her part was given back to her by the audience, and the thrill of acting consumed her.

The play flew by. The transformation scene was a resounding success; when Brooke threw off the cape, the audience audibly gasped at her "sudden" transformation. Brooke even felt beautiful in the sparkling, royal blue gown she wore for the second half. Before she knew it, opening night was over and the cast greeted the audience as they exited the theater. Brooke thought she would feel awkward shaking the hands of perfect strangers and accepting their compliments, but it felt perfectly natural, as if she had been an actress all her life, and had done this very thing hundreds of times.

"Thank you so much," Brooke said over and over again, tucking the compliments into her heart for safekeeping.

CHAPTER 19

Brooke had performances Thursday and Saturday nights, and her days were busy as well. In August she began attending teacher workshops and meetings, and in other ways getting ready for school to start at the end of the month. Even so, her mind continued to race with questions about her role in Greg's and Angela's lives.

After a training meeting one afternoon, Brooke headed down the half-lit school hallway to her classroom. As she walked, she went down a catalog of mental questions: Did she love Greg Stevens? Absolutely. Did she love his daughter? Yes. In fact, probably too much. Could she marry Greg, step in as Angela's mother, and live her life without feeling guilty for taking Heather's place? She didn't know. On the other hand, could she walk away from the two people she loved most because of what someone who was dead might or might not think? She shook her head to brush off the thought. She needn't worry about Heather's feelings in all this. After all, if Greg was fine with it, Brooke figured, she should be too.

She opened her classroom door to see a figure standing by her desk. "Can I help you with something?" She flicked on the lights. "Oh, hello, Jane. I didn't expect to see you here."

Jane hobbled closer. Brooke noticed she was wearing a walking cast. "Yeah, well, I don't go many places these days with this cast, but . . . We need to talk. I mean . . ." Jane struggled for words for a minute. "Why did you try to sabotage my relationship with Christopher? Do you hate me that much?"

"Jane, I don't hate you. I was honestly trying to warn you."

"I can't believe Christopher is dangerous. How can you know?"

"Like I told you, he threatened me with a gun and broke into my house. His sister warned me too."

Jane chewed her cheek for a minute.

"Ask Greg. He saw it. I have no reason to be making this up." Brooke sat on a student desk. "I don't hate you," she said again. "I thought you hated me."

Jane looked at her hands, then shoved them into her pockets. "All right, fine. I admit you're not my favorite person in the world."

"I never wanted to be your favorite person."

"And there's no way you could be. My favorite person is dead."

"Heather," Brooke whispered.

Jane nodded, her lower lip trembling. "Listen, I'm sorry I've been so . . . well, rude, I guess. The first time I met you something told me that you weren't going to be anything temporary. I could tell that you'd be around for some time, and to be honest, I didn't like the idea."

Brooke nodded with a wan smile. "I gathered as much."

"I want to apologize. I just didn't want you putting your nose in my business. Anyway, Christopher and I aren't seeing each other anymore. I brought Angela along on a lunch date on Saturday, and I didn't like how he treated her. She didn't like him either, for what that's worth." Jane sighed heavily, and then continued, "I couldn't forget what you told me about him. He hasn't changed. He blew up when I suggested we not see each other anymore. I realized I couldn't be with someone who wasn't willing to try, who would only drag me down. It still frightens me to think of what he may have done . . . and what he's capable of." Jane's gaze descended to the floor as she spoke the last phrase. Slowly she looked up and continued, "Really Brooke, I don't hate you. I've got a temper, and I don't hide it well, but I don't actually hate you. It's nothing personal. I'd resent anyone who tried to step into my sister's place."

This wasn't exactly the kind of apology Brooke was accustomed to, but it was more than she had ever expected from Jane. As long as they respected each other and agreed to keep their distance, they could probably both be happy.

Jane turned to hobble out of the classroom, and Brooke bit her cheek. "Jane?"

Jane turned around slowly. "Yeah?"

"Let's do lunch sometime."

A tentative smile spread across Jane's face. "I think I'd like that." She looked down at her cast for a moment, then back to Brooke. "You know what made me come today?" Brooke couldn't imagine what it might have been. "I met your musical director at the hospital. She kept saying what a great person you were, how you two had become close friends. Kathy was so great herself, I had to believe that you're a pretty decent person."

"I'll have to thank her for that," Brooke said. "You know, she said the same thing about you."

"She did?" When she smiled, Jane seemed almost a different person.

Brooke nodded. "That's when I decided to talk with you, but you beat me to it."

* * *

When Brooke got home that night, the phone rang. Brooke saw the number on the caller ID as her parents' and almost didn't answer. She just didn't want to deal with the usual discussions about all her friends who were married, which one had just had her fifth child, "Why aren't you married yet, Brookey," and "Are you still seeing that Greg boy?" Brooke picked up the phone reluctantly. In her typical fashion, Brooke's mother started right in with the local news.

"Brookey, did you hear that Amy Norton—you remember her, don't you? Well, she's having twins. I ran into her mother at the store today, and she says they could be here anytime now. They're not due for another month or so, but you know how twins always come early."

"That's great. I'm happy for her," Brooke said, rubbing her feet, which had gotten sore from standing in the classroom for so long. She wasn't used to it anymore and had forgotten to wear comfortable shoes. "So is there anything new with you and Dad at home?"

"Heavens, no. Just the same old stuff. Except that Dad was released from the Explorers and was put in as Cub Master." She laughed. "Can you picture that? He hasn't done anything with the Cub Scouts since your brother was that age!"

Brooke gave an obligatory laugh, hoping that the conversation would stay in these areas, but not having much hope about it. "Does he enjoy it?"

"Well enough. At least the younger boys aren't as cheeky as the teenagers since they haven't decided they have to be 'cool' yet. But that's not why I'm calling." Brooke braced herself as her mother went on. "How are *you* doing, Brooke? I haven't heard much from you lately. Are you and Greg still seeing each other?"

"Yes, we're still seeing each other," Brooke echoed, unwilling to volunteer any additional information.

"Great. From what Pat's told me, he seems like a great catch. Provided you don't mind the daughter thing."

"No, I don't mind Angela at all. She's a great girl," Brooke said, growing defensive at Gee-la being called a "thing."

"I suppose it's best that her mother died when she was so young. She'll be more willing to accept you as her mother."

"Mom, please," Brooke said. "If and when I have news, I'll let you know." Of all people, she couldn't tell her mother what was going on inside her, someone whose sole purpose in life was to see her oldest daughter married.

* * *

Greg had promised to pick up Brooke from the show on Thursday. He had also promised to bring Angela to Saturday's performance, but now he wasn't so sure. He had been thinking all day and dreaded what he had to do next. He arrived at the theater just as the audience finished shaking hands with the cast and Brooke headed for the dressing room. As she entered the stage area she saw Greg.

"Hi. You're right on time," she said. She gave him a quick kiss, squeezed his hand, and headed for the dressing rooms. "I'll be right out."

Greg held her hand tightly. "Just a minute."

Brooke looked back. Her expression grew concerned when she saw his. "Is something wrong?"

Greg glanced around at Jeremy and several cast members who stood watching. He rubbed his forehead with his fingers. "Can we go somewhere more private?"

Brooke nodded and led the way to the greenroom, where she closed the door behind them. "What is it?"

Greg sat heavily on the couch, his hands clasped. "It's about Heather."

"What about her?"

Greg's heart began to pound. He could hardly get himself to speak the words he had practiced for the last half hour. It was too painful. "I have come to love you more than I ever thought possible," he began slowly.

Brooke took a deep breath, as if she'd heard something in his voice that warned her what he was about to say. "But?"

Greg exhaled heavily and clasped his sweaty hands together. "But . . . lately I can't stop thinking about how Heather hated the idea of my ever remarrying. I even promised I wouldn't. I see her watching me, seeing how much . . . how much I love you. How much Angela loves you."

Brooke looked at him with disbelief. "I wondered how she might feel too, but since you seemed fine with it, I wrote those worries off."

"I know. I'm so sorry." Tears sprang to Greg's eyes. His chest felt heavy. "But I can't hurt Heather like this. She was first." He looked at her helplessly.

Brooke swallowed hard. "So do you need some time to work through this, or? . . . "

"I don't know." Greg ran his fingers through his hair in frustration and pressed his eyes with his fingers to stop the tears. He took Brooke's hand in his and rubbed his thumb across the top. Her skin was so soft. "It's not fair to make you wait around for something that might not ever happen."

Brooke shook her head. "So that's it? You and Angela are going to vanish from my life just like that?"

"I'm so sorry," Greg said again. He stood and wiped at his cheeks with the back of his hand. "I guess I should go." He reached for the doorknob.

"Will you and Angela still come to the play on Saturday?"

He turned back and stared at the carpet. "Angela will be there. She's had her heart set on it for so long."

"What about you?"

He looked up to Brooke's eyes. They looked as miserable as he felt. "I can't."

"You don't work Saturday nights."

He looked at her evenly. "I can't come, Brooke. I *can't.* I'll ask Jane to take her. The department almost always needs someone to cover a shift." He opened the door, then paused. Looking at the floor he whispered one more time, "I'm so sorry."

CHAPTER 20

Brooke didn't hear from Greg on Friday or Saturday, but the silent telephone didn't hurt nearly as much as the empty makeup counter in the dressing room before Saturday's performance. Not only did a rose belong on the counter, but Greg should have been in the audience with Angela. Instead, Jane would be with her, and Greg would probably be working.

"Hey Brooke, looks like your Romeo's late today," Rapunzel said. "But don't worry. I'm sure he'll get your flower here before you go on."

Jack's Mother grunted as she tied her apron. "Unless that was a fight you two had the other night. What happened?"

Brooke hung her purse on the coatrack and forced a smile. "Oh, nothing of interest." She glued on her nose without the enthusiasm she'd had for past performances.

When she could hear the audience arriving, she tried to find some energy for the performance. She needed to do well tonight, if not for the sake of the show, then for Angela.

* * *

"Ten-four." Greg turned on his lights and sirens, then turned his patrol car around to head for the address that dispatch had just given. Of all calls, he disliked domestic ones the most. Emotions were hottest at those ones, and more officers went down at them than at any other kind. That's why they always called for backup. Officer Berry had already arrived on the scene and taken a defensive position to wait for Greg to arrive and back him up. Dispatch said this husband had a shotgun. Greg prayed he wouldn't be too late.

He arrived at the run-down home minutes later and took a position across the property from Officer Berry. The husband peered through the screen door.

Berry called out. "Police. Let me see your hands."

The husband opened the screen door and came out, waving his shotgun. With his other hand he dragged his wife behind him. He thrust her down to her knees, then aimed the gun at her chest.

"I'll do it!" he yelled out in the direction of Berry. "I will!"

Greg suddenly envisioned Heather with a gun at her chest. He gripped his nine millimeter tightly with both hands and concentrated on the man's every movement.

Berry called out again. "Put down the gun. Now!"

In a sudden, swift movement, the husband lifted the shotgun toward Berry. Greg yelled, "Put it down, or I'll shoot!"

The shotgun abruptly changed targets. Suddenly the barrel stared at Greg. His training kicked in. He aimed and pulled the trigger. At the same moment, a shot rang out from the porch. A fiery pain struck his leg and he collapsed to the ground.

One final thought entered his mind before darkness overtook him completely. *Please, God, don't take me yet. I have to stay for my baby girl.*

* * *

For the first time the play dragged. Brooke could have sworn that the music played at a slower tempo than normal, lengthening each song. It was a relief when her character was finally killed and she didn't have to go back on stage until the curtain call. Shaking hands after the performance was almost physically painful. All Brooke wanted was to go home and curl up in bed.

Jane and Angela waited near the end of the line of audience members. Brooke was grateful to Jane for that; Angela wouldn't want to be ushered out the door quickly, but would want to talk with them longer. Brooke eyed the line, which was gradually growing shorter, but not fast enough. Jane and Angela were only fifteen feet away now. Suddenly a phone rang, and Jane dug into her purse for her cell.

Brooke breathed a grateful sigh that no one had called during the show; Jane should know better than to keep her phone on during a theatrical performance.

As Brooke thanked a few more audience members for coming, she heard a gasp. Her head jerked toward Jane, whose face had drained of all color, her hand pressed against her mouth.

"We'll be right there," she said. "Thanks, Dad." She hung up and shoved the phone back into her purse. She leaned down and whispered something to Angela, whose eyes grew wide and frightened. Jane gave the suddenly pale Angela a hug, then took her hand and turned toward the back exit. When she stopped and turned back, Brooke broke from the cast greeting line and ran towards her.

"What's wrong?"

"Greg's been shot. He's at the hospital."

Brooke felt like someone had hit her in the gut and knocked the wind out of her. "Will he be all right?"

"They don't know yet. He's in surgery. He was shot by an angry husband or something. I thought I should tell you before I left."

"Thank you for coming back to tell me," Brooke said, putting a hand on Jane's arm.

Jane smiled awkwardly. "You're welcome."

"You two go ahead. I'll be right out as soon as I get out of this dress." With that Brooke raced to the dressing room, oblivious of the stares of exiting audience members.

She didn't bother hanging up her dress or putting her wig away properly. With her costume off, she threw on her street clothes, grabbed her purse, and raced out the door.

She arrived at the emergency waiting room shortly after Jane and Angela. Greg was still in surgery. The family knew nothing more than that he had been shot in the upper leg and had lost a significant amount of blood from an artery. More than once someone had come to say they could wait in another wing, where families waited for patients in the operating room once they were stabilized in the ER. But since Greg's parents hadn't been reached yet, Jane and Russell insisted on staying in the emergency room lobby.

Angela sat restlessly in one blue upholstered chair in the small alcove, then hopped to another. Then she pressed her face against the fish aquarium and stared at an orange fish with black and white stripes. Her face was pale, her eyes red and puffy when she turned to her grandfather. "Can we see him yet? Is Daddy going to be okay?"

"I'm sure he'll be fine," Russell said. "But we can't see him until they come tell us we can. I'll make sure you're the first to know anything. Deal?"

Angela nodded without a word, as if her worry had choked off her vocal chords. She climbed into Brooke's lap and leaned her head against her chest. The group had been sitting in silence for several minutes when Angela lifted her head.

"Brooke?"

Brooke stroked Angela's flaxen hair. "What is it, Gee-la?"

"If Daddy dies . . . will you be my mom and take care of me?"

Brooke caught her breath. She looked to Russell for help, but he hadn't heard the question. She held Angela a bit closer. "You don't need to worry about that. Your daddy is going to be just fine."

"Are you sure?"

"Sure I'm sure," Brooke lied.

"Will he just have a cast like Aunt Janie?"

"I don't know. It's something different with his leg. But I'm sure everything will be fine."

"Will you take care of me while he's sick?"

"I think your grandparents and Aunt Janie might want to help with that," Brooke said. Her heart ached; if only she could reassure Angela. But as it was, the seven-year-old had seen more death than many people three times her age. Anxiety overwhelmed Brooke too. It took a lot to keep herself smiling for Angela, pretending that nothing was wrong, that Greg's injuries were no worse than Jane's had been. Everyone tried to distract Angela, for their own sakes as well as hers. Russell bought her some chips and pop from the vending machines.

When the snacks were gone, Jane dug around in her purse for a minute and found a notebook and a pen. Putting them on the small plastic children's table in the center of the alcove, she said, "Here, Angela. Why don't you draw for a few minutes? You can copy those paintings of the lion and giraffes." Jane pointed to the pictures on the walls.

Angela reluctantly sat on the bench and drew, but the activity didn't keep her distracted for long. She turned to Russell in frustration. "Grandpa, when will they let us see Daddy? I bet if I held his hand he'd feel better."

Russell gave her a warm smile. "I'm sure he would, Gee-la." He glanced at his watch, knowing that trauma surgery could last hours, and Angela couldn't take much more of the waiting. "You know what I need you to do?" Russell asked. Angela shook her head. "I need you to do two things for your daddy." He held up his index finger. "First, get some real food in that tummy of yours." He brought up another finger. "And second, take a little nap. Your daddy will need you nice and strong. Okay?"

"Okay," Angela said weakly.

Russell looked up to Jane. "Would you take her to the cafeteria? It's upstairs." He pulled out his wallet and handed her a twenty. "Get both of you anything you want. Under the circumstances, I don't think Greg would mind her eating junk food at this hour. And try to reach his parents again."

Jane nodded and took Angela's hand. "Let's get you some food," she said, and led her away. Angela stopped and peeked around the doorway.

"Grandpa, if the doctor tells you about Daddy, come find us, okay?"

"I will," Russell said.

"Promise?"

"I promise. I know where the cafeteria is."

Angela turned, satisfied, and let her aunt take her away. When they rounded the corner, Russell stood. "I'll be back in a minute. Got to go to the restroom."

Brooke sat alone for a few minutes, every second feeling like an eternity. She went to the desk and asked for an update.

"Are you family?" a young man asked.

"Not exactly," Brooke said.

"Then I'm sorry, but I can't give out any information." He turned back to his papers as if Brooke no longer existed. She groaned inwardly and returned to her seat.

A few minutes later, when Russell returned, Brooke asked, "Would you ask them for an update? Any news at all. At least how much longer it might be."

"Sure," Russell said, and headed for the same man Brooke had just spoken to.

After a few moments, Russell pulled up a chair beside Brooke. "Still in surgery. Had to give him a few transfusions, so it may take a while yet. They don't know whether he'll pull through, and even if he does, he may still lose his leg. They have to 'ligate' the artery. That means sew it up."

Brooke nodded and tried to picture Greg with only one leg. Greg, who lived for activity of any kind. Country dancing came to mind, quickly followed by pictures of Greg hiking through the Uintahs and walking down the school hall in his uniform. What would he do if he couldn't return to his patrol duties? She pushed the thoughts out of her mind. At least she knew *something*. Knowing sketchy and possibly dismal facts was better than not knowing anything at all, which would have been the case without Russell.

"I asked for an update, but they wouldn't give me anything since I'm not family. The waiting is driving me crazy. I hope Greg's parents get here soon."

"Jane's left a couple of messages at their house already. We don't know where else to contact them. I suppose they'll come here as soon as they listen to their machine." They sat in silence for a few minutes, until Russell suddenly let out one of his rumbling chuckles.

"What's that for?" Brooke asked. This didn't exactly seem like the time for jokes.

Russell cocked his head. "I just had an idea. I don't know for sure, but maybe they'd consider you family if . . ."

"If what?"

"Well, they might be willing to give information to a *fiancée.*"

Brooke looked away. "I don't fit that description, Russell." He eyed her intensely, and Brooke found herself shifting in her seat under the weight of his gaze. *"What?"* she finally burst out with exasperation.

"Why aren't you his fiancée?"

Brooke's head dropped. "I thought you knew."

"Knew what?"

"Greg broke it off between us on Thursday."

Russell's mouth opened, then shut again. He stood up and paced ten feet off in the direction of the vending machines, then turned and strode back. "What was he thinking? Did he give you a reason?"

"Heather."

Russell sat down and shook his head. "This isn't right." His eyes narrowed, and he appeared lost in his own thoughts for a few minutes. Then he patted Brooke's leg. "Don't you worry. I'll set this straight."

Brooke appreciated the sentiment, but had little hope. An older man in scrubs walked toward them, and a sinking feeling hit her stomach. What if Greg didn't survive? Would she even get a chance to marry Greg? Fatigue lined the doctor's face as he approached. Russell and Brooke stood, and the doctor held out a hand.

"I'm Dr. Monson. I understand you're Greg's father-in-law?"

"That's right."

"Have his parents arrived yet?"

Russell shook his head. "No, not yet."

He held out a hand to Brooke. "Are you Greg's wife?"

Brooke flushed. "I'm a friend."

He turned to Russell. "Would you prefer that I talk with you in private?"

"Not at all. Brooke here is practically family." Russell put an arm around Brooke. She smiled gratefully up at him. "Please, tell us how he is."

The sound of running sneakers rounded the corner, and soon Angela appeared, with Jane following close behind. Angela threw herself at Russell and eyed the doctor with combined fear and anticipation. "Will my daddy be all right?"

Russell leaned down and picked up Angela. "The doctor was just about to tell us," he said. "Please, Doctor. Go on."

Dr. Monson didn't waste any time with small talk. "For now it looks like he has a slim chance of keeping his leg," he said. "That's the good news. He's still in critical condition, especially because of his blood loss, so he'll be in ICU for a while yet. They're moving him up there now. It's on the second floor of the east wing."

"So he'll live?" Jane asked quietly.

"It's too soon to tell," Dr. Monson said. "The next few hours will be the most critical."

Russell nodded heavily as Angela piped up. "Can I see him now?"

Dr. Monson smiled. "Not yet, I'm afraid. He's still sleeping from the operation," he answered, addressing himself directly to Angela before turning back to the rest of the group. "When he wakes up, we'll let you all know. But he'll be very groggy and weak. He shouldn't have more than a few minutes every hour with family members tonight, and no one under the age of ten."

Angela's eyes grew wide. "I'm only seven. You mean I can't see my dad?"

Dr. Monson patted her shoulder. "I'll see if we can work something out."

Another tight knot formed in Brooke's throat. When would *she* be able to see Greg? With only family allowed in ICU, she would have to wait until—*if,* she corrected herself—Greg recovered and was moved to a regular room. How long might that be? And would Greg even want to see her? She hugged her arms about herself to keep her emotions at bay. Dr. Monson answered a few more questions, promised to keep them updated, and walked back toward the OR.

Right then an older couple raced in, hair windblown and worry written all over their faces. John and Linda Stevens looked around frantically and nearly ran headlong into Dr. Monson. Mumbling an apology, they searched the room, their eyes finally resting on Russell. Linda's face was ashen, her eyes haunted, as she rushed over and practically clung to Russell's sweater. "Is he alive?"

Russell took her hands in his and gave them a gentle squeeze. "He made it through surgery."

Linda turned to her husband and collapsed in tears against his chest. John wrapped his trembling arms around his wife and gave a sob of relief as he pressed his face against her hair.

CHAPTER 21

Brooke spent most of the night on the second floor of the hospital, watching family members take their turns going through the swinging double doors to ICU. Every hour someone went in. Greg's mother, followed by his father, then Russell. Each time someone came out, Brooke jumped to her feet for any news. Everyone had something different to say. Linda Stevens mentioned how helpless her son looked and wished she could take his pain away. John Stevens came out a bit shaken, but pleased at the good care Greg was receiving. Russell said little except that he was sure Greg would be fine, then pulled Brooke to the side to tell her that Greg had asked about her before nodding off.

Brooke closed her eyes and swallowed hard, hardly able to trust her legs. She wanted nothing more than to be with the man behind those doors, to be with him forever. Greg loved her, but even if he recovered, that wouldn't be enough for him. More than once she stood at the doors and peered through the small square windows at the top. Russell had told her that Greg's room was the third one on the left. She couldn't see anything but his door. No one manned the small desk. She could probably get in without anyone knowing. Or she could get kicked out.

The following hour Jane got permission to bring Angela in to see her father, and Brooke had to walk away in frustration. The waiting area was beginning to feel claustrophobic, and the swirl pattern in the blue carpet was making her dizzy. So she went to the elevator and back to the ground floor, where she wandered the halls and wondered if Greg would want to see her if he could. She finally found some privacy in the waiting area for patients in surgery. It was nearly empty thanks to the late hour, but a few people sat around reading newspapers or watching the news on television. She put her head into her hands and let out all the tears she had been keeping back all night.

People eyed her oddly, and Brooke suddenly remembered that she still wore her stage makeup, fake eyelashes and all. She hadn't bothered to do more than change her clothes and take off her wig, so she must be a sight. She wiped at her cheeks, covering her fingertips in stage makeup. She was reaching into her purse for a tissue when a heavy hand touched her shoulder. Brooke jumped in surprise to see Russell. She quickly wiped her tears and put on a smile, but she didn't fool him.

"What are you doing down here?" she asked.

"I came to find you. Didn't think you'd leave without telling someone." Russell sat down beside her. "You need to go in there, don't you?"

Brooke nodded mutely. "But I don't know if Greg would want to see me."

"I think he would. I'll see if I can pull some strings and get you in."

Brooke gave a wan smile. "Thanks, Russell, but I doubt even you could charm the nurses enough for that."

She took a deep breath, then stood up and wiped at her cheeks. "I'm not doing anyone any good by being here, including Greg."

"You go home and get some sleep," Russell said.

She slung her purse over her shoulder. "I'll be back tomorrow. Thanks for everything, Russell." She gave him a hug, and he held her tightly in his strong arms.

Then she headed down the tiled entryway toward the parking garage, tearing off her fake eyelashes as she went.

* * *

The following day Greg's condition remained about the same, and the day dragged on until she went to bed, disappointed from the lack of news. When Brooke came back Monday morning no one was there to tell her if anything had changed this time. So she sat down and began crossing off the events listed for the day in her planner.

The elevator dinged, and Russell emerged. "Are you all right, Brooke?"

"I'm okay. Just a little tired." She shrugged. "I've never missed a training meeting until today. I've attended every one. But today I don't really care what I miss." She crossed off another hour block on her schedule.

Russell sat down beside her. "You look beat. You need something to do. Staying here is killing you."

"I was gone most of the night. I wanted to be back in case anything happened. Besides, I got six hours of sleep, so I'm fine." Brooke's eyes started to tear up. "What if I leave and he . . ."

Russell put his hand over hers. "He won't. I got an update an hour ago. He was in the same condition as he was last night. Go on to your meetings. I think you need a distraction."

"But—"

"If there is any change or news, I'll call you right away on your cell phone."

"What about Angela?" Brooke asked, not willing to leave right away. "Does she need someone to watch her?"

"Linda's got her all day. I think they went shopping or something."

"Oh."

"Go ahead to your meetings. I'd hate for you to miss something important there. I'll call you, I promise."

"All right. Thanks, Russell."

Brooke charged her phone as she drove to the meetings, just to be safe. She spent most of the day lost in her thoughts, unable to pay attention to her meetings anyway. Wishing she could hold Greg, missing Angela, wondering what the future would bring.

Shortly after the lunch break, Brooke's phone rang. She jumped from her seat and raced to the hallway to answer it.

"Russell? How is he?"

Russell's voice cracked as he spoke. "Brooke. It's . . . it's not Greg. It's Angela. She's missing."

* * *

Angela sat in the passenger seat of the car, her shirt wet from spilled root beer. Her whole body trembled as the car screeched around another corner. Through tears blurring her vision, she looked out the back window, but knew that the McDonald's where her Grandma Stevens had taken her was too far away to see anymore.

She buckled her seat belt, wishing it could keep her safe from whatever lay ahead. She tried to remember all the things her dad had taught her about using her brains to stay safe. She knew never to go with strangers, no matter how nice they seemed.

But this angry man driving hadn't given her the chance to run away. When she had come out of a slide in the Play Place, he grabbed her and ran out of the exit. He had held his hand on her mouth, so she could barely breathe, let alone scream. She bit his fingers, and he had relaxed his grip for just a second, so she managed to let out one small cry, but he had hit her in the stomach, and she didn't try it again. She wondered if anyone had heard her.

She tried to stop herself from trembling so he wouldn't know she was scared. She thought back to all the discussions she and her father had had about things like this. He had drilled her and role-played with her, and she thought she knew everything. But now she strained to remember. What had he said? Something about talking with the kidnapper so they get to know you. She forced herself to speak.

"Where are we going?" Her voice quivered, and she bit her tongue so her tears wouldn't fall.

"To a park." His voice sounded odd. Cold, almost like ice. Angela shivered and pulled her knees up to her body and hugged them tightly. They drove all over the city, and at first Angela thought he was lost. When they passed North Park, she spoke up again. "This is one of my favorite parks. I don't get to go there too often 'cause I don't live that close to it."

He didn't respond. Instead, he continued down the street until he drove into another park, one without playground equipment. He stopped the car.

"Get out."

Angela did as she was told, looking around for a place she could run away. The parking lot alone was too big; he would catch her if she tried to run, and there wasn't any place to hide either. He snatched a blue duffle bag from the car, then grabbed her hand and dragged her into the park.

She had to take two steps for every one of his. Her mind raced. What could she do? Suddenly her father's voice came back to her mind. "Keep him talking," she heard him say.

Angela saw a duck pond and a bridge. "I like ducks," she said suddenly. "Do you?"

"No."

He turned into an area thick with foliage, less visible from the normal walkways, and plopped onto the grass under a tree. Then he dumped out the contents of the bag. Several medicine bottles rolled out, two cans of beer, and one can of orange pop. Other odds and ends fell out and littered the grass too—old receipts, several rolls of Smarties candies, a chewed pencil, an empty pack of gum, a small flashlight, and a piece of narrow rope. He took the rope and tied Angela's legs together, then tied the end of the rope to his own leg.

Next, he proceeded to open the bottles and dump their contents onto the bag. Angela thought the two oversized bottles looked like the jumbo Tylenol bottle in her father's top dresser drawer. The other ones looked like the orange bottles in Grandpa Miller's bathroom, which her father had warned her not to touch because they could make her sick.

He busied himself with sorting his pills. He did it methodically, counting and arranging them in piles for several minutes, all the while muttering something about if everyone wanted him to take pills, he would take them all right. As she watched him, Angela thought back to the lunch she had had with Aunt Jane and this friend. He hadn't seemed to like her, and she didn't like him then either. She couldn't understand why he had taken her away. She couldn't remember doing anything wrong. Her stomach ached from fear.

She suddenly felt an odd, calm sensation, and the impression that she should take the Smarties and hold them in her lap. Without knowing why, she reached out slowly and slid a roll toward her. Intent on sorting the pills, Christopher didn't notice. She took another roll of candy, then another and another, until she had all five rolls in her lap. Then she opened them as quietly as she could. As she finished opening the last one, Christopher turned to her. She jumped, afraid he had heard the wrapper. Instead he handed her a can of orange pop.

"I got you this."

He brought the duffle bag between them. The pills sat in two piles, one twice the size of the other. He pointed to the smaller pile. "This is yours. You will swallow all of these. Understand?" Angela nodded silently. "I've got a gun in the car. The kind your daddy takes with him to work. I could do it that way. First you, then me."

Angela's eyes grew wide. "Don't. Please don't."

Christopher didn't seem to hear her. "But I thought taking these might be easier for both of us." She stared at the piles, wondering if they were enough to kill her, like he said they could.

Just then a man and woman crossed the bridge, laughing and holding hands. Christopher grabbed Angela's wrist and whispered menacingly, "Don't you dare make a noise, or I won't bother with the pills. You hear me?"

Angela nodded, her entire body trembling again as her hands had last winter when she played in the snow without her mittens. She watched the couple walk out of the park and a moment later drive away. Her heart sank. If only they would have seen her, perhaps she could have gotten them to understand that something wasn't right.

She looked back at her pile of pills, not knowing what she should do. Christopher selected four or five from his own pile, popped them into his mouth, and washed them down with beer. "Your turn."

Angela reached forward and took some pills from the pile, then stared at them in the palm of her hand.

"Well? What are you waiting for? Eat them."

Angela gripped the pills in her hand, unwilling to swallow them, but afraid of what he would do if she didn't. He held her arm and squeezed tightly. She let out a yelp. "Eat them now."

Angela put two pills into her mouth and tried to chew them up, but they were hard and bitter. She took a swallow from the soda can. Christopher let go. "That's better."

As he turned back to his own pile, Angela remembered the candies. She put two in her right hand before he turned back. "All right, your turn again," he said.

This time she took three pills from the pile, but instead of eating them, she popped the candies into her mouth, keeping the pills in her palm, and took another drink. When Christopher was satisfied and turned back to his pile, she hid the pills under her leg. They repeated the routine over and over, with Angela praying all the while that her candies would last long enough. She began taking more pills each time so the pile would disappear faster.

They took turns for what felt like hours, though it couldn't have been more than twenty minutes or so. Each time Christopher got slower taking his turn.

"Are you feeling it yet?" he asked groggily. "It shouldn't be long now."

"My stomach hurts," Angela said. And it did, but from fear, not pills.

He blinked slowly and looked at her. "This is it, kid. Let's lie down and wait for the end. Move over."

Angela's heart skipped a beat. If she moved at all, he would surely see her pills and force them down her throat. "I'm fine here."

"You're going to move over," he said, his arm raised, when his speech suddenly slurred. He shook his hands. "I can't feel my hands!" He clawed at his ears. "My ears!" He reached for Angela and grasped her arms. She tried not to scream out in pain. He stared at her with wild eyes; she closed her eyes to block out the sight. She knew she would have bruises on her shoulders.

"Help me! I'm dying!" he screamed. She tried to jerk her arm free, but his hold was too great. "Call 911! I don't want to die!"

Angela wished with everything in her that she could call 911. Christopher kept shrieking in fear, his grip on her arm getting tighter some minutes, then looser at others. Her heart beat wildly. She tugged at the ropes, but instead of getting looser, they only dug into her leg harder.

After several minutes of raving Christopher squinted and blinked, then collapsed on the grass. Angela screamed first in fright, then for help, but no one heard her. All the tears she had been holding back fell freely. She rubbed her arms where he had grabbed so hard and prayed aloud that someone would find her. She tried to untie the rope, but she couldn't budge the knots.

Against her will, she watched his chest rise and fall. She couldn't pull her eyes away from the sight. Sometimes his breaths seemed awfully far apart, and more than once Angela held her own breath and waited.

Hours passed. Daylight turned to dusk. The lights in the parking lot turned on one by one. The moon rose, bright and nearly full, and Angela's reserves finally gave out. She buried her head in her knees so she couldn't see Christopher lying on the ground, his leg still attached to hers. She kept whispering prayers as her body gave out and she fell asleep.

When the sound of a car reached her, she sat bolt upright, peering at the parking lot through the shrubbery. The movement sent a jolt of pain through her stiffened muscles, but she didn't care. She could see a patrol car in the parking lot.

"Daddy!" Angela screamed. She tried to stand up, forgetting about the rope at her ankles. She fell back to the ground, her skin chafing against the ropes. "Daddy! Daddy! I'm here!"

* * *

"I called the hospital as soon as the paramedics got here," Officer Berry told Brooke by her car. "When she told me her name, I realized she was Stevens's daughter, so I called the hospital right away."

"Thank you." For the moment, Brooke couldn't find any other words. She just held Angela tighter.

Jane came up, holding an old blanket she had retrieved from the trunk. She wrapped Angela in it, then gave her a big hug. "Are you hungry? I think there's still some Doritos in the car."

Angela gave a weak smile and nodded.

"How did you find her?" Jane asked.

Officer Berry shrugged. "I just came to clear the park. Do it a lot after curfew when there's a car in the parking lot. I expected the usual bunch of teenagers hanging out, but then I heard her calling for her daddy," Officer Berry said, nodding toward Angela.

Jane returned a minute later with the chips and a drink.

Angela piped up. "What about . . . him? Will he be all right?"

"The man who took you? I don't know. I think he was still alive when the paramedics arrived."

"So he didn't die?"

"I don't think so."

Brooke held Angela tighter, grateful that even if Christopher didn't pull through, at least he didn't die beside Angela. The young girl had been through plenty already, and would have a lot to deal with for some time without the additional nightmare of a dead body being attached to her leg by a rope. Brooke left Angela with Jane and followed Officer Berry to his patrol car to finish filling out the necessary paperwork. She then returned to Jane's car, where Angela sat eating chips in the passenger seat.

"Are you feeling better?" Jane asked Angela, whose fingers were orange from the chips.

Angela nodded slowly, then looked intently at Brooke and her aunt and said, "I tried to do what Daddy taught me. I didn't say I'd go with him, I promise. He just grabbed me."

Jane and Brooke each reached for one of Angela's hands.

"We know, Gee-la," Jane said.

"You did good," Brooke agreed. "Your daddy will be proud."

"At first I thought it was my fault, that maybe the Holy Ghost had tried to warn me and I didn't listen." Angela looked at them earnestly. "But you know what? He helped me. The Holy Ghost told me what to do, just like in the mountains. So I didn't have to eat the pills. I didn't know why I should take the candies, but I listened. I heard Him, and I listened."

"You sure did, Gee-la. And we're so glad you did," Jane said. The three of them held each other close, tears streaming down everyone's faces. For the moment Jane and Brooke cared for nothing more than that their little girl was safe.

Linda Stevens pulled into the parking lot, having finally been reached at home about Angela's recovery. Linda jumped out of her car and raced over to them, sobbing. Angela went to her grandmother and held her tight.

"I'm so sorry, Angela! It's all my fault. I should have been watching you closer."

"It's okay, Grandma. I'm all right."

Standing beside Brooke, Jane watched Linda for a moment before a sob caught in her throat. Jane turned away and Brooke reached for her.

"Jane, what is it?"

"It's not Linda's fault. It's mine. Christopher wouldn't have known about Angela if I hadn't brought her to lunch with us. You said that when you broke up with him he came after you. I've been worried about him coming after *me*. But . . ." Her hand covered her mouth. "I never expected him to go after *her*."

Jane turned to Brooke and sobbed against her shoulder.

CHAPTER 22

When Russell returned to the hospital, he debated whether or not to tell Greg about the abduction and decided against it. He would tell Greg when he was stronger. Right now there was no point, since Angela was safe and sound. But he wanted to talk to Greg about something else.

Russell planned to wait until Greg was alert and strong enough to listen. Really listen. It was almost lunch before that happened. Russell sat on the chair beside the hospital bed and waited until Greg looked fairly alert.

"Greg, I've got something important to tell you. Something I should have said a long time ago. You'd better listen close, Greg. Because you're making a terrible mistake."

Greg's brow furrowed. His voice was hoarse as he whispered, "What do you mean?"

"I mean Brooke. You'd better put it right soon. I'm sure Heather's getting antsy for you to finally take the plunge."

"No." Greg shook his head. "She didn't want me to remarry. She said so over and over when we were first married."

"I heard Heather say that too. But she doesn't feel like that anymore. She would want you to marry Brooke."

Greg licked his dry lips weakly. "How can you say that?"

"Because she loved Angela more than anything in the world." Russell put his hand on Greg's. "Trust me on this one. I know because she told me herself," Russell said, his eyes growing moist at the memory of his final moments with his eldest daughter. Then he told Greg about it, lost in the images and emotions of that day. He could remember it as if the scene were being played out right before him . . .

In the ambulance Heather had held Russell's hand as she cried out for Greg.

"Dad, I have to see him before I die."

"You'll be fine," Russell reassured her. "You're stable now. They'll get you patched up at the hospital, and next thing you know, Greg will be there with you in the recovery room."

But Heather cried out again, tears streaming down her face as she lay there. Russell squeezed her hand, wishing he could take away the pain. But as he looked into her eyes, he realized it wasn't her physical pain that caused such agony.

She gripped his hand tightly with a sudden surge of strength. "Dad, Greg has to find a mother for Angela. He has to. Someone really good. An honorable woman. I wish I could tell him myself, but I won't get to."

"You aren't dying," Russell insisted.

"Yes, Dad. I am. And Angela needs a mother. But Greg—"

Russell blinked back his own tears. "But you made him promise to never remarry," he finished speaking for her.

She made a valiant effort to smile. "Don't worry, Dad. I won't be jealous. Not if she loves my little girl as much as I do, and raises her as I would . . . I would embrace such a woman."

Those last moments with his daughter faded out as Russell looked at the ceiling with shining eyes, brought back to the present. "That's when she left, and we couldn't revive her. So Greg, it's about time that you fix this. If you give Angela a mother again, Heather will be more than happy. I know it."

Tears filled Greg's eyes and slipped onto his lower lashes. "She said all that?"

Russell patted Greg's hand and blinked several times to keep the tears in his own eyes from falling. He nodded hard, then swallowed a few times before he trusted his voice. "That's exactly what she said."

* * *

Instead of spending her free time at the hospital over the next few days as she would have liked, despite being barred from ICU, Brooke ended up spending much of her time with Angela. For once Jane didn't seem to mind; Angela's desires and safety were everyone's focus these days. If Gee-la wanted to be with Brooke, that was fine with everyone. As she tended Angela, Brooke was grateful she wouldn't have to go on stage until Thursday night, which gave her a couple of days to get her life and emotions under control.

One day Brooke and Angela spent the greater part of the afternoon setting up Brooke's classroom, followed by dinner, which Brooke made in Greg's kitchen as she had every night that week. It felt natural to be there, reaching for the spatula in that drawer, pulling out the garlic powder from this cupboard. But Greg wouldn't be coming in the front door, and she wasn't his wife. His mother would be back soon to spend the night with Angela. As much as Brooke wanted Greg well, she knew if and when that happened, she would probably have to say good-bye to him and Angela.

After dinner Angela disappeared to get ready for her ballet class while Brooke cleaned up the dishes. Five minutes later she came back, dressed in a black leotard and pink tights, but with a panicked look in her eyes. "I can't find my ballet slippers!" she cried. "And my hair isn't in a bun either. Have you seen my slippers?"

Brooke wiped her hands on a dish rag. "No, but I'll help you look for them." They scoured the house, but to no avail, when suddenly Angela jumped to her feet and clapped her hands.

"I bet they're in the truck!" she exclaimed. "Sometimes Daddy forgets to take them out when we get home. Sometimes he throws them in the back seat."

"Then that's where we'll look," Brooke said, taking Greg's car keys from their hook and heading for the garage in search of the missing slippers. The garage seemed painfully empty without Greg's patrol car. The slippers weren't in the back seat of the family truck, but when Brooke opened the trunk, there they were, sitting on top of a large box with silver wrapping paper and a white bow. Brooke leaned closer to see the writing on the attached card, which wished Brooke a happy birthday. She lifted the box and leaned against the back of the car, holding the box before her. She had nearly forgotten that her birthday was next week. Greg must have gotten her gift before he decided he couldn't go against Heather's wishes.

Without wondering if she should put the box back where she found it, Brooke opened the gift. Inside she found a beautiful pair of tan cowboy boots. She lifted one from the box and ran her finger across the design on the slick leather. She pressed her fingers to her eyes and tried not to cry. Would she and Greg ever go dancing again? If he survived, would his leg heal enough to let him dance on it? She kicked her sneakers off onto the garage floor, pulled the other boot from its box and tissue paper, and slipped the boots on. She wiggled her toes. They fit perfectly. She swayed to imaginary music, all the while her eyes watering as she pictured Greg leading her through dance moves on their first date.

"Brooke, did you find them?"

Angela's voice tore Brooke out of her thoughts, and she almost tripped on the lawn mower at the side of the garage. She swiped at her eyes, then reached for the ballet slippers in the back of the car. "They're right here, just as you thought," she said. "Ready to go?"

"I still need my bun."

"That's right, I forgot," Brooke said. "Let's see what we can do about that."

* * *

Brooke wore her boots to the hospital the following morning. None of Greg's family was there yet, so she read a book in a back corner of the ICU waiting area, still wishing she could go inside, or at least get an update from someone. Last she had heard, Greg was alert more often and getting some strength back, but he wasn't out of the woods yet. A police officer stepped off the elevator and talked with the woman at the desk by the doors. He seemed to be insistent about something, but the woman kept shaking her head.

"I'm sorry, Officer, but only family is allowed in the intensive care unit. You can leave a message for him if you like, and I'll make sure he receives it."

"But this isn't the kind of message you can write down," the officer said.

The woman did not answer, but instead returned to her work. The officer beat the desk with his fist once, and let out a frustrated breath, when he caught Brooke watching him. She stood up and took a step in his direction.

"Do you work with Greg Stevens?" she asked.

"That's right. He came as my backup when . . . it happened. Are you his sister?"

She held out a hand. "I'm Brooke Williamson," she said, avoiding any title.

He shook her hand and nodded. "I remember him mentioning you." The nurse glanced up at the two of them, then went into ICU. "I'm Rich Berry. How is he?"

Brooke's shoulders lifted, then fell. "From what I've heard, it's still touch and go, but if he survives, they hope he'll have his leg."

"What about returning to work?"

"The jury's still out on that one."

Rich nodded thoughtfully. "I came to tell him what happened that night, but they won't let me in to see him."

The woman returned to the desk and interrupted them. "Did I hear you say that you are Brooke Williamson?"

"Yes," Brooke answered, looking around the hospital for any of Greg's family who might have mentioned her. "Is there a message for me?"

"Sort of. Russell Miller left just a few minutes ago. He said you're Greg's fiancée and haven't had a chance to see him yet. He's awake now, so if you'd like to go in, you're welcome to."

The statement took her off guard to such a degree that she didn't know how to respond. "Uh, thank you," she said as the nurse gave her a smile and left to answer a call.

Rich's eyes widened. "I didn't know Greg was engaged. Congratulations. Hey, would *you* give him a message for me?"

"Sure, anything." He didn't give Brooke a chance to clarify her and Greg's relationship, and she didn't go out of her way to do it either.

"Tell him he saved the woman's life, and probably her son's life too."

Brooke's eyes widened. "How?"

"Domestic violence calls are always scary—we always call for backup. We've been to that address more than once, but the wife never pressed charges. This time when the fighting got bad, her son called 911. The husband stood on the porch and aimed his shotgun right at his wife. I tried to warn him to put it down, and he aimed it at me. Then Stevens—I mean Greg—fired. The husband fired his weapon at Greg at the same time. They both went down."

Brooke found her pulse beating rapidly as she pictured the moment. "What happened to him? I mean the husband?"

"He didn't make it. Greg saved the wife's life by what he did. Mine too." Officer Berry got a pensive look on his face. "It's easy to replay an incident over and over and wonder if you did the right thing. I didn't want Greg worrying about whether he made the right choice."

"I'd probably wonder the same thing . . . like whether the man would have really killed his wife."

"Oh, he would have. That's what I wanted to tell Greg. Turns out the man's done it before. He was living under an alias and was wanted in California for murdering another wife and a stepdaughter. There's no question. He would have killed this family too." He looked toward the ICU doors, then back at Brooke. "Will you tell him that?"

She nodded, emotion filling her throat. "I will," she managed to say. "Thank you for telling me."

"I probably shouldn't have. Don't mention it to anyone but Greg."

"Don't worry, I won't. Thanks again. This will mean a lot to him." She reached out her hand in a gesture of gratitude.

"You're welcome," the officer finished with a smile.

Officer Berry turned toward the elevators as Brooke pushed open the ICU door. He stopped and called back, "Brooke?"

She turned with raised eyebrows. "Yes?"

"I hope you get to have your wedding day real soon. He's a good man."

Brooke gave him a small smile. "Thanks."

"We'll all miss him if he can't come back on the force." With that, Officer Berry turned on his heels and headed down the hall to the elevators.

Brooke's heart began to beat harder as she pushed open the ICU doors. She half expected someone to stop her, that by merely looking at her they would know she wasn't really engaged to Greg Stevens. She prayed he would be happy to see her.

She looked down the long hall and walked past two rooms on each side, trying not to look at the patients in the other rooms, as if that would encroach on their privacy. She wondered what stories were behind their illnesses, what loved ones were praying for them as she was praying for Greg. Brooke stopped one step before Greg's room and gathered her nerves, hardly able to wait until she could see him, speak to him, touch him.

She took a step into the room, where Greg appeared to be sleeping. He had a healthy beginning of a beard, and his skin looked sallow. Something dripped into his IV. Brooke hoped it was something to keep him out of pain. Careful not to touch his leg, she eased to the side and sat down on a chair. Gently, she took his limp hand in hers. It was cold, and she put her other hand on top to warm it. As she stroked her thumb across the top of his hand, she began to speak.

"Greg, it's me, Brooke. You're going to be just fine. Russell says the doctors think—"

Greg's head slowly turned toward her. "Brooke, is that really you?" His voice sounded gravelly, as if his throat was sore. A weak smile broke across his face at seeing her.

"I didn't know whether you'd want me here," Brooke said.

"Oh, I do! I've wanted to see you, but—how did you sneak in?"

Brooke shrugged with a grin. "Your father-in-law sort of used his charms."

He nodded with a smile. "Trust Russell." Greg's eyes clouded over. "I guess you heard what happened." Brooke nodded, and Greg spoke quietly. "Did he die? I haven't been able to get anyone else to tell me." Brooke nodded reluctantly.

Greg closed his eyes tightly. "I killed a man," he said under his breath. "I killed a man."

Brooke shook her head and squeezed his hand tightly. "You didn't kill a man," she said, unwilling for him to focus on that part of the story.

"But you said—"

Brooke tried to find a way to explain so he would understand. "Yes, the man died." Greg closed his eyes, and his face turned away. "But Greg, it was more than that. You don't know the rest. I just ran into Rich Berry in the hall. He wanted to talk to you himself, but the nurse wouldn't let him in to see you. So he told me."

Greg turned back to face her and opened his eyes. "What did he say?"

"The man was wanted in California for killing another wife and a stepdaughter. They would have been just two more on his list. So you didn't kill a man. You saved a family."

Greg's lower lip trembled slightly as a tear squeezed out of each eye. "I finally did it? I saved a mother?" He turned to Brooke, his dry lips curving into a weak smile. "I've made up for Heather's death."

Brooke shook her head and stroked his cheek with her hand. "But you never had to pay anyone back for anything," she whispered.

Greg nodded, then put his hand over hers on his cheek. "But it helps. I made a difference for one family. For a mother and her child." He took a deep breath. "It doesn't matter if I can't go back to the force."

Brooke sat up straighter. "Did the doctors say you won't?"

Greg shook his head weakly. "No. But I can tell my chances aren't good." He took in a deep breath, and Brooke realized that she had worn him out with the excitement of the story.

"I should go and let you rest," she said, giving his hand a squeeze.

But before she could leave, he squeezed her hand in return, if a bit weakly. "Brooke," he said. She turned back. "Thanks for coming. I needed you. And I love you. I always will."

Brooke leaned in to hold him as best she could. When she pulled away, his cheek was wet with her tears. "I love you too, Greg."

As Brooke came out, she saw Russell, a candy bar in hand. She went directly to him, her hand on her hip in a pretext of indignation. "You told them I'm Greg's fiancée?"

Russell's warm, rumbling laugh filled the waiting room. "And I see you didn't exactly correct them." Brooke opened her mouth to protest, but Russell went on. "Doesn't matter. It wasn't a lie, exactly. I figured one of these days Greg will propose and you'll say yes. So it's just a technicality that you're not his fiancée now. You will be."

CHAPTER 23

Closing night arrived without Greg ever getting to see the play. His father-in-law got permission to videotape the closing performance so Greg could at least see that. Russell came to the play two times before taping it so he would know how best to film it, and on closing night he arrived well before the doors opened to the general public and set up a tripod in a back corner.

"Thanks, Russell," Brooke said on her way to the dressing room. "It'll be nice to have some evidence of my theater life, just in case I never do this again."

Kathy folded her arms and leaned against a doorway. "And why wouldn't you do this again?"

Brooke shrugged. "You never know what's going to happen," she said, thinking how quickly Greg's life had changed with a single gunshot. Life was so fragile.

The final performance of *Into the Woods* proved to be one of the best. No one missed a cue or forgot a prop, and Rapunzel hit every b-flat on the nose. When it was all over, Brooke sat in the dressing room and stared in the mirror at her red hair, which she planned to dye back to her normal shade just in time for school to start. She thought back over the past few months and how much things had changed. She thought of all the new people in her life, from Greg and his family to her friends in the cast.

She twisted her finger around a lock of her bright, curly hair. Somehow it represented all of those changes. Greg liked it, but more than that, she felt stronger with the color, even though she knew it was silly. She took her wig off and fluffed her own hair with her fingers.

* * *

Too soon Brooke was back at school with a new crop of starry-eyed fourth-graders. For the first time since her first year of teaching, the days dragged by. Each day she waited for the bell to ring so she could go to the hospital and visit Greg. He had moved out of ICU sooner than anyone expected, although it wasn't fast enough for Brooke. He insisted that paying back his debt to Heather made the difference. Whenever Brooke came to visit, he was in great spirits. Neither mentioned their breakup or what the future might hold.

Each time Brooke asked him when he would be discharged, but he always shrugged.

"I still have to do a lot of therapy on my leg," he'd say.

"But they don't have to keep you in a hospital bed for that, do they? Can't you ask the doctors to even guess at when you'll be discharged? All I want is a ballpark figure: are we talking days, weeks, months? You've been here for over two weeks already."

Greg would simply smile and shrug, and Brooke would groan in frustration. "It'll come," he'd say.

The following week Brooke was helping individual students with math problems when the classroom door opened. Russell poked his head in the room, then caught Brooke's eye and grinned. Then he disappeared for a moment to pull the door all the way open. But instead of coming in himself, he held the door and let a pair of crutches through first. Brooke almost dropped her pencil at the sight.

"Greg!" Her voice cracked with surprise.

The hum of working students silenced immediately as the children looked from their teacher to the intruder, wondering who he was and what he was doing in their class. Brooke crossed the room and threw her arms around him.

"You're out!" she cried. Greg hopped on his good leg to catch his balance, then laughed as he hugged her back. "Why didn't you tell me you were getting discharged?"

"Because I wanted to see that expression on your face."

Brooke was suddenly aware of twenty-one pairs of nine-year-old eyes watching them. "So why did you decide to surprise me here?" she whispered.

"This was where I asked you out on our first date. I thought it would be an appropriate place to make the result of that date official." He looked around at the students. "Would you all like to see something?"

"Are you Miss Williamson's boyfriend?" came a high voice from the back of the room.

Brooke surprised herself by flushing. Greg grinned. "Watch and see." He reached into his pocket and pulled out a velvet box. Russell came up behind him with a chair, and Greg sat on it. "I can't kneel very well, so this will have to do."

A couple of boys began to whistle, and girls tittered. Greg opened the box to reveal a glittering solitaire.

Holding the ring higher, he said, "Brooke Williamson, will you marry me?"

The room was still, and a rush of thoughts and emotions came over Brooke. "Of course I will," she assured quietly. The room rippled with young laughter and squeals of excitement. Greg managed to get back to his feet, then he leaned close and gave Brooke a deep kiss.

The room erupted with exclamations ranging from, "Eeew, gross!" and, "Whoo-whooo!" to, "How romantic!"

Greg promised to call that night, then left the chaos he had created, but Brooke didn't mind. She might have had a zoo for a class for the rest of the day, but with the sparkling diamond on her left hand, she didn't mind in the least.

* * *

They spent that evening talking in Greg's living room. "So between being able to make up for Heather's death, and Russell telling me about her final wishes, I felt free to go after what I wanted most." He took Brooke's left hand and looked at the ring. "Do you like it?"

"I love it."

"Do you want to set a date? I don't want to wait, but I know it can take time to plan a wedding."

"Oh, I don't want a big wedding. My mother will fight me on this one, but for me, the smaller the better. The kind of wedding I want won't take more than a few weeks to plan."

"Are you sure?"

"I admit, ten years ago, I would have wanted a huge production, but not now. The celebration isn't the important part anymore. I don't need a big reception, just a small get-together with our closest friends and family."

"Whatever you want is fine with me. I have just one request."

"And what's that?"

"Can the cake be chocolate? White frosting, of course, but chocolate inside?"

Brooke laughed aloud. "I think that can be arranged. It probably won't be anything elaborate. Not one of those four layer things with real flowers and columns."

"As long as it's chocolate."

"You can count on it."

That night before going to bed Brooke looked at the phone and decided she needed to call her mother and break the news.

"I have something to tell you about me and Greg," Brooke said when her mother answered.

"You broke up? Who did it this time?"

"No, Mom, we didn't break up."

"Then what did you want to tell . . ." After a pause, the other option dawned on her, and she squealed so loud into the phone that Brooke had to hold the receiver away from her ear. "Don't toy with me, Brookey," her mother finally said in a warning tone. "Are you really engaged?"

"Yes, Mom. I'm really getting married."

"Do you have a date yet? I hope it's not too soon. We'll need at least four or five months to plan it. Do you want to go dress shopping on Saturday? The other day Carol told me of a great wedding photographer. He's pricy, but worth every penny. Where do you want your reception? The Historic County Courthouse is gorgeous, and it doesn't need much decorating—"

"Mom," Brooke interjected. "I don't want a big reception. Just a few friends. I want the whole thing very simple. I don't know that I'll even bother with announcements, and I may wear my temple dress instead of getting a fancy new one."

Brooke heard a gasp on the other end. "Don't do this to me, Brookey. Please. I've waited so long."

"I've waited just as long, and all the fluff doesn't mean much anymore."

"Can I at least buy you a dress? And order a cake?"

Brooke could hear the strain in her mother's voice, the effort at acceptance and compromise. If the fuss didn't mean much to Brooke, it did to her mother. She wouldn't give on the size of the wedding, but she could at least give her mother a dress and a cake. "Sure, Mom. We can find a dress together, and Greg would love a fancy cake, as long as it's chocolate inside."

"What about a photographer?"

"I'd love some pictures of the day," she admitted.

"Then I suppose I can live without the rest, if you're sure that's what you want."

"I'm sure. And thank you for being willing to do all of that for me. I love you, Mom."

* * *

Autumn leaves lined the city streets by the time Greg returned to work at his new desk job at the police department. He said he enjoyed it, although he had already decided to go back to school so he would have a greater chance for promotion to administrative positions. He still had a lot of physical therapy before his leg would get its strength back, but now that he was home and doing well, he and Brooke were eager to move on with their lives together. Angela pestered them every day about when Brooke was going to come live with them as her mommy.

So on a crisp fall day in October, Greg, Brooke, and their families went to the Provo Temple. The temple matrons flitted around Brooke in the bride's dressing room almost as much as her mother and Pat did. As Brooke looked at herself in the full-length mirror, she was glad she had dyed her hair back to normal. Because of the damage from the perm and hair coloring, she had trimmed her hair shorter than normal, but it was nice to see the old color back. Besides, she felt more like herself without the red hair. And of all times and places, this was one where she wanted to feel like her best self. She saw her mother's glowing face beside her, and she was glad she decided to get the dress, for her mother's sake. She looked almost as happy as Brooke felt.

Her mother gave her a big hug before leaving with a temple worker to join the other guests. "My little Brookey!" she said, tears in her eyes. "It feels like yesterday that you were my chubby baby that Dad called 'Butterball', and here you are getting married! The years went so fast! I love you so much."

"I love you too, Mom," Brooke said.

Pat, whose belly bulged with pregnancy, adjusted Brooke's dress one last time, then gave her a long hug. "I'm so happy for you. It's been a long time coming, hasn't it?"

Brooke looked into the mirror at her reflection. If finding Greg took ten years longer than her original dreams, she could accept it. "He was worth the wait," she said. *And so is Angela.*

A few minutes later an elderly temple worker led her into a hall. There she saw a young groom standing with a male temple worker. The young man's cheeks were flushed with nervousness, and when he caught sight of Brooke, he spoke up. "She's not mine," he said in a panic.

Brooke grinned, amazed at herself for feeling so calm and collected. "Don't worry," she said to him. "I've got my own groom." The young man, probably twenty-two or so, visibly sighed with relief. Brooke was excited, but not a nervous wreck like this young groom. She wondered if Greg had been anything like that when he and Heather had married.

Before she knew it, Brooke knelt across the altar hand in hand with Greg, who knelt on his right knee, his left leg sticking out since it couldn't bend well or handle much weight yet. The workers assured him he could sit on a chair, but he insisted on kneeling as best he could. It had to be exactly right, he said. Brooke gazed into his eyes and held his hand tightly in her own, trying to commit every detail of the moment to memory.

Following the ceremony, they had their first married kiss. Brooke couldn't help but thinking of another bride who had shared such a moment with Greg. But this time when she thought of Heather, she didn't feel envy, only peace and acceptance. For a brief moment she could even picture the two of them embracing. She knew that somehow everything was fine, that she and Heather would grow to be wonderful friends.

Greg and Brooke stood by the altar as family and friends congratulated them one by one until the newlyweds were left with only a few temple workers, who ushered them toward the door. Greg leaned in for another kiss, then took her hand and led her out.

Brooke turned for one last look at the room, intending to preserve the memory of the day. The room was empty, but she heard a voice speak clearly to her mind. *Thank you. My family was lost without you.* Brooke suddenly caught her breath as reverent tears sprang to her eyes.

"Are you all right?" Greg whispered.

Brooke looked at him, then back at the sealing room. She nodded and smiled at her new husband with pure happiness, warmth radiating through her soul. "I've never been better."

ABOUT THE AUTHOR

Annette Luthy Lyon has been writing ever since the second grade—when she began piling pillows on a chair to reach her mother's typewriter. She wrote (and a year later almost published) a non-fiction children's book at age twelve. In high school she collaborated on a screenplay, and in college she and the same friend completed a fantasy novel together. She has written on her own seriously since the fall of 1994, in which time she completed six other novels.

She has published dozens of articles in a variety of publications, and received several awards from the League of Utah Writers, including a publication award and second place in consecutive years for novels. Annette has also served on the League's Utah Valley Chapter board for three years, including as president for the 2001–2002 year.

Annette was born in Provo, Utah, and spent most of her childhood there except for three years spent in Finland with her family, where she learned to love her mother's homeland. She is the third of four children. She graduated cum laude from BYU in 1995 with a BA in English. She currently serves in her ward as a Primary teacher.

Annette enjoys scrapbooking, knitting, camping in the Uintahs, singing, and spending time with family. She lives with her husband, Rob, in Spanish Fork, Utah with their three children.

Annette would appreciate hearing from her readers. They can write to her in care of Covenant Communications, P.O. Box 415, American Fork, Utah 84003-0416.